Catherine Cookson was born in East Jarrow and the place of her birth provides the background she so vividly creates in many of her novels. Although acclaimed as a regional writer – her novel THE ROUND TOWER won the Winifred Holtby Award for the best regional novel of 1968 – her readership spreads throughout the world. Her work has been translated into twelve languages and Corgi alone has over 20,000,000 copies of her novels in print, including those written under the name of Catherine Marchant.

Mrs Cookson was born the illegitimate daughter of a poverty-stricken woman, Kate, whom she believed to be her older sister. Catherine began work in service but eventually moved South to Hastings where she met and married a local grammar school master. At the age of forty she began writing with great success about the lives of the working class people of the North-East with whom she had grown up, including her intriguing autobiography, OUR KATE. More recently THE CINDER PATH has established her position as one of the most popular of contemporary women novelists.

Mrs Cookson now lives in Northumberland, overlooking the Tyne.

## Also by Catherine Cookson

KATIE MULHOLLAND
THE ROUND TOWER
FENWICK HOUSES
THE FIFTEEN STREETS
MAGGIE ROWAN
THE LONG CORRIDOR
THE UNBAITED TRAP
COLOUR BLIND
THE MENAGERIE
THE BLIND MILLER
FANNY MCBRIDE
THE GLASS VIRGIN
ROONEY
THE NICE BLOKE
THE INVITATION
THE DWELLING PLACE
OUR KATE
THE INVISIBLE CORD
THE GAMBLING MAN
THE TIDE OF LIFE
THE GIRL
THE CINDER PATH
PURE AS THE LILY
FEATHERS IN THE FIRE
THE MAN WHO CRIED

### The 'Mary Ann' series

A GRAND MAN
THE DEVIL AND MARY ANN
THE LORD AND MARY ANN
LIFE AND MARY ANN
LOVE AND MARY ANN
MARRIAGE AND MARY ANN
MARY ANN'S ANGELS
MARY ANN AND BILL

### The 'Mallen' Trilogy

THE MALLEN STREAK
THE MALLEN GIRL
THE MALLEN LITTER

### By Catherine Cookson as Catherine Marchant

HOUSE OF MEN
THE FEN TIGER
HERITAGE OF FOLLY
MISS MARTHA MARY CRAWFORD
THE IRON FAÇADE
THE SLOW AWAKENING

and published by Corgi Books

Catherine Cookson

# Kate Hannigan

CORGI BOOKS
A DIVISION OF TRANSWORLD PUBLISHERS LTD

# KATE HANNIGAN

## A CORGI BOOK 0 552 11370 0

Originally published in Great Britain by
Macdonald & Co. (Publishers), Ltd.

PRINTING HISTORY
Macdonald edition published 1950
Corgi edition published 1969
Corgi edition reprinted 1970
Corgi edition reprinted 1970
Corgi edition reprinted 1972
Corgi edition reprinted 1972
Corgi edition reprinted 1973
Corgi edition reprinted 1974
Corgi edition reprinted 1975
Corgi edition reprinted 1976
Corgi edition reprinted 1977
Corgi edition reprinted 1978 (twice)
Corgi edition reissued 1980
Corgi edition reprinted 1980 (twice)

This book is set in Baskerville 10 pt.

Corgi Books are published by Transworld Publishers, Ltd.,
Century House, 61–63 Uxbridge Road,
Ealing, London W5 5SA.
Made and printed in Great Britain by
Hunt Barnard Printing Ltd.,
Aylesbury, Bucks.

*To*
*MY MOTHER*
*who has found*
*her expression through me*

## AUTHOR'S NOTE

The characters in this book are entirely fictitious and have no relation to any living person.

Although the setting is Tyneside and several actual place names have been used, 'the fifteen streets' are entirely imaginary.

Owing to difficulty in comprehension by the uninitiated, the Tyneside dialect has not been adhered to.

## CONTENTS

# KATE HANNIGAN

# THE BIRTH

'I shall want more hot water, and those towels there will not be enough.'

'Glory to God, doctor, you have every towel there is in the house!'

'Then bring sheets, old ones, and we can tear them.'

'Old ones, and we can tear them,' mimicked Dorrie Clarke to herself. 'New brooms sweep clean. By God, if they don't! Old Kelly would have more sense, drunk as he might have been. The way this one's going on you would think sovereigns were as thick as fleas and there was a father downstairs to welcome the brat.'

'There's no more sheets, doctor,' she said, rolling her already tightly rolled sleeves further up her fat arms. Speak to her like that, would he! She'd been bringing bairns into the world when his arse was still being washed! For two hours now he had said: 'Do this, do that,' as if Kate Hannigan on the bed there was the Duchess of Connaught, instead of a trollop going to bring a bastard into the world; when it made up its mind to come, which wouldn't be for another couple of hours. And here she'd been hanging around since tea-time; and it was Christmas Eve and all, and not a drop past her lips; an' couldn't get away for this young swine saying: 'Lend me a hand here, Mrs. Clarke,' 'Let her pull on you, Mrs. Clarke,' 'Get that damn fire to burn, Mrs. Clarke!' ... Yes, he even damned her. Now Doctor Kelly, rest his soul, could be as drunk as hell, but he'd never swear at you; more likely to say, 'Have a drop, Mrs. Clarke; you need it.' There was a gentleman for you. This one wouldn't reign long; but he was reigning tonight, blast him! and get out for a wet she must, or die.

Into Dorrie Clarke's agile brain flashed an idea; she'd trade Sarah Hannigan a pair of sheets for the chiffonier downstairs; she'd always had her eyes on that. Begod! she'd get the best of this bargain, and get out of this young upstart's sight for five minutes.

Her fat, well-red face rolled itself into a stiff, oily smile. 'There's not a rag in this house but what's in the pawn, doctor; but I've a pair of sheets of me own that I'll gladly go and get this minute, for I couldn't see this poor thing want.' She nodded pathetically down at the humped figure on the bed.

The doctor didn't raise himself from his stooping posture over the bed, he didn't even raise his head, but he raised his eyes, and his eyebrows shot into the tumbled, thick black hair on his forehead. And his black eyes stared at Mrs. Clarke for a second in such a way that she thought: 'Begod! he looks like the divil himself. And he might be that, with his black eyes in that long face and that pointed beard; and him so young and handsome. Holy Mother of God, I must have a drink!'

Whether it was she slipped, or it was the doctor's remark that momentarily unbalanced her she couldn't afterwards decide; for she was stamping down the narrow dark stairs, in a rage, when her feet ... just left her, as she put it, and she found herself in a heap in the Hannigans' kitchen, with Tim Hannigan sitting in his chair by the fireside, wearing his look of sullen anger, only more so, and not moving to give a body a hand up, and Sarah Hannigan, with her weary face bending above her, saying: 'Oh, are you hurt, Dorrie?' She picked herself up, grabbed her coat off the back of the kitchen door, pulled a shawl tightly around her head, and, with figure bent, passed out through the door Sarah Hannigan held ajar for her and into the driving snow, without uttering a word. She was too angry even to take much notice of the pain in her knee.

She'd get even with the young sod. ... Begod! if it took her a lifetime she'd get even with him.

'Mrs. Clarke,' he had said, 'I don't allow intoxicated women to assist at births. And, if you bring the sheets, we won't tear them. They will only be a loan, Mrs. Clarke.'

Dorrie Clarke suddenly shivered violently. And it wasn't a shiver caused by the snow as it danced and swirled about her; it wasn't a cold shiver at all. 'Jesus, Mary and Joseph! How did he know? He could have heard I take a drop, but he couldn't have known about the sheets. My God! it's what Father O'Malley said.... The divil walks the earth, he has many guises.... He's the divil! Ah! but as Father O'Malley would say, he's got to be fought, and, begod! I'll fight him!'

Back in the bedroom of 16 Whitley Street Doctor Rodney Prince stood with his elbows on the mantelpiece. He had to bend down a considerable way to do this as it was only four feet high and merely a narrow ledge above the bedroom fireplace. He kept pushing his hands through his hair with a rhythmic movement.... God! but he was tired. Wasn't it ever going to come? What a Christmas Eve, and Stella likely sitting in a blue stately fume, cramming herself with pity . . . the beautiful, talented, brutally treated (he gave a soundless laugh at the thought) and neglected wife of a slum doctor! Well, he had telephoned her and told her to go on to the Richards. And he had also telephoned the Richards and told them; but they had said, 'Well, you know Mrs. Prince! She won't come without you.' Clever Stella; playing the part of the dutiful wife, awaiting her husband's return with coffee and sandwiches and a loving smile. Clever Stella.... Oh, my God, where was it going to end? Four years of it now, and perhaps ten ... fifteen ... twenty more.... Oh no! If only he didn't love her so much.... Christmas Day tomorrow; she would go to church and kneel like ... one of God's angels, somewhere where the choirboys could see her. Poor choirboys! He knew the feelings she would send through them. How could they think of the Trinity? sing their little responses? when the great God Nature, he who gave you concrete proof of his presence, was competing against the other God, who, as far as they understood, wasn't introduced to them until they were dead.... Oh, Stella! What was he thinking? He was so tired. If only he could go home after this was over and find her there, soft and yielding, wanting something from him. . . .

'Doctor! Doctor!'

He turned swiftly towards the bed and gripped the hands outstretched to him. 'There, there! Is it starting again? Try hard now.'

'How much longer, doctor?'

'Not long,' he lied; 'any time now. Only don't worry; you'll be all right.'

'I don't mind . . . I don't mind.' The tousled head rolled to and fro on the pillow. 'I want to die . . . I hope we both die . . . just go out quietly. . . .'

'Kate, here, don't talk like that!' He released one of his hands from hers and brought her face round to look at him, his palm against her cheek. 'Now, we want none of that nonsense. Do you hear?'

Her great blue eyes looked up at him, quietly and enquiringly, for a second. 'What chance has it?' she asked.

He knew she wasn't enquiring after the child's chance of being born alive, although about that he was beginning to have his doubts, but of its chance to live in her world, handicapped as it would be. 'As much as the next,' he answered her. 'And more,' he added, 'seeing it'll be your child.'

Now, what had made him say that? For, if it inherited her beauty and was brought up in these surroundings, it was doomed from birth. How the feelings of kindliness made one lie, made one tactful and insincere! Only when you hated someone did you tell the truth.

He pulled up a rickety chair and sat down, letting Kate, in her spasms, pull on his arm. . . . Where the deuce had that drunken sot got to? . . . The room was cold; the fire that had glowed for a little while had died down under its heap of coaldust . . . If that old hag didn't come back he'd be in a nice fix; the mother downstairs was less than useless, scared to death of her man, and of this event, and of life in general. . . . If that Clarke woman didn't come back. But why was he harping on about her not coming back? She was a midwife . . . of sorts; it was her job. But he had had a little experience of her during these last few months, and he had come to recognise her as a fawning leech, picking her victims from among the poorer of her own kind.

'Oh, doc ... tor! Oh, God!'

Easing the bedclothes off the contorted figure he moved his hands quickly over her. Then he covered her up again and banged on the floor with his heel. In a few seconds the door was opened quietly, and the mother stood there, clutching her holland apron in both hands.

'Has Mrs. Clarke come back yet?'

'No, doctor.'

'Then will you kindly get this fire to burn? Put wood on it.'

'There's no wood, doctor; there's only the slack.'

'Can't you break up something?'

She looked at him helplessly; her lips twitched, and her tongue seemed to be moving at random in her mouth. He couldn't meet her eyes. He thrust his hand into his pocket and handed her a sovereign. She looked at it, lying bright and yellow on her palm. Her tongue ran wild races between her teeth, but she made no sound.

'Get what's necessary,' he said gruffly. 'And perhaps a chicken; Kate will likely need it tomorrow.'

She nodded slowly at him, while her tongue, darting from side to side, caught the drops as they ran down her cheeks.

Kate was moaning; she could hear herself. The moans seemed to float around her, then rise up to the ceiling and stick on the mottled plaster. Most of them were right above her head, gathered together in the dark patch that formed the three-legged horse which had been her companion and secret confidant since childhood. He wouldn't mind having her moans; he thought all about her, her sins, the secret things she thought and was ashamed of, even her feeling sometimes that there couldn't be a God. It was, as she had once read, that people like Father O'Malley were only put there to stop people like her from thinking; for, if she once started thinking, she and her like wouldn't put up with things as they were. Jimmy McManus had lent her that book, but she had understood hardly anything at all of it. Yet, it was after reading it that she had gone and got the place

15

in Newcastle, in the best end ... Shields wasn't good enough for her. And it was after reading that very book that she had taken off all her clothes and had stood naked before the mirror, swinging its mottled square back and forth so that she could see every part of herself; and glorying in it as she did it, and knowing that she was beautiful, that she was fit to marry anybody. It was only her talk that was all wrong.... But she would learn; she was quick at picking things up.... Of course, she had suffered for this. Her conscience had driven her to confession, and, in the dark box, with face ablaze, she had confessed the greatest sin of her life. The priest had told her she must guard against the sin of impurity by keeping a close watch on her thoughts; and he went on to explain how a great saint, when sorely tempted by the flesh, had thrown himself naked into a holly bush, or was it a bramble? she wasn't sure now.

The moans floated thick about her.... Where was John now? ... Did he know he was soon to be a father? ... Had he ever been a father before? ... He wasn't a husband, she wasn't a wife; yet she was having a baby.... It was all her own fault, she couldn't blame John; he had never mentioned marriage to her. Her inherent honesty had told her so a thousand times these past months.

'John!' she called out sharply as the doctor wiped the sweat from her face.

'It's all right, Kate, it's all right; it won't be long now.'

It won't be long now! It won't be long now! the moans said. John's baby, with his slant eyes and beautiful mouth.... It was as near as yesterday when she had first seen him, seated in the Jacksons' drawing-room. Since two of the maids had been sent into town, she had been told that she was to serve tea ... wee cakes and china cups. Something had happened inside her when their eyes had first met. She had been glad to get out of the room and into the coolness of the hall. He had been there only three days when he slipped a note to her, asking her to meet him.... Oh, the mad joy! the ecstasy of love before its fulfilment! Even when she had given herself to him, it had not compared with the strange delight of knowing she was wanted; and by him, a gentleman who had travelled the world. Twice he had taken her; only twice; and both times within a month, on her half-day. Right up Lanesby way they had gone; and he had told her she was the most beautiful thing he had ever seen, that he loved her as she'd never be loved again, and that she'd always be his. . . .

'Oh, doctor! Doctor!'

'It's all right,' he assured her, as he went out of the room. 'Mrs. Hannigan!' he shouted to the frightened face, framed in the shawl, already at the bottom of the dim stairs, 'get me Mrs. Clarke here at once!'

'I'm here, doctor!' cried a voice, 'an' I can't come up them stairs.' Mrs. Clarke pushed Sarah Hannigan to one side, and stood glaring up at him. 'Something's happened to me knee with that fall I had down the bl—down the stairs. I'm beside meself with the pain of it. I don't know if I'll be able to get back home through this snow, the drifts are chin high.'

'Mrs. Clarke, I've got to have help! You'll come up here if I have to carry you up!'

'Begod, an' I will not! Look at that!' she cried.

He bounded down the stairs towards her. She had pulled up her skirt and was disclosing her knee, already laid bare for inspection.

He looked at it. . . . Well, that settles that. The damned woman, you would think she had done it on purpose. . . . He thought a moment . . . 'Nurse Snell, that's it! She'll come. How can I get . . . ?'

'It's no use. She's in the heart of Jarrow this very minute after a case; I saw her go only a couple of hours ago.' Mrs. Clarke was triumphant. 'It's nobody you'll get this night. Now, Doctor Kelly used to——'

'Be quiet, woman!' He glared at her, the point of his beard thrust out.

Begod, if she could only strike him down dead! Him to speak to her like that, and to call her—woman! . . . She that was looked up to and respected for her knowledge all round these black buildings, all fifteen streets of them. They had even sent for her from Shields and Jarrow to deliver, before today, and Doctor Kelly had said she was every bit as good as himself. Yet this young snot . . . with his big, new-fangled motor-car and his fine clothes, and his voice like a foreigner ... would tell her to shut up! Even Tim Hannigan there, who put the fear of God into everybody in the fifteen streets with his swearing and bashing, when the mood was on him, even he had never dared to tell her ... Dorrie Clarke ... to shut up. Her blood boiled. She fastened the top of her stocking into a knot and rolled it down her leg to make it secure; she pulled her coat tighter about her and limped to the kitchen door, before turning to him. 'You may be a doctor ... yet that's got to be proved ... but yer no gentleman. You can strike me off your club; and I wouldn't work on a case where you are to save me the workhouse; I'm a particular woman. And take my word for it, you won't reign long!' The snow whirled into the kitchen as she pulled open the door.

'Keep that leg up for a few days,' he called after her.

'You go to Hell's flames!' was the rejoinder.

A fleeting shadow, that could have been amusement, passed over Tim Hannigan's face. Throughout the conversation he had sat immobile in the straight-backed, wooden arm-chair dead in front of the fire, staring at the glowing slack which the good draught of the big chimney kept bright.

Sarah Hannigan stood near the bare kitchen table in the centre of the room, picking at her bass bag and her shawl alternately, and her pale, weary eyes never left the doctor's face. She watched him think a minute after Dorrie Clarke had banged the door, then swiftly wrote something on a piece of paper which he took from a notebook.

'I'm sending for Doctor Davidson, Mrs. Hannigan,' he said, as he wrote. 'Perhaps your husband will get this note to him as soon as possible?'

'I'll take it, doctor,' said Sarah, breathlessly.

'No, you have your shopping to do, and you must get something to keep that room warm. Your husband can take it.'

She looked helplessly from the back of her husband's head to the bearded face of this strange doctor.... He didn't know; he was so cool and remote; from another world altogether; didn't the sovereign prove that? If it got round he threw his money about he'd have no peace. And him speaking to Dorrie Clarke like that, and now asking Tim to go a message.... Oh, Holy Mary! ...

'I'll go on me way, doctor....'

'Certainly not! Mr. Hannigan,' he addressed the back of Tim's head, still immobile, 'will you kindly get this message to Doctor Davidson at once? Your daughter is a very sick woman.'

Only Tim Hannigan's head turned; his pale eyes, under their overhanging, grizzly eyebrows, seemed to work behind a thin film. They moved slowly over the doctor and came to rest, derisively, on his black, pointed beard. 'Hell's cure to her!' he said slowly. His upper lip rested inside his lower one and his eyes flashed a quick glint at his wife before he turned his head to the fire again.

'Sir, do you know that your daughter might die?'

Tim's head came back with a jerk as if he was silently laughing.

'Doctor, please ... let me. Oh, please! I'll get there in no time.'

Sarah grabbed the folded note from his hand, and he let her go without a word. The back door banged again, and he still stood staring at the back of Tim Hannigan's head. He felt more angry than ever he had done in his life before.... These people! What were they? Animals? That frightful, fat, gin-smelling woman, and this man, callous beyond even the wildest stretches of imagination. He would like to punch that beastly mouth, close up those snake eyes.... Oh, why get worked up? He'd need all his energy.... He turned and went back up the stairs, groping at the walls in the dark.... As Frank had said, it was a waste of sympathy; for what little he would achieve he would not assist their crawling out of the mire one jot, ninety per cent of them still being in the animal stage.... Not that he took much notice of anything his brother might say; but he had upset his family and dragged Stella to this frightful place . . . for what? To express some obscure feeling that came to the surface and acted as a spoke whenever he was bent on following a sensible course ... at least sensible to his people's way of thinking. Had he followed the course laid out he would now have his London surgery and a definite footing in one of the larger hospitals, and at this minute he would have been at Rookhurst; likely just going in to dinner with the family. Oh, what a fool he was! He couldn't pretend to an ideal urging him on, or love for these frightful people. Obstinacy, his father called it; a form of snobbery was his mother's verdict; cussedness and the desire to be different, Frank said, with a sneer. Only his grandfather had said nothing, neither of approbation nor of condemnation; he had just listened. But there was a peculiar expression in his eyes when he looked at Rodney, which might have been mistaken for envy.

This room was freezing. If this girl didn't die of childbirth she would of exposure. Bending over Kate, he felt her pulse. Davidson should be here within half an hour, if he were at home; the sooner they got this job over the better, for it promised to be an awkward job. . . . He must try to do something with that fire.

Kneeling down on the small clippy mat, he blew on the pale embers. This resulted in his face and hair being covered with coaldust. . . . Damnation! . . . He stood up and shook himself. Temporarily blinded, he stumbled towards the half-circle of marble, supported on a three-legged frame, standing in the corner and poured some water out of the enamel jug standing in the tin dish. He washed his face, and the yellow soap stung his eyes more than the coal dust had done. . . . What a night! And likely his car was half buried by now; it had been snowing for hours. . . . In the ordinary course he would have left his patient earlier, to return later. But this fresh fall of snow, on top of twelve inches already frozen hard, had warned him that this would have been easier said than done, and the condition of this girl made it imperative that he should be on the spot. . . . Pulling the cream paper window blind to one side, he looked out, but he couldn't see down into the street, the window being a thick, frosted mass of snowflakes. He turned towards the bed and sat down on the chair again.

Kate was lying inert, breathing heavily. He looked

around the room, ten by eight at the most; the three-quarter-size iron bed, adorned with brass knobs, the marble-topped wash-hand stand, and a large wooden box, end up, with a curtain in front and a mirror on top, was all the room held in the way of furniture; pegs on the door supported an odd assortment of clothes, and a patchwork quilt and two thin biscuit-coloured blankets covered Kate; the floor was as white as frequent scrubbing could make it, and the whole was lit up by a single gas jet.

Rodney Prince looked at this gas jet flickering on the turned-up end of a piece of lead piping. Its power was, he thought, about one-hundredth that of the chandelier above the dining-table at home.... Home, to his mind, was Rookhurst, not the place he shared with Stella; that was 'the house'. He had a sudden nostalgia for all the things he had known and had taken for granted for so many years, but most of all, at this moment, for the dining-room at Rookhurst, for its dim, worn red and golds, for its long, wide windows, forming a frame for the sweeping downs beyond, and for the old furniture polished by time and handling to a delight for the eye. And there was a strange longing for his people; for his greying and stately, slightly cynical mother, whom, temperamentally, he resembled too much to be on good terms with, for the easy tolerance of his father, even for the jealousy of Frank.

It was Christmas Eve, and, in spite of all their differences, Christmas Eve had always been a gay day at home. But from ten o'clock this morning he had been trudging in and out of tiny houses, some clean, some smelly, but all seeming to be filled with the same type of people, coarse-voiced and wary. Then there was Stella. The row they had had last night might have been patched up tonight had he been able to take her to the Richards. As much as he knew she despised them, their flattery would have helped to smooth the plumage that he had so brusquely ruffled, and perhaps put her into a tender frame of mind. But wasn't she always tender? Dreamy and tender, that was Stella. Then how could she be the cold, outraged beauty? How could she make a man feel like a wild beast? Last night she had snuggled, and nestled, and purred like a contented kitten, while he fondled her hair, murmuring into it, telling her of the magic she cast about him. He had kissed her eyes and her ears, and had stroked her arms, and she had lain, docile and beautifully sweet, as if awaiting final consummation. And his mind had cried, 'Ah, now!' And then, as always, like a snowflake on a hot log, she had melted away from him.

'Stella,' he had cried to her ... actually cried to her! ... 'Don't! You are torturing me.' He had crushed her body under his, but she was far withdrawn. He had been furious that this should be happening again, and had renewed his efforts to solicit her affections.

Her voice had come as a whisper, which might easily have been a hiss, when she had said, 'Why must you always want the same thing? Why are you so beastly? We have had all this out before. I'm just not going to put up with it, night after night.'

'But, darling, it's nearly ... it's so long...' he had stammered, in his pain.

'Oh, don't be so coarse! You talk like ... well, like one of these dockers.'

At that he had let her go, her long, white limbs in their crumpled chiffon whirling out of the bed and into the dressing-room. It was only when he had heard the key turn in the lock, and he knew that she meant to spend the night on the couch, that the torturing desire in his blood seemed to gather itself into one hard knot in his head, which beat with sudden hate of her. He was banging on the dressing-room door and hissing words he would never have believed possible. She made no answering sound.... When he dropped into bed, shaking and limp, he had to bite into the pillow to stifle the tearing emotion that wracked him.

Stella could reduce him to that because he loved her, because he could not stop loving her. She had the power to change in a flash his six feet of virility into a shamed, trembling heap. He knew the course he should have adopted long ago; but he could never see himself touching anyone but Stella. He had loved her from the age of five, when she had walked between Frank and him and had been the cause of their first serious quarrel.

This morning they had met at breakfast; Stella, a little white, but smiling and talking of the snow and the Christmas doings, in front of the servants.... Stella was very well bred; she would keep up appearances in hell, he thought.... He knew he had looked ghastly, the blackness of his beard accentuated the pallor of his face. He had scarcely spoken and had eaten nothing, and, on the plea of outstanding calls, he had hurriedly excused himself after drinking three cups of coffee. Without looking at her he knew that her whole bearing was one of sad and gentle reproach.

What the servants had heard last night from their distant rooms didn't trouble him; he was used to servants knowing as much about his life and that of his family as they did themselves. He forgot to take into account that the servants of thirty and forty years' standing, who were like one's own friends, were a different proposition from chance maids of three months.

The knocker of the front-door banged twice. It brought back Kate from far-away regions. She opened her eyes wide. 'Who's that?' she asked. Then, grabbing his hand, 'You're not having me sent to the workhouse?' She looked around wildly. 'Where's Mrs. Clarke? Oh, don't send me! Please don't send me. I can easily pay you when I'm up.'

'What on earth are you talking about? Don't be silly, Kate! What put such an idea into your head? That is likely Doctor Davidson; Mrs. Clarke can't help me, she's hurt her knee. There, now, lie down.' He pressed her gently back into the pillow.

The knocker banged again, quicker and louder this time. Rodney went to the stair-head. Surely that brute wasn't still sitting there and making no attempt to open the door! He heard the poker rattle against the bars of the fire. By God, he was! Of all the swine!

He ran down the stairs. 'Are you deaf, sir?' he shouted at Tim Hannigan's back, as he hurried through the kitchen and into the front-room, from where the front door led into the street. The knocker banged once more as he pulled open the door, letting in a whirl of snow.

'I thought you were all dead.' The big muffled figure was kicking his feet against the wall. 'Phew! What a night!' He stepped into the room, and Rodney closed the door without a word and led the way through into the comparative brightness of the kitchen.

'Oh, hello, Tim! You deaf?' The easy familiarity of Doctor Davidson surprised Rodney. He gave the big, bony man a quick glance; no annoyance showed on his face at being kept waiting; there was about it that lingering half smile that had so baffled Rodney on the few previous occasions when they had met.... He had felt at first that Davidson was laughing at him; laughing gently, but nevertheless laughing. And he had thought, how dare he! He had soon learnt all about Davidson, who was the son of a Jarrow grocer. The grocer had made money, and had spent it on his son. And the son, instead of taking himself and his career to a far distant place, as far away as possible from Jarrow, had returned, bought a practice in the worst quarter, near the ferry, and married a Jarrow girl. They lived in an ugly house overlooking the muddy Don, where it poured its chemical-discoloured water into the Jarrow slacks and so into the Tyne. But all this had not wiped that quaint smile off Peter Davidson's face. And, through time, Rodney had found that the smile was not for him alone; Davidson seemed to handle life gently and with that half smile; he never seemed to hurry, nor to be impatient. Rodney wondered what he was really like. He had felt Davidson would be worth knowing, but at the same time knew it was impossible; they met seldom in the course of their rounds, and the only other way would be through social visiting. For himself, he wouldn't mind in the least, but Stella! Well, he couldn't imagine her and the Jarrow girl, somehow.

They were in the bedroom before Rodney spoke. 'I'm sorry, Davidson, I've had to ask you to turn out on a night like this; Christmas Eve, too.'

'Oh, don't let that worry you, it's all in the game. Hello, Kate!' he said, bending over the bed, with his hands on his knees. 'You're going to have a Christmas baby, eh?'

Again that tone of familiarity. Rodney watched Kate's

24

face; she smiled as one would at a friend. Rodney felt a little stir of professional jealousy; she hadn't smiled at him like that; nor would any of his patients, he thought, treat him as they did Davidson. He had tried for three months to get below their wary surface; he had tried, indeed he had, to put them at their ease, little guessing that his voice alone put him in the category of 'The Class' and that, in their fierce independence, they resented the necessity for what they unwordingly thought his condescension.

With great reluctance he took off his coat and rolled up his sleeves; the chill of the room seeped through his fine wool shirt and vest. As he opened his case and picked out what he required, voices from below the window came to him like words spoken through a thick towel:

'Hello there, Joe! Merry Christmas.'

'Same to you, Jimmy. Same to you.'

'Coming for a wet?'

'Ee, lad, no; ah haven't been yem yet. The missis'll likely bash me over the heed when ah puts me nose in the door!'

Muffled laughter, then the thick silence from the street again.

Davidson was still talking to Kate, and a feeling of utter and absolute loneliness suddenly flooded through Rodney. He seemed divorced from every human contact and feeling; everyone he knew, his family, and Stella all stood aloof and condemning ... sending out their displeasure through the bleak stares of their eyes. He saw them all as a hillside covered with sturdy oaks, and himself a little stream at their feet, bent on winding his own way past them. They were so powerful, but helpless to stop his meandering. And he had wound his way into the valley where there were these people ... those men in the street, this girl on the bed, this big, burly doctor who held life steadily by the reins; they were all one. He was in their midst, but he couldn't get near them either; and, oh, he wanted the touch of some friendly hand. He was lost in that vast, unknown and terrible continent of loneliness; it stretched on and on, very white and hopeless, and quite bare.

Good heavens! he thought, this won't do. I'm light-headed. No breakfast, no dinner; must have something as soon as this is over.... He looked across at Davidson who was still talking to Kate. 'Well, there it is,' he was saying. 'If you want the place it's yours. Their own girl won't be leaving for a month, and it's five shillings a week. So there you are, Kate; you're all set up and nothing to worry about.'

Rodney nodded to him, and Davidson came round the foot of the bed to the wash-hand stand. 'Afraid it's going to be a bit of a job; I think it advisable to give her a whiff.' He handed Davidson a bottle and a pad of cotton wool. Davidson nodded and walked back to the bed.

'Two old boys nearly eighty and their sister about seventy, and only eight rooms. When they told me today their girl was leaving I thought of you right away, Kate; and it's a lovely little house, down Westoe. If you go there you'll be set up. Now just breathe steadily, Kate. That's it, th ... at's it. Now we are all set,' he addressed Rodney. 'That'll have eased her mind a bit; the main part of their worry is to get into a good place. Poor little beggar! She's only a child herself.'

'Do you know her?' asked Rodney, pulling the prostrate form into position.

'Yes. Watched her grow up. Everybody knows Kate Hannigan; she was too beautiful to miss. By! she was a lovely kiddy. It always struck me as odd how old Tim Hannigan could have a child like her. I didn't know she had got into this mess until yesterday; it surprised me. Somehow she always appeared different; quiet, a little aloof, as if she didn't quite belong around these quarters. Didn't run round with the lads, either; kept them at their distance. And if she hadn't, old Tim would have.... And now this. Poor Kate!'

Doctor Davidson gently lifted one of the long, nut-brown plaits off Kate's face with his free hand, while with the other he felt her pulse. 'Not as strong as it should be,' he muttered. 'How is it to time? Was it due?'

'Yes, as far as I can gather. But I couldn't get much out of her,' said Rodney. 'She didn't come home until the day before yesterday. She had been working in some lodging house in Newcastle; the mother thought she was still in service. She hasn't been home for months, having made one excuse after another. Then she turns up like this. Knowing that beast downstairs, you can't wonder at her being terrified to come home; but I should have thought the workhouse would have been preferable to facing him. Yet she seems to have a horror of it.'

The smile disappeared from Doctor Davidson's face as he asked. 'You don't know much about the workhouse, do you?'

But Rodney didn't answer, he had started upon his job. His hands moved swiftly; he braced himself and pulled, gently pressing ... easing.... He worked for some minutes, and Davidson, who watched his every move, thought: Good hands, no quivers there. Yet he's as strung up and as taut as a bow. Wonder what brought him this way . . . funny fellow. Why did he take old Kelly's place when Anderson's was going up Westoe end? Could have had a couple of titles on his books there. But still, apparently it isn't money he wants; old windbag Richards says he's got at least two thousand a year private income.... Whew! Two thousand a year! ... Davidson had a vision of a bright shining clinic, fitted with the latest appliances.... Wonder what he does want; he's certainly not the welfare type. Whatever his aim, I bet it doesn't meet with his lady-wife's ...

'No use,' said Rodney, raising his eyes to Davidson; 'it's wedged.... I'll have to cut.' He nodded towards his case.

Davidson handed him an instrument. There was a sharp snip, snip, a quick dabbing of spirits, and his hands were once more pulling, easing, pressing. He was no longer cold; beads of sweat ran down his forehead, falling from his brow on to his hands. His chin was drawn in, his beard lying like an arrow on his shirt front.... A little more, a little more, he encouraged himself.... Ah, the head! ... Now then ... now then ... easy, but make it quick. She can't stand much more; Davidson is anxious about that pulse.... There, there ... a little more.... Oh, hell! don't say it's going to be obstinate now!

Pulling, easing, pressing, it went on. The sweat was

running into his eyes now and his shirt was no longer white.

Davidson's expression became pitying.... Poor Kate! It was practically up. Still, this fellow was good; if she were paying hundreds she wouldn't have had anyone better.... But these things happened....

'A ... ah!' It was an exclamation of triumph as much as relief. Rodney slowly withdrew the red body covered with silvery slime. For a second it lay across both his hands, a girl child ... to be named Annie Hannigan, and who was to help make and to almost mar his career.

# THE KITCHEN

The kitchen was bright and gleaming. From the open fireplace the coal glowed a deeper red in contrast with the shining blackleaded hob, with the oven to its right and the nook for pans to its left. It sent down its glow on to the steel-topped and brass-railed fender, where its reflections appeared like delicate rose clouds seen through a silver curtain. The fire glinted on the mahogany legs of the kitchen-table and on the cups spread on the white, patched cloth. It shed its glow over the red wood of the chiffonier standing against the wall opposite, and over the brass-knobbed handle of the staircase door. The hard, wood saddle, standing along the wall to the left of the fire-place, took on an innocent deception from the glow; its flock-stuffed cushions looked soft and inviting. Even the sneck of the door that led to the front room had glints of white along its black handle. But it was to the window that the fire lent its most enchanting grace. With its six red earthenware pots of coloured hyacinths, and framed in the dolly-tinted lace curtains, starched to a stiffness which kept their folds in perpetual billows, it looked like a startling, bright painting. Never had that window-sill upheld such beauty.

Hyacinths at any time of the year were things one just dreamed of. But at Christmas! and in her kitchen! they made Sarah Hannigan feel that life was changing, that it was becoming easier, and that before she was really old she would know peace ... she didn't ask for happiness, just peace. And she asked herself, as she looked out over the bulbs to the tiny backyard and to the backs of the houses opposite, hadn't she had more peace this last year than she had had for the previous seventeen years. ...

She had thought life would become unbearable when Kate had come home like that last Christmas. And it was unbearable for nearly a month after Annie was born. But when Kate got that place in Westoe things had seemed to change. It wasn't only that Kate gave her four-and-six a week out of her five shillings and God alone knew what a difference that had made—it was that things had seemed to happen to keep Tim off her, that his eighteen years' persecution of her was easing at last.

First, the baby had been fretful, and for most of the winter she had had to keep it downstairs in the warmth of the kitchen. So she had slept, thankfully, on the saddle. Then she had been covered with that rash, and the smell of the ointment the doctor had given her had been nauseating to Tim. He had sworn and raged, and she had thankfully left the feather bed and her husband's side for the hard comfort of the saddle again. But a rash doesn't last for ever, although she had lengthened its stay by weeks, until he had begun to get suspicious. When she had returned to the feather bed the old nightmare began again. Sometimes she would wait a week, or even two, until, blind with rage at his own impotence and the caducity of his passion, he would repeat the old cry, 'She isn't mine! Tell me, or I'll throttle it out of you. Is she? Is she? She's the artist's bastard, isn't she? Tell me!'

Sarah knew that it was only the fear of hell as painted so realistically by Father O'Malley that had saved her life on more than one occasion. Three times, when Kate was but a few months old, she had flown with her into Mrs. Mullen's, next door. Things like that soon got around the fifteen streets, and one day Father O'Malley came and had a talk with Tim up in the bedroom, and an equally long talk with her down in the kitchen. The result, in her case, had been that she never went to confession again without a dire feeling of guilt, whereas, up till then, her great sin, as it would be called, had been something between God and her alone. She could not put it into words, for the result of it was the brightness of her life. But Father O'Malley's probing had reached her very soul, only some instinct, not yet beaten into submission, warning her to risk hell's flames rather than entrust it to any human, even though he be an agent of the Almighty.

The effect on Tim was to make him attend mass regularly, even Benediction on a Thursday night. He could get sodden drunk on a Saturday and beat her up, but he'd go to mass on the Sunday. There were worse things than having your eyes blacked and being kicked around the room, as Sarah knew; and when he was drunk, strange as it may seem, he made no futile demands on her.

So, taking things all in all, she didn't mind him getting drunk as long as she could get the money out of him beforehand for the rent. And he usually let her have that; for she knew he had the fear of being turned out on to the street and of having to go to the workhouse. To provide their food she could always do a couple of days cleaning or washing. She had managed somehow, up till last year. But then things in the docks became worse; sometimes he would only get one shift in in a week. When he returned from his twelve-hour shift, his moleskins red and wet up to the thighs, she had it in her heart then to feel sorry for him ... unloading iron ore all day, and only bone broth, thickened with pot stuff, to set before him. And the three-and-six he got for the shift had to go for the rent, not even twopence for baccy, let alone a pint. With Kate's four-and-six a week and what she could pawn they had existed. They hadn't yet gone on the parish, for they both knew that, before they could get a penny, they'd be told to sell the chiffonier, the saddle and the spare iron bed upstairs that was kept for Kate.

Her mind wandered back and forth over the past, as she stared out into the dark day. Eleven o'clock on Christmas Eve, and you really needed a light, the sky was so low and heavy. Christmas had always brought trouble; she had never known a happy one, and you always seemed to remember your troubles more at Christmas. She and Tim had been married in Christmas week. She couldn't remember why she had married Tim; perhaps because he was big and quiet. And she had taken his quietness for kindness ... never had she been so mistaken. Or perhaps because she had wanted to get away from Mrs. Marris's, where she worked for sixteen hours a day for seven days a week for the sum total of half a crown. She hadn't known Tim very well when she had married him; it was difficult to get to know a man when you had only half a day off a month. She was then eighteen and Tim twenty-seven. Now she was forty-two and he was fifty-one; and of all her life she'd had only three months happiness ... stolen moments of ecstasy and terror; but no one could take them from her ... no one. She'd kept them for over eighteen years; she'd manage to keep them till she died.... And now things were changing, she could feel the change. It wasn't that Tim had been a prisoner up-stairs for six weeks, or that there was a baby in the house; it was rather a premonition....

She'd better mash some tea and take him up a cup. And she'd ask Maggie in for one; they'd be quiet, he wouldn't hear. She turned from the window and put the black kettle on to the centre of the red fire. Then, with a preliminary rattle of the bars to cover her signal, she gave two sharp taps on the back of the grate. After a short pause it was answered by a dull thud. Sarah put the poker down and went to the cupboard at the right-hand side of the fire-place and took from one of its scalloped-edged newspaper-covered shelves the brown teapot. After placing it on the hob, she went quietly through the front-room and gently opened the door, leaving it ajar. She returned to the kitchen and, drawing up the wooden chair near to the clothes-basket at the side of the hearth, she sat smiling wanly down on the sleeping baby lying therein. Presently her gaze wandered around the kitchen. It was all beautifully clean for Kate's coming. Any min-ute now Kate would come in, and for a whole week she'd be here with her in the kitchen.... No Tim; just her and Kate and the baby. Her hands, as they lay one on the other in the lap of her white apron, relaxed, her body relaxed, and she slumped, staring unseeing at Tim's arm-chair on the other side of the hearth. Never had she known such a Christmas Eve; there was nothing to dread.

Sarah started slightly when a little dumpy woman with grey hair and twinkling eyes stepped noiselessly into the kitchen from the front-room. Mrs. Mullen came to the improvised cradle and nodded, smiling down on the baby.

'By! she's lovely, Sarah,' she whispered. 'How's he?' She jerked her head sharply towards the ceiling.

'He's just the same. I'm expecting doctor today,' Sarah whispered back. 'Sit down, Maggie.'

Mrs. Mullen, making a wry face, refused the proffered arm-chair and pulled up a small cracket to the fire. 'This'll do me; I mustn't stay long. I've just sent the whole bang lot of them out to draw their Christmas clubs. They've got twenty-five shillings on their cards between the six of them; God knows what they'll buy. But I say, let them buy what they like, they're only young once. But it'll be hell let loose when they bring all their ket back; so I won't stay long, Sarah, for we'll have him'—she nodded again to the ceiling—'banging on the wall and cursing like old Harry.'

'The kettle's boiling, I'll mash the tea now,' said Sarah. 'Tell me, what are you putting in their stockings?'

'Oh, all kinds. Mick's had a few good weeks. And the things he's bought! You'd never believe. Come in the night, when we're filling them, and see. By! you're all done,' she said, looking around the room. 'And don't your window-sill look grand! I've never seen owt like them flowers; they weren't in bloom when I was in last.'

Going to the window, Sarah lifted two pots. 'I want you to have these for a Christmas-box, Maggie. I can't give you anything else, but I'd like you to have these.'

'No, lass. No. Kate brought them for you.'

'Sh!' said Sarah warningly. 'Take them, Maggie; they're so little for all the kindness you've shown me.'

'Well, thanks, Sarah ... I do like a flower. By! they're grand.'

'I'll take this up first,' said Sarah, filling a pint pot with tea, and adding four heaped teaspoons of sugar. She disappeared up the dark stairs, leaving Maggie Mullen sitting on the cracket comparing the seeming spaciousness around her with her own cramped quarters next door. Ten of them in four box-like rooms, and two of the eight children nearly young men; it was such a crush. But still, please God, give her her lot any day before Sarah's, with her four rooms for two people and a baby. By God, yes; any day!

Sarah re-entered the kitchen, closing the stair door softly behind her. She poured out two cups of black tea and handed one to Mrs. Mullen.

'Thanks, Sarah,' said Maggie. 'By the way, did you hear Big Dixon's got her other one?'

'No! When?'

'Eleven o'clock last night. Another boy. That's the sixth; she'll be all right for money later on. By! the place won't hold her when they all start working; you can't keep her down now since she's got her Mary in place at the doctor's. Do you know she bought a gramophone only last week?'

'No!'

'Yes, with a horn on it the size of a poss tub; you'd think she'd have plenty noise with six wee'ns round her, wouldn't you, now?'

'Who has she got looking after her?'

'Oh, Dorrie Clarke, of course! She can't afford a gramophone and Nurse Snell!'

Here the two women chuckled and sipped their tea.

'Very few people are having Dorrie Clarke now,' continued Mrs. Mullen. 'Can you blame them? She reeks of gin. And how she has the nerve to go to the altar rails every Sunday morning, God alone knows—and He won't split!'

'Oh,' whispered Sarah, 'don't make me laugh, Maggie.'

'Laugh!' said Maggie; 'I wish I could. I'd like to see you laugh until you split yer stays.'

Sarah's weary face took on a sudden glow, and she smiled across the hearth at her friend. 'I've got a funny feeling today, Maggie; as if life was going to change for the better. That is, as if something was going to happen ... perhaps it's only Kate coming home; I don't know ... Oh, here she is!'

The back-door opened and Kate came in, carrying a heavy suitcase. She put down the case, closed the door, and then stood looking at her mother and Mrs. Mullen who had both risen and were staring back at her, with eyes wide and mouths agape.

34

Kate lifted her arms from her sides and smiled at her mother. 'Do you like them, ma?' she asked.

'Name of God, Kate, where did you get them clothes?'

'Do you like them?' persisted Kate.

'Hinny ... you look ... oh, Kate! ...' Sarah could find no words.

'Aye, Kate, you do look luvly. My, I've never seen owt like them before!' put in Mrs. Mullen.

Sarah went to her daughter. They didn't kiss, but stood for a second cheek pressed against cheek. Then Sarah stepped back. 'Where did you get them, lass?' A trace of anxiety showed in her voice.

'Miss Tolmache gave them to me for a Christmas box. Aren't they lovely, ma?'

'Lovely,' murmured Sarah, 'lovely.'

'By! lass, you look like a real ...' Mrs. Mullen had been going to say 'lady', but, on the face of what had happened last year, felt it would be a little out of place; so she added, 'toff.'

'Miss Tolmache had the costume and hat specially made for me, and she took me out yesterday and bought me the shoes. Look at the fur round the bottom of the coat?' Kate held up the bottom of the three-quarter-length mole-coloured coat for her mother to inspect the trimming of dark-brown fur. 'And feel how thick the material is, ma. And look at my hat; she had it made to match, and trimmed with fur too.'

For the moment Kate was not the mother of a year-old child, she was an eighteen-year-old girl, wearing the first new clothes of her life. 'She's sent you a Christmas box, ma, but you're not getting it until tomorrow. And material to make dresses for Annie; oh, and heaps of other things!'

'Ee, Kate!' was all Sarah could utter, for the tears were choking her ... her Kate to be dressed so ... like ... like the class: and she'd never seen any of the class look half so lovely as Kate did. Oh, she was beautiful, beautiful.... Thank God Tim was upstairs.

'You won't half make the tongues wag in the fifteen streets when they see you in the rig-out, Kate.... I think you've fallen on your feet in that place, lass.'

'Oh, I have, Mrs. Mullen! Miss Tolmache is wonderful; and so is Master Rex, and Master Bernard. But, here I am, ma'—she turned to her mother—'talking about my clothes and forgetting all about Annie. How is she?' Kate knelt down by the clothes-basket.

'Now leave her be, Kate, and let her sleep, for she's the devil's own imp when she's up,' said Sarah.

Kate gazed down at the sleeping baby; the dark lashes lay upcurled from the pink cheeks, the silver hair gleamed on the pillow. A rush of feeling, so intense as to be suffocating, swept through Kate; her thoughts encircled her, shutting out all but her desire.... John! John! If you could only see her; she's so like you. Oh, where are you? I must know whether you are at home. I won't make any claim on you, I'll never mention marriage; only I must see you, I must show her to you. I've got a whole week. I'll phone the Jackson's today, they'll know if you're back; you said about eighteen months. And when you see me in my new clothes, and see how different I am in other ways, too....

'My God, listen to that!' exclaimed Mrs. Mullen, in a hoarse whisper, as a hullabaloo sounded through the thin wall of the kitchen. 'Cowboys and Indians! ... Oh, Sarah, hinny, I must be off. See you later, lass.' She patted Kate's shoulder as she hurried out.

'Come on, lass, get your things off and have a cup of tea,' said Sarah.

'Never mind the tea, ma,' said Kate, getting up; 'just look what I've brought. Clear the table.'

She took off her hat and coat, and lifted the case on to the corner of the table. When it was opened Sarah exclaimed, in amazement, 'But, hinny, she didn't give you all that stuff?'

'She did, ma. Look! A chicken, tinned peaches, a tongue, a box of cheese'—Kate named each article as she took it out of the case—'dates, a pudding, a cake....'

'You're sure she gave you them all, Kate?'

'Ma!'

'Oh, I'm sorry, lass. I know you wouldn't touch anything that didn't belong to you; it's only I can't imagine anybody so good.'

'Yes,' said Kate, stopping the process of emptying the case and staring, unseeing, at the picture of Lord Roberts hanging on the wall above the chiffonier; 'it took me a long time to get used to it. At first I couldn't believe that anyone could be so kind and not want something back. I feel terrified, ma, when I think they'll soon die; Miss Tolmache is the youngest, and she's seventy!'

'But the old gentleman must be hale and hearty to look after greenhouses and grow bulbs like them,' Sarah pointed to the window-sill.

'Oh, yes; they are all very healthy, but some day they must die,' said Kate.

'Oh, lass, don't be so mournful. There they are, off to Newcastle to spend their Christmas in an hotel so as to see a bit of life, and you talk of them dying. Folk like that seem far from dying to me.'

'Yes, I suppose so; this is the tenth Christmas they've spent in that hotel. You know, ma, when I set them to the the train this morning they waved to me just like three schoolchildren.... Do you think money keeps you young, ma?'

'I don't know, lass; I only know that work and worry can make you old before your time. But, hinny, don't let's get doleful.'

Sarah looked hard at her daughter.... There was something different about her Kate; it wasn't only that she was taller, it was her manner, and the things she said, and the way she said them.... Kate gave her part of the explanation in her next words: 'I haven't told you, ma, but I've been having lessons.'

'Lessons?' queried Sarah.

'Yes, from Master Bernard. I've had an hour each night. He's teaching me English, how to read and write it, and how to speak it.'

'But, lass, you can read and write better than the next, and you've always talked better than them around these doors.'

'But, ma, this is different; I'm learning grammar ... nouns and pronouns, adjectives and adverbs....'

'Adjectives and adverbs!' Sarah looked at her daughter in amazement. 'But what good is it going to do you,

hinny? Don't let them put ideas into your head, lass ...
you've got to work for your living.'

'Oh, ma, don't worry.' Kate smiled tenderly at her
mother, and touched her rough cheeks with her fingers.
'It's only that you can understand things better when you
can read properly and when you know what books to
read.... Look!' She went to her purse and took out two
sovereigns. 'One from Master Bernard with which to buy
books ... he says he'll know how much I've learned by my
choice of books ... and the other from Master Rex, who
says I've to stuff myself with chocolates and to forget
about the books.'

'Two pounds! Oh, lass!'

'Yes, ma; and here's one of them ... that's my Christmas box to you, and I must keep the other to get the
books.'

'Kate, lass, I'll not take it.'

'Don't be silly, ma; I don't want it. With all my new
clothes and everything, there's nothing I want.... And
I've another bit of news ... I'm getting a two-shilling-a-
week rise next year.'

'No!'

'I am.'

Sarah sat down on the kitchen chair. 'You know, lass,
all the good things are happening together. God's good,'
she added. Then, as if to question the Deity, her thoughts
swung to Tim upstairs. But even the thought of him
could do nothing to dim her gladness this day; it even
evoked a spasm of pity. 'Would you mind, lass,' she asked,
'if I bought him an ounce of baccy out of this?' She
motioned to the sovereign in her hand.

'No,' said Kate, without looking at her mother. 'How is
his leg?'

'Just about the same; it doesn't seem to heal up. The
doctor said he should be in hospital; but you know he
won't go because they'll send him to Harton. The doctor
explained it wouldn't be the workhouse side, but it's no
use, he just won't go.'

'Will he walk again?'

'Oh yes; the bone isn't broken; only the dirt got in,
with him dragging himself home from the docks and

having to wait until the doctor came.'

They both started slightly as a knock sounded on the front-door.... 'That's the doctor, now,' said Sarah, running her hand over her tightly drawn hair and smoothing her white apron.

Kate stood by the table and watched her mother go through the front-room. She felt embarrassed and shy; she had not seen the doctor since a fortnight after Annie had been born, when she sat, swathed in a blanket, before the bedroom fire, and here she was now all dressed up.

The front-door opened and a voice said, 'Morning to you, Mrs. Hannigan.'

Sarah answered, 'Oh, good morning, Father,' in a toneless voice.

The priest entered the kitchen, and the pin-points of his eyes through the thick glasses took in all before him in their slow movement from right to left. They saw the table laden with food, and not ordinary food; they saw the fur-trimmed coat and hat lying on a chair; and, in the centre of the kitchen, dressed in rich cloth and silk, with the fire-light playing on the shining coils of her hair, piled high in no respectable fashion, they saw a tall girl, who had sinned, and who, doubtless, by the evidence of his eyes, was still sinning. The thin lips parted.... 'Well, Kate!'

'Good morning, Father,' said Kate, her colour rising slowly under his cold stare. Sarah had no need to look at the priest's face, or to hear his tone, to know what was in his mind.

'Do have a chair, Father, and have a look at all the lovely things Kate's mistress has sent us for Christmas; and look, Father,' Sarah said, holding out Kate's coat and hat across her arms. 'Miss Tolmache had this costume made, and the hat too. And look at the shoes that she bought, and the blouse.'

The priest did not take his eyes from Kate. 'Your mistress bought you all these things, Kate?'

'Yes, Father.'

'She is indeed kind; a most unusual mistress. No, Mrs. Hannigan, I won't sit down.' He motioned away the chair that Sarah held out. 'Is she a Catholic, Kate?'

'No, Father.'

'No? Then of what religion is she?'

Kate glanced from the priest's face to her mother's, then back to the priest's again. She straightened her back and lifted her head from its respectful droop. 'No religion, Father.'

There was a pause during which the priest and Kate stared at each other, and Sarah tried to signal Kate to silence by the entreaty of her eyes.

'No religion! An atheist! And you are content to work there?'

'They are very kind, Father.'

'So is the Devil, when he sets himself out.'

'They are good, Father!' Kate's voice had risen. 'They are wonderful people; they are better than anyone I've ever known.'

'Kate means they are kind, Father,' Sarah put in anxiously; 'she means . . .'

'I know what Kate means, Mrs. Hannigan,' answered the priest, without looking at Sarah; 'I know quite well. When were you last at confession, Kate?'

'Three months ago, Father.'

'Three months! Father Bailey and I myself will be hearing confession from six until eight tonight. I'm just giving you the times in case you've forgotten, Kate. Perhaps I'll see you at the altar rails at Midnight Mass, and I hope you will have a happy and holy Christmas. . . . And now, Mrs. Hannigan'—he turned to Sarah—'I will go up and see Tim, for, with all his faults, it will be a great sorrow to him not being able to attend Midnight Mass.'

The priest opened the stairway door and his short, spare figure disappeared into the dimness. Sarah watched him climb the stairs, and when he reached the top she softly closed the door and turned to Kate, who stood now, with one foot on the fender and her arm along the brass rail below the high mantelpiece, staring down into the fire.

'Oh, lass!' said Sarah, 'you should have said you didn't know what religion they were; you know what he is. Now, if it had been Father Baily, he'd have understood.'

'Classing them with the devil!' muttered Kate. 'They're the kindest and best people on earth.' She

40

turned to her mother: 'Mr. Bernard talked to me about God one night, ma. And he said if I found faith in God through the Catholic religion, I had to hang on to it with all my might; for the greatest disaster in life was to lose one's faith. And then, him a priest, speaking of them like that!'

Sarah stared at her daughter.... Yes, Kate was changing; she was talking differently already.... A little shiver passed through her, and she uttered a silent prayer that in the change her child would not drift away from her.

'Miss Tolmache said if I wanted to go to mass on a Sunday morning I could.'

'And have you gone, hinny?'

'No.'

'Ah, lass. And he never asked you that ... he likely will when he comes down.' Sarah glanced uneasily at the stair door. 'Look, hinny; go on down to Shields and buy your books.'

'Ma, I'm not afraid of him; I can't imagine now why I ever was ... I'll tell him I haven't been.'

'Oh, God in Heaven, don't do that! He'll tell Tim, and then ... Oh, lass, go on out! I don't want any more rows.'

'But, ma, I haven't seen Annie yet.'

'Oh, she'll sleep for another hour, she was up at six. Go on, lass, and get your books; go on before he comes down.'

Kate looked steadily at her mother. 'All right, ma.' She picked up her coat and hat. 'But why should a man like that be allowed to scare the wits out of people? He's terrified me for years, in fact up to this last few months. After all, he's only a man, ma.'

'Hinny!' The horror in Sarah's voice conveyed itself to Kate, and she said, 'Oh, don't look so shocked, ma; I didn't mean anything.'

'He's a priest, lass,' said Sarah, with as much reproach as she could find it in her heart to use to her daughter.

'Yes, I suppose he is,' said Kate dully. She put on her hat and coat. 'But why should he have the power to frighten people?' she asked, looking at her mother through the small mirror hanging on the wall. 'All right,'

41

she added, as Sarah clasped and unclasped her hands, 'I won't say any more; I'm going.' She turned, and smiled suddenly, a soft, illuminating smile, and, bending forward, kissed her mother swiftly on the lips. 'Ta-ta, ma; and don't worry, I'll go to confession and communion tonight.... But I'll not go to confession to him,' she added, pulling a face.

From the front door, Sarah watched Kate go down the long narrow street; she watched her until she was lost in the muck and gloom of the day. Then, with a sigh, she turned indoors. There was all this food, she had a whole sovereign, she had a present that Kate wouldn't let her see until tomorrow, and she had Kate. It's funny, she thought, as she cleared the table, I had a surprise sovereign last Christmas Eve too.

Immediately Kate was outside, one thing, and one thing alone, filled her mind: how was she going to word her telephone call to the Jacksons. She turned into the main road from which the fifteen streets branched off; walked between the tram sheds and the chemical works, and came to the Jarrow Slacks, with the great timbers, roped together in batches, lying helpless on the mud like skeletons unearthed in a graveyard. She passed the New Buildings opposite, similar in design to the group she had just left, and walked on down the long road connecting East Jarrow and Tyne Dock, past the saw-mill, through the four slime-dripping arches, and into the heart of the docks. She passed the dock gates and stood on the pavement, waiting for a tram that would take her into Shields; and she wasn't aware of standing there, so familiar was the scene and so urgent was the need to make a choice of words for the telephone call. Trimmers stood in groups, a little apart, as befitted their superior position; men gathered in batches, awaiting the choice by gaffers for the unloading of grain or ore boats; strings of coolies, in single file, passed up and down the dock bank, bass bags, full of fish, swinging against their thin, shining legs; sturdy, brass-buttoned captains strolled, with conscious insolence, into the dock offices, or across the road to one of the line of public houses, that stood wall to wall, filling a whole street, even continuing up the dock bank; sailors of all nationalities pushed in and out of their doors; and Kate stood among this seething life, utterly unconscious of anything but her own great need.

Heads were turned towards her; remarks passed between men; women, some of whom knew her, stopped and stared.... That's young Kate Hannigan. You know, her who got dropped last year. Look at the way she's got up! My God, like the Duchess of Fife! It must be a paying business.... A chief engineer, catching sight of Kate as he crossed the road, changed his course and came and stood within a few feet of her, presumably waiting for a tram, his eyes devouring her hungrily.

Even when Kate reached the Shields post office, and had passed her money across the counter, and had waited until her call was through and was directed to the nearer of the two boxes which stood in a corner, even then she was still not clear in her mind what she would say. She was quite used to this wonderful invention, for Miss Tolmache had a telephone, and it was part of Kate's pleasant duty to answer it; whereas at the Jacksons the housekeeper had allowed no one of the staff but herself to touch the instrument.

She heard a buzz at the other end, and a voice said, 'Hello! Who's speaking?' Kate was stricken dumb; it was Mrs. Hanlin, the housekeeper herself. 'Hello!' the voice said again. 'This is the Jackson residence.' Alter your voice; try to speak like Miss Tolmache, said Kate, wildly, to herself.

'Hel-lo!'

'Yes?'

'Er ... is Mr. Herrington ... at home?'

'Mr. Herrington?'

'Yes. I mean, has he returned from abroad yet?'

'Oh yes.' Kate leaned against the side of the booth for support. 'He came home three weeks ago. Who's speaking?'

'I'm ... I'm a friend of his. Is he at home now?'

'At home? Oh no. He's on honeymoon; he was married by special licence last week.... Are you there?'

'Yes.'

'They've gone to America, where Mr. Herrington is going to lecture.... What did you say?... Oh, who did he marry? Why, Miss Scott-Jones, of course, they were engaged before he left for Africa, the year before last.... Can I give his sister, Mrs. Jackson, any message?... Hello!... Hello!'

Kate hung up the receiver and walked out of the booth. An old woman in a long black coat and bonnet touched her arm: 'What's the matter, hinny? Are yer not feeling well?'

'I'm all right, thank you,' said Kate, and walked away.... Oh, John! John!... Miss Scott-Jones! You never said; no one ever said; and she was so ugly. Oh, Holy Mary, help me! He'll never see Annie now. He couldn't have even loved me, after all he said; not even when he.... Oh, I must sit down....

She went into a café, and sat in a corner, with her back to the room, oblivious of the stares and chatter of the Christmas shoppers. She ordered a cup of tea and sat sipping it.... The purpose had suddenly been taken out of living, and the sick hopelessness of the period before Annie had been born returned. Her efforts of the past year had been for nothing; for she admitted to herself now that there had been but one aim in her desire for knowledge; to be different; one aim that made her such an apt pupil and evoked the praise and encouragement of Bernard Tolmache.

She felt very young and helpless; all the magnificent feeling of the morning had fled. She wanted to cry.... She mustn't cry here, she told herself, she must wait until she got home. But then, she mustn't give way there, either; for what would her mother think? She knew nothing about John. She had asked her only once who the man was, and, on her stubborn silence, had not pressed the point. And it was strange, she thought at this moment, that her da, of all people, had said nothing; only glared at her silently. And always his glance had left her and rested on her mother, with an expression for which Kate could find no words to define.... No, she mustn't go home and cry, because it would upset her mother; and she had looked happier this morning than Kate had ever remembered her looking before. She'd have to wait until she was in bed.... And then there was Annie. Gone now was the hope that she would have a da. This disappointment added to her own wretched feelings, and she realised how much she had been banking on that.

She didn't buy her books, but instead took the tram back to Tyne Dock; the Jarrow tram terminus was within a few yards of the dock gates. A tram was in, and she hurried towards it, dodging the groups of men so carefully that she didn't know how she managed to knock the case out of the young man's hand as he, too, hurried towards the tram. Kate's apology was laughingly brushed aside, the young man saying there was certainly nothing to be sorry about. He sat beside her on the long wooden seat. 'Mild weather we're having for the time of the year,' he remarked.

'Yes, it is,' answered Kate.

'I like to see a bit of snow myself at Christmas; don't you?' said the young man.

'Yes, it's more seasonable, I suppose.'

'You're Miss Hannigan, aren't you?'

'Yes, I am Kate Hannigan.' She wished he would be quiet and would stop talking.... It was with relief when she stood up and said, 'Goodbye, and a happy Christmas.'

He was a little taken aback at the coolness of her; he had not expected her to be so composed.... After all, she'd no need to put on airs. Anyway, he'd made a start, and she'd likely be at Midnight Mass tonight.... He stretched his five feet four inches, patted his bow tie, and pulled down his celluloid cuffs. Together with the interested spectators of the little scene, he watched Kate alight from the tram and, lifting her skirt, step lightly over the puddles in the road and on to the pavement.

Now, Kate thought, as she walked slowly up the street, I must say they hadn't the books I wanted, and that I've got a bad head; she'll believe that. But, whatever I do, I mustn't spoil her Christmas.

The front door was ajar. She pulled up abruptly at the kitchen door. Her mother was by the window, with Annie in her arms, and, standing near the table, drawing on his gloves, was Doctor Prince.

The last time Rodney Prince had seen Kate she had looked what she was, a very young girl, and one who had narrowly escaped death. Staring at her now, in unfeigned amazement, he vividly recalled that night a year ago when he had had to put up a stiff fight for her life, only Davidson's help preventing him from losing. How they had worked on her! Now he felt grateful to her for being the medium through which he and Davidson had become such firm friends. And he wondered how he would have got through the past year without Davidson and his wife and the haven the grim-looking house on the Don had become.

But this girl, Kate Hannigan; she looked amazing ... and so utterly out of place in her surroundings.... What was it?... Not only her warm, glowing face, or that hair.... Of course, it was her clothes! Good Lord, she was got up in style; and good style at that!... But where?... A sadness crept into his eyes.... What a pity? Oh, why couldn't some man take her and marry her? ... Instead of that! She was so fresh, so unusually beautiful, and she looked ... yes, unspoiled, in spite of the fact ...

'Good day, doctor.'

'Good day, Kate!' He finished drawing on his gloves. 'You're looking well, Kate.' To himself he sounded pompous.

Sarah came forward; she hadn't missed the doctor's scrutiny any more than the priest's. 'She does look grand, doesn't she, doctor? And it's all thanks to Doctor Davidson for getting her that place; her mistress bought her that whole rig-out for a Christmas box.'

Rodney suddenly smiled. He had heard of the Tolmaches and their kind eccentricities from Davidson. 'You look very smart, Kate.'

'Thank you, doctor,' said Kate, walking to her mother and taking Annie into her arms; the child bounced and gurgled with glee. Kate knew why her mother had informed both the priest and the doctor so quickly of the source of her new clothes, and felt both hurt and annoyed.... I'm not bad ... I'm not, she thought. I could never do a thing like that for money ... or anything, but ... she couldn't even say to herself the word 'love'.

'She's a lovely child, Kate.'

'Yes, she's growing, isn't she?'

'Your mother has her hands full with her, haven't you, Mrs. Hannigan?'

Sarah smiled. What a grand man he was! She had been a little afraid of him at first, but not now. And he loved children; he had even nursed Annie, here in the kitchen.

'She gave me some trouble a year tonight, did this little madam,' he said, bending towards the child and poking her playfully with his finger. Annie opened her mouth wide, showing six white stumps, and beat her fists delightedly on Kate's face. Then, with a swift movement, she bent towards the black head, so temptingly near, and burrowed her two hands in its depth.

'Oh, good lord, you little imp!'

Rodney eased his head towards her and put up his hands, trying to unclasp the tiny fingers.

'Annie, let go this minute, you naughty girl!' said Kate.

'Oh, my goodness!' cried Sarah. 'Who'd have believed she'd be so sharp. Oh, dear me! Pull her off, Kate!'

'No, don't pull her off,' pleaded Rodney; 'you'll hurt her hands.' He went nearer: 'Unclasp one hand at a time, Kate, and I'll hold it.'

As Kate's fingers moved in his hair they touched his, and he felt their cool firmness.

Sarah stood irresolute, her hands wavering.... Not to save her life could she have touched the doctor's hair.

The three of them were so engrossed that they did not hear the knock ... if there had been one ... nor the kitchen door opening.

But when they heard a familiar voice say, 'I'm sorry, Mrs. Hannigan, I'm sure; I didn't know you had company. I'll give you a look in later,' they turned as one.

Rodney screwed round his head to look at the figure in the doorway; his hands were covering one of Kate's. As she turned, their faces were within an inch of each other, with the laughing face of the child behind.

They stared at Dorrie Clarke; and she stared back, genuinely surprised at the domesticity of the scene before her.... By God, she had stumbled on something now! Would you believe it? Carrying on openly like that.... Jesus strike her down this minute, she never suspected it. No wonder the upstart had ordered her about. No wonder! ... Canoodling openly in the kitchen here, brazen as brass the both of them! And look at the way she was got up.... He could spend money on her yet he'd deprive another woman of an honest living.... Big Dixon was the first case she'd had in months, and she wouldn't have got her if he'd had anything to do with it.... Why'd this carry-on not struck her before?... By the God above, she'd make it hot for him! So damned hot he'd be sorry he ever crossed her.

'I'll see you later, Sarah.' Her eyes darted a malevolent glance at Rodney, and she withdrew her grim-lipped, fat face and closed the door.

In making Rodney the father of Kate's child, Dorrie Clarke did not dream that she was defeating her own object; for he would become, for the mass of the people, a lad ... someone human; in spite of him being a toff and different he would be one of themselves; various sections of the poor community would view his action in different lights, but most of them would want his attendance on them ... and the reasons would have horrified some of the more respectable of them had they faced the truth, in their minds; her scandal was to enlarge his practice as hard work would never have done.

'That was Mrs. Clarke,' said Sarah lamely. She had an uncomfortable feeling, although she could not explain why. 'Are you all right, doctor? Would you like a comb?'

'No, thanks, Mrs. Hannigan; I have one.... And, yes, I noticed that was my friend, Mrs. Clarke,' he laughed, as he ran the comb through his hair; 'but we're not on speaking terms. And it's all through you, madam,' he said, pointing the comb at Annie. 'You lose me a friend, then you pull out my hair.... Well, I must be off.'

He took up his case. 'A happy Christmas to you, Kate. And to you, Mrs. Hannigan.'

'A happy Christmas, doctor,' they both said.

As the door closed behind him they looked at each other.

'Isn't he a lovely man?' Sarah said.

'Yes; he seems very nice,' Kate replied quietly.

'I wonder what brought Dorrie Clarke here,' mused Sarah; 'she's no friend of mine.'

'Nor of him, by the look she gave him,' said Kate.

# THE DRAWING-ROOM

A narrow lane off the rural Harton road led to Conister House; at least, to one of the walls which surrounded it. A wrought-iron gate in the wall led out of the lane into the lower garden, a long sloping lawn, studded with ornamental trees. The upper garden, which was also on a slight rise, was another lawn, with a lily pond in the centre and bordered by flower-beds. Shallow steps led from this to a terrace, on to which two sets of broad french windows opened from the house. But so gentle was the rise of the ground and so high the surrounding creeper-covered walls that nothing but the garden was to be seen from any part of the ground floor of the three-storied, red-brick house. This, Stella Prince told herself, was the only thing that made life bearable in this vile town. When they had first arrived in Shields there had been no suitable house vacant in the best end of the town. Some that were offered were open to the gaze of passers-by or of neighbours; these were not to be even considered. So, when she saw Conister House, although not actually in the upper quarter, she felt that, in all this cesspool of ships, coal mines, mean streets and impossible people, this was an oasis. Here, in the summer, she could sit in the garden and write, as undisturbed as if she were a thousand miles away from all this grimness; only the far-away sound of ships' horns penetrated the garden, the soot and smuts which dared to invade it and the house being soon dealt with by two gardeners and three maids. She was determined that if she had to live here it was going to be bearable.

Stella had spent a lot of thought and time on the inside of the house, but most of all on the drawing-room. The walls were of a delicate silver-grey, not a picture marring their virgin surface, and the woodwork was painted black. The windows were draped in long straight folds of dull-rose velvet, and the plain carpet, of heavy pile, was a tone darker. Standing on the carpet, one at each side of the bog-oak fire-place, were two superb Hepplewhite elbow chairs, and two occasional chairs, oozing preserved antiquity, rested nonchalantly at given distances. A Queen Anne walnut bureau bookcase stood against one wall, while a china cabinet of the same period stood against the other. The black wood of the mantelpiece lent a deeper lustre to the three Bow figures which had its long length entirely to themselves. A cabriole-legged settee faced the fire, and opposite the french window, stood a seventeenth-century writing-desk.

The room at any time would have appeared unusual, but at this period of chair-backs, mantel-borders and heavy mahogany it was rebellious. Visitors to Conister House were impressed, as they were meant to be. The order of the room was rarely disturbed. If there were more than six people present, chairs were brought in from other parts of the house, to be removed immediately the visitors had departed . . a little subdued at the splendour and more than a little awed by the creator of it all; for who would think a gentle, fragile creature, such as Mrs. Prince, could arrange a house like that, and give such dinners! But of course, she wasn't just an ordinary woman, no one who wrote poetry was.

Stella knew herself to be absolutely in line with the room; she herself had chosen each article in it, replacing the more homely pieces she and Rodney had chosen together at the beginning of their married life.

She sat now at her desk and read again the letter she had received by the mid-morning post. Her deep-set eyes glowed, and the creamy pallor, usual to her heart-shaped face, was tinged with the flush of excitement.

What would Rodney, who had thought her writing only a pose and who had no belief in her ability, say to this? At first he had called her his clever little girl and had treated her work as a joke, or, at best, as a hobby. But lately he had been absolutely hostile to it; even going so far as to say she spent too much time scribbling, and hinting that there were more useful occupations. She hadn't put the question, 'Such as what?' telling herself she was too wise to make that mistake; one of his answers might have been, 'Raising an adopted family.' She had enough to endure, she thought, without this horror. Of course, had she known that Rodney would insist on practising in these slums, she would never have married him; she had thought it would have been Harley Street at least, and then, perhaps, a title. Her sister had managed that for herself, and she had always been inclined to look down on Annabel. She knew she could certainly have done better for herself than she had done; but it had been the two Prince boys constantly fighting over her that had seemed so exciting at the time, and Rodney had appeared so romantic when he had returned from college with that beard. Still, Frank, she now realised, would have been the more sensible choice, especially since at that time she liked him nearly as much. She felt certain he would have been easier to manage, much easier; for one thing, he was staunch to his class, he had no revolutionary ideas; and for another, she couldn't imagine Frank being beastly in the same way as Rodney was ... Frank was more ... yes ... more cultured; there was a coarse streak in Rodney. Still, she smiled inwardly, she had managed very well to avoid all unpleasantness, such as children. After all, men were such fools, and Rodney, a doctor too, was no exception. In fact, the whole thing was laughable; it paid one to finish off abroad. Of course, the knowledge had been of little use to her there, for she wasn't inclined that way. But it had stood her in good stead since her marriage, and Rodney had never guessed. He had always underestimated her intelligence; it was just as well, in that direction, at any rate.

Hearing the 'chunk-chunk' of his car behind the house, she rose and went out of the drawing-room, across the hall and into the dining-room, opposite. A glance at the table told her everything was in order. She rang a small hand-bell, and when a smartly dressed maid appeared she said, 'Tell cook not to serve dinner for fifteen minutes, Mary.' She returned to the drawing-room, picked up the letter from the desk, and stood near the fire-place, waiting. As she listened to the side-door opening, she was at a loss to account for what she heard. Who on earth was he talking to?

'Here we are, then. Let me take your hat and coat off. What a fine young lady! Now we're all ready.'

When Rodney stood in the drawing-room doorway, holding by the hand a child, the most startling blonde child she had ever seen, her surprise could not have been more genuine had he appeared sprouting horns out of his black head.

'I've brought a little lady to see you, Stella.' He advanced across the room, suiting his steps to the child's.

'Who on earth ... ?' began Stella.

'Now, Annie, say, "How do you do, Mrs. Prince?" Go on; like Kate showed you.' Rodney squatted down beside the child, his head level with hers. Annie gazed at him, her green slant eyes full of trust and adoration; her flaxen hair, dropping straight on to the shoulders of her white, frilled pinafore, lay in little tendrils; her mouth was wide, and when she smiled two gaps showed in her lower set of teeth.

She turned from him, quick to obey his command, and, thrusting her hand up to the very clean lady, said: 'How ... do ... you ... do!' in a soft voice, thick with the Northern accent.

'There! Isn't she a clever girl?'

As Stella's fingers touched those of the child, she thought, 'Of all the impossible incidents! What does he mean?'

Seeing the expression on his wife's face, Rodney straightened himself, and, under pretext of poking the fire, murmured, 'Just thought I'd give her a treat, Stella. Hope you don't mind me bringing her; she waits for me nearly every day at the end of the fifteen streets; it's pathetic. And if you could see where she lives! The surroundings are dreadful....'

'Who is she?'

'Kate Hannigan's child; you know, the one I nearly lost four years tonight ... in fact, I nearly lost the pair of them.'

'Won't her mother miss her?'

'Oh, she's in service in Westoe; I told the grandmother I was bringing her.'

Stella looked at her husband in amazement.... Of all the unorthodox, undignified people! ... 'What do you intend to do with her, now that she's here? You can't let a child run wild around the house!'

Rodney's black brows contracted, and his beard took on a slight forward tilt. 'I intend to give her some lunch!' he answered, in what she termed his stubborn voice.

'Very well! I'll ring for Mary to take her into the kitchen.'

'She's not going into the kitchen!'

'You don't propose to sit her at table with us?'

'That's just what I do propose!'

'Doctor!' Annie was gripping the bottom of his coat and staring up at him, the laughter gone now from her face, her eyes timorous. She sensed the warning element; her granda's voice was sharp like that when he pushed her out of the way or frightened her grandma.

'It's all right, my dear. It's all right,' said Rodney, picking her up in his arms.

Stella's eyes were like pieces of blue glass. 'There is a hand-worked lace cloth on the dining-table; there is cut-glass and Spode! Why, even I wasn't allowed in the dining-room until I was ten, and then only on ...'

'All right! all right!' he snapped. 'Say no more about it.' He walked out of the drawing-room, down the passage, and into the kitchen, forcing himself to laugh and chat to take the look of fear from the child's face. The look had wrung his heart, for he knew that she had had, and would have, many occasions for fear in Tim Hannigan's house; but that she should have it in his was unthinkable!

The three women in the kitchen were not unprepared for his entry, for they had stared, in various degrees of astonishment, some minutes earlier when they had watched him, from the kitchen window, lifting the child from the car. Mary Dixon had simply gaped ... Kate Hannigan's bairn! ... and him bringing it here! Dorrie Clarke mightn't be so far wrong with her hints and 'My, there are things I could tell you if I had a mind!' She hadn't taken much notice of her, for she was a bitter old pig, and a Catholic at that, so you couldn't believe a word of what she said. But now, when you put two and two together ... and all the grand clothes of Kate Hannigan's ... well, what a kettle of fish! ... She looked at the doctor through new eyes.

'I've brought you a visitor, cook. Would you like to give this little lady some lunch?'

'With pleasure, doctor. With pleasure.' Mrs. Summers looked at the dark and fair heads close together; she gave an apt description of them to herself.... He looks like a kindly divil holding a wee angel. It's bairns that man wants; he'd be a different man if he had bairns. But he'll never get any out of that 'un. She's got ice in her veins; I don't need to have fallen seven times to know that. I bet that's what half the rows are over, too....

Annie's lips quivered as she watched the doctor back towards the door. 'I want to come with you.'

'I won't be a minute, Annie; I'm just going into the other room.'

'Will you come back?'

'Of course I will.'

'Now just look what I've got for you.' Mrs. Summers took the situation in hand, and Rodney went out and into the cloakroom off the hall, and washed his hands.... It had been a mistake to bring the child here, but she had looked so pathetic, standing at the end of that grim street, waiting patiently for him to pass down the main road. And on a Christmas Eve, too; Christmas was made for children.... He had had a vision of himself playing with her on the rug before the fire, and perhaps Stella laughing down at them from her chair ... the perhaps had obliterated the vision.... Annie's childish love, born of his kindness to her, had struck an answering chord in him. He wished he could do something for her, make her lot easier without causing comment.... In his dis-appointment at Stella's reception of the child he realised that his intention had been to arouse her interest. There was so much she could do; there were so many like Annie. If only ... Oh, it was hopeless! Every move he made, every suggestion, was tactfully turned aside. . . .

When he re-entered the drawing-room Stella was still standing by the fire-place, her face like a cameo against the black bog-oak. She gave off an air of delicacy, which made him wonder anew at the strength of so fragile a creature. . . . Why had things gone wrong between them? Right from the beginning their temperaments had warred; not only in their physical relations but in their mental and everyday relations there were jarring notes. He wanted children; she couldn't have any. Yet, after having had the necessary examinations, she had been found quite normal. He had seen to it that the fault didn't lie with him; but still, never a mention of one. He had wanted a home, a place where he could at least have a dog, but she had made this beautiful shell. He wanted someone to talk to, someone who could enter into the desolation that was himself, or bring him out of it by their sympathy and understanding. He did not want to be led into the realms of mental phantasy by description of even the most commonplace things, which was the turn any conversation with her took. He liked poetry; but his poets were of a nature, so beefy, or style so simple, as to bring laughing derision on them. If only he and Stella could agree to differ; but this would seem to be the most difficult task of all.

Stella, still holding the letter in her hands, was impatient to give him the news. But she could not do it effectively while the atmosphere of the silly incident still prevailed; so she prepared her ground. 'Rodney, I'm sorry, dear, but children are so awkward. It would have upset us both if she had spilt or broken anything. You would then have blamed yourself for bringing her. . . . Don't you see?' She went to him and held up her face to be kissed. 'There! Am I forgiven for not wanting my Spode to be broken?' she said, laughing up at him. 'You're not angry with me any more? When you are angry you look like a black demon; it's a wonder children aren't afraid of you, instead of waiting at street corners for you.' She had succeeded; he even looked gratified at her playfulness. 'Come on!' she urged, tweaking his nose.

He smiled at her, hope rising in him, anew, and he

began to clutch wildly at straws again. 'I'm sorry, dear, I was nasty. But if you could see how some of those children live; twelve to fourteen people herded together in four rooms. Annie's lucky, in a way, there are only three of them; but she's got a beast of a grandfather. I attended him for eight months when his leg was smashed up. I used to loathe the thought of touching him; he always gave me the impression of being a gigantic snake; it's his eyes, I think. I can never understand how he came to be the father of....'

'Look, darling,' Stella broke in gently, 'Mary's taking the dinner in, and I want to tell you my little bit of news.... Read that!' She thrust the letter towards him, and stood, her hands behind her back, gazing up at him in a little-girl attitude while he read it.

'Why, Stella, I didn't even know you had sent the book away. Oh, I am glad.'

Guessing how much this meant to her, he tried to appear thrilled at the news, thrusting down the dread that it would create another milestone between them. Taking her into his arms, he kissed her. 'Congratulations, my dear.... Well!' he said, reading the letter again while standing with one arm around her shoulders. 'And they would like another at your leisure! I say, you're famous!'

'Rodney, don't be silly!'

'But it's no easy thing to get a book of poems published. Stories, yes; but publishers are very wary of poems.'

'But they are so simple.'

'Simple or not, they like them.'

To Stella's chagrin, she realised that his amazement was not so much at her writing the poems as the publisher accepting them.... Simple or not! he had said. Would Herbert Barrington have given that retort? Never. But in Rodney's estimation Herbert Barrington was an effeminate sop. He didn't know that it was on Herbert's advice that she had sent the book away, and that the publisher was Herbert's cousin. Were she to tell him, he would likely imply that influence was the main factor on which it had relied for publication.... Hiding her annoyance, she smilingly led the way into the dining-room.

In an endeavour to hold fast to the new ground they were on, Rodney burst out, 'This calls for a celebration. Let's go somewhere tonight! We'll dash up to Newcastle; I'll order a table. . . .'

'Rodney!' Stella's voice was patient. 'Do you really mean to say you have forgotten we are giving a dinner tonight?'

'Good lord! So I had.'

'Even with your friends the Davidsons coming?'

'Now, now, Stella. No sarcasm.'

'But I'm not being sarcastic. You are for ever talking of them, so it surprises me that you have forgotten you invited them.'

'I had forgotten about tonight, but only for the moment. I wanted us to have a little fling to celebrate your success.'

'That's very sweet of you, dear, but we'll have to reserve it for another time. Tonight we entertain the locals' . . . all but one, she added to herself.

At her reference to the locals Rodney gave her a quick glance. Then he lapsed into silence; for he knew they were no nearer. Her success had made her more pleasant for a time, that was all, and had saved him from having another dose of her patient suffering that would have surely followed his latest indiscretion of bringing the child to the house.

Another of Mrs. Prince's dinners was drawing to its close. Clara Richards, sitting at her host's right hand, looked down the long, glittering table to where her hostess sat talking to that pasty-looking young man who kept flinging his hands about as though they did not belong to him. Mrs. Richards was inwardly seething. At her last dinner, when the Princes were there, she had served seven courses; it had taken days to look up books and think out dishes. Now that china doll up there had served only five and had everyone exclaiming over them . . . her and her hors d'œuvres, and her finger-bowls and candles on the table. Who was she, anyway? Only a doctor's wife, like herself. And look at him, there, laughing with Peggy Davidson. . . . Looking at Rodney, she wondered what it was about him that had trebled his practice within four years; he had more than half the Tyne Dock patients and all East Jarrow; and then that Lady Cuthbert Harris sending for him right from yon end of Westoe. It was easy for Joe to say she was a neurotic and hoped to get a sensation out of his beard. Joe had lost quite a number of patients lately, mostly women; and why? Well, he certainly wasn't her idea of handsome. It's his la-la manners and haw-haw voice they go daft over, I suppose. Something would have to be done; but what? She didn't know. She certainly couldn't see her Joe mincing around women, and perhaps that was something to be thankful for. She had enough trouble with him, as it was; the money he spent on drink, and with three girls to bring up! Which brought her back to her hostess. . . . It paid you to hold a candle to the Devil. Stella Prince had a sister married to a lord; not one of these newly made ones, either. She had looked up this particular one's lineage, and had been deeply impressed. They had visited here last year, and would likely visit again; and if her girls could obtain an introduction to a lord—well, everything has to start, hasn't it. . . .

Across the table, Peggy Davidson was now listening to Doctor Richards's pompous voice and thinking, How soon can we leave? I hope the kiddies are asleep. But they won't be . . . they'll be playing old Anna up. Fancy having a dinner on a Christmas Eve! Oh, I hate leaving the house tonight; and I've got their stockings to fill. I wonder if we could go about nine o'clock. No, that would be too soon. And it would likely hurt Rodney; he's so anxious for me to be friends with her; but I can't. Still, I mustn't let him see. He sounds very gay tonight, as if he has been drinking. But he seldom touches anything. She cast a quick glance at him. It's all put on; he's not happy. And this house! It's like a showpiece. What he wants is a home. I used to wonder how he could be comfortable in our sitting-room, with the mess it's usually in, but I don't wonder any longer after having seen this.

The rather squeaky voice of the young man broke in upon her thoughts. He had risen and was holding a glass of wine in his hand: 'Ladies and gentlemen! I ask you to drink the success of our gifted hostess. I don't know whether you are aware of it, but our hostess is the author of a book of very fine poems which is soon to be published.'

Rodney frowned. How dare he! Damn him! What right has he, anyway? And how does he know? . . . He came late. It's not likely she's just told him. . . . The muscles in his cheeks worked rapidly.

Amid exclamations of surprise and congratulations, the toast was drunk. Stella sweetly acknowledged their congratulations, and playfully admonished the young man for giving away her little secret. While he was insisting that she read the poems to the company in the drawing-room, Rodney's voice broke in on her pleasure: 'Let's celebrate,' he was saying, looking from Peggy Davidson to her husband. 'What do you say, Peter?'

'Anything you like, Rodney. Suits me.'

'We'll do a show in Shields . . . there's a pantomime on somewhere. . . . That's it, let's all go to the pantomime!' He looked round the table, like an excited boy.

Mrs. Richards nodded laughing assent. . . . Anything, she thought, is better than listening to that madam blowing her horn over a book of poetry. . . .

'A little childish fun won't do us any harm,' said Doctor Richards, easing his stomach away from the table. 'If the ladies are agreeable, I'm for it.'

The plain young woman who had come with Herbert Barrington looked relieved, even animated for a moment.

Herbert Barrington looked at Stella, and she, striving to keep the signs of her anger from her face, looked down the table towards Rodney. . . . How dare he! What did he mean? Breaking up her dinner party like this! And to suggest celebrating her success by going to a pantomime . . . a pantomime of all things! . . . She took a small, cold vow to herself: She'd make him suffer for this, as only she knew how. Her time would come.

'I think we're too late for the pantomime,' she temporised.

'No we're not. It's just turned eight o'clock, and the first house doesn't come out until half-past,' said Rodney, without looking at her. 'If we go now we'll have plenty of time.' With the exception of Barrington, he took in the rest of the company in his glance: 'Don't you think so?'

There were murmurs of assent.

'I think we'll leave the decision to our hostess,' said Herbert Barrington, whose bulbous eyes were sending messages of sympathy and understanding to Stella.

Stella allowed a little expectant silence to pervade the table before graciously answering, 'By all means. If we are all of the same mind, let us go.'

'And you will read your poems when we return?' Herbert Barrington's long white hands hovered before her beseechingly.

Stella smiled at him: 'If you wish.'

The ladies got into their wraps, with the exception of Peggy who was wearing a plain grey coat. There were repeated warnings from Doctor Richards to wrap up well, for there was snow coming and he didn't want any of them on his books. Peter Davidson stood aside in the hall, looking on, the half smile playing on his face. He wondered about Rodney.... Why this sudden burst of animal spirits? He didn't like it. If only he'd come out, and talk about things. Something was worrying him; that was evident.

The party divided themselves into Rodney's and Doctor Richards's cars, and drove off amid laughter. Within fifteen minutes they were in Shields and had parked the cars in some stables off the market-place. The big, open market was thronged with shoppers, a number of them, by the sound of the singing and laughter, three seas over; paraffin flares threw into relief the gesticulating chocolate 'kings', medicine-men and other 'auctioneers'. The party skirted the market and walked down King Street, and ran into a throng of people coming out of the theatre.

'Keep together,' called Rodney; 'first house just coming out.'

Stella shuddered.... He was acting as if he were drunk. But she knew he wasn't drunk; he was doing this just to annoy her ... well!

Having piloted the company to a comparatively clear corner of the vestibule, Rodney said, 'I'll see if I can get a box. Stay there!'

They stood together, awaiting his return, Peter and Mrs. Richards keeping up a bantering flow of small talk. A little distance away a queue for the second house passed quickly in front of the ticket box as the last of the first-house audience were leaving the theatre.

Rodney was near the foot of the staircase talking to the manager—who was assuring him he was very lucky; there was one box left, and it would be a pleasure—when a childish voice shouting 'Doctor!' made itself heard above the din.

Turning quickly, Stella saw the child who had caused her so much annoyance earlier in the day evade the detaining hand of a tall girl and dash towards Rodney.

'Oh, doctor,' cried Annie, hurling herself against his legs, 'I've seen the goose and all the great big eggs and the funny man and the beautiful ladies ... !'

'Why, Annie,' said Rodney, 'you've been to the panto-mime!' He took the hands held up to him: 'Who brought you? ... Hallo, Kate!' he exclaimed, as Kate, accompanied by a stocky young man, pushed her way to his side.

'Good evening, doctor. I'm so sorry,' she apologised.... 'You're a very naughty girl, Annie. Come along this min-ute!'

'Now don't scold her, Kate. Is it her first pantomime?'

'Yes; and she's been so excited we've hardly been able to keep her in her seat.'

Rodney's hands were cupping Annie's upturned face, but he was looking at Kate.... It must be three years since he last saw her. She was much taller.... How fine she looked ... stately; and what a figure! She had been a lovely girl.... She was lovely now, but in a different way, for she had an air about her.... Yes, that was it, she had a strange air about her.... 'How are you getting on, Kate?' he asked her.

'Oh, very well, doctor, thank you.' Even her voice seemed different.

'Still at the Tolmaches'?'

'Oh yes!' She hesitated and cast a swift, sidelong glance at the young man at her side.

The young man looked at her with a possessive glint in his eye, and seemed to stretch himself to reach her height, as he spoke: 'Not for much longer, though; you'll soon be leaving there.... We got engaged today, we'll soon be married,' he said to Rodney.

Rodney looked from Kate to the young man with the aggressive voice, then back to Kate again. 'Congratulations, Kate! I'm so glad.' His hand went out and she hesitantly put hers into it. It was the second time her fingers had touched him, and he was conscious of the fact. Her deep blue eyes, with that soft kindness in their depth, seemed to float mistily before him.

The young man stretched his neck and moved his chin from side to side, and Stella, standing amid her guests watching the scene, was livid with fury. Twice today Rodney had made a spectacle of himself with that child, and now, to stand there in a public place holding that girl's hand! It was just too much. She guessed who the girl was....

'Doctor Prince has met some friends,' Mrs. Richards remarked, to no one in particular; the expression on Stella's face had not escaped her, and she was beginning to enjoy herself.

'She was a patient of my husband's, and, as far as I can gather, is a maid in Westoe.'

A signal look passed between Peggy Davidson and her husband: 'And a patient of mine, too; for one night, at least,' said Peter. 'You know, I always had my eye on Kate Hannigan; she's the best-looking girl in the county. And if it hadn't been for Peggy here getting her hooks into me ... well, you never know!'

Peggy smiled broadly; only she knew how much this great, lumbering man was hers.

Stella looked at Herbert Barrington and slowly closed her eyes. 'Oh, these people!' her expression said.

'I must go and have a word with Kate. Excuse me just a minute.' Peter ambled over to the other group, hoping that his comments had made the scene before them appear more general.... Rodney seemed to be storing up trouble for himself with every step he took tonight....

'Hello, Kate! Hello, Annie!'

'Oh, hello, Doctor Davidson.'

'How are you, Kate? But why need I ask! You're looking fine; and this young lady too!' He patted Annie's cheek.

'For which I have to thank you, doctor.'

'Me, Kate?'

'Of course. I should have never met the Tolmaches but for you.'

'They are grand folk, aren't they, Kate?'

'The most wonderful on earth.'

'Don't you think she's grown into a very grand young lady, Rodney?'

'Very grand indeed!' said Rodney, not taking his eyes for one second from Kate's face. 'And she's going to be married!'

'Married! And this the lucky young man?' said Peter, turning to the man, who now stood a little apart, uncontrolled jealousy burning in his eyes. 'I should know you, shouldn't I? You're a Jarrowite like myself, surely?'

Somewhat mollified by the personal note, the young man replied, 'Yes, Doctor Davidson; I'm Alec Moran. I'm the agent for The New London Insurance.'

'Yes, yes, I thought I should know you. So you and Kate are to be married. Well, I hope you'll both be very happy.'

'And what does my little girl say about all this?' said Rodney, stooping down to Annie. Annie's fingers traced themselves over the white scarf hanging from his neck, as she said, 'Santy Clause is bringing me a doll and a shop.'

'Have you got our box, doctor?' Herbert Barrington's voice broke in, with studied politeness.

'Be with you in a minute,' said Rodney without looking up, his tone expressing total indifference.

'This way, sir,' said the manager to Barrington; 'if you'll just follow me.'

Stella, with neither a glance to right nor left, passed the group at the foot of the staircase. Rodney looked up from Annie's glorified countenance to the cold beauty of his wife, whose displeasure was evident from the point of

her fine kid shoes to the floating tulle on her head. . . .
Great lady, he said to himself; she couldn't be expected
to speak to the common people. . . . His eyes hardened.

Turning to Annie again, he said, 'That's not all Father
Christmas is going to bring you. I saw him this afternoon,
and what do you think he told me? . . . You don't know?'

Annie shook her head, her eyes, like dark green pools,
adoring him.

' "Well," he said, "I'm away off now to Africa to see if I
can get a black baby for Annie Hannigan!" '

'A black baby?'

'Yes, with curly hair.' Peter made accompanying sounds
of delight.

'Doctor, it was most kind of you; it's really beautiful,'
said Kate softly.

'Nonsense!' His eyes came back to her face again.

'We must go now,' said Kate hurriedly. 'Good night,
Doctor Davidson. Good night, Doctor Prince. Say "Good
night, and a merry Christmas" to the doctors, Annie.'

Annie suddenly flung her arms up and around Rodney's
neck; her young mouth pressed on his, and then she
laughed in high delight, 'Your beard tickles.'

'Good night,' said Kate again, forcefully dragging
Annie away to where Alec, now glowering, awaited them
from a distance.

Rodney and Peter walked up the stairs to the circle.
Rodney was strangely stirred by the child's kiss; it opened
the old desire, the ever-present desire for a child of his
own. . . . By God, he would have a child! He would make
her have a child!

'Kate's quite a grand-looking girl, isn't she?' Peter remarked. 'The Tolmaches think the world of her. I heard
old Bernard had ideas for her, but this marriage will
knock them on the head.'

'He looks a surly devil; I can't see her being happy
with him.'

'Oh, I don't see why not; the most odd-assorted couples
generally make the best go of it. Anyway, it's the best
thing for her, and he'll be a father to the child.'

5                                   65

A deep, inexplicable sadness enveloped Rodney ... a new sadness, a new emptiness. For some time now he had felt that he owned nothing, possessed nothing, beyond his work; but it would seem there were still things which could be taken from him.... 'He'll be a father to the child!' he repeated to himself.

# THE RIDE

Peggy Davidson sat hunched up on a lop-sided pouffe in front of the fire between her husband and the dark, sombre man who had, in some strange way, become part and parcel of their joint lives. The busy day was nearly over, and for the past two hours they had sat, talking in spasms or sunk in companionable silence. But as the time of quietude was almost spent and she must arouse herself to get ready for her journey into Jarrow she returned to the attack she had waged on, and off, all evening: 'Why be so pig-headed, Rodney? You have no need to go home. Now, have you? You can telephone Mrs. Summers and tell her you are staying the night, and, as you are coming to dinner tomorrow, doesn't it seem silly to go back to an empty house?'

'Woman, won't you be convinced? You cannot talk me round,' said Rodney. 'If I were to stay, old Peter there would miss Midnight Mass, and there I'd be, sitting in torment, knowing I had imperilled his immortal soul,' he laughed; 'and the face of Father O'Malley would haunt me for weeks afterwards.'

'Isn't he a fool!' said Peggy to her husband.

Peter laughed at the seriousness of her thin face, and nodded.

'Don't be silly, Rodney; there are no Father O'Malleys in Jarrow church. If you met Father Patterson, you'd change your mind about priests,' said Peggy.

'Nothing will make me change my mind about one priest, at least. Do you know, Peggy, I've had three cases of hysteria in children during the past month. And I've traced it all to the fear of Hell and Purgatory that damned priest has put into their little heads. Of course, the parents are staunch Catholics, and they won't have that it is anything to do with the church at all. It's no use trying to explain even the weakest psychology to adults who are eaten up with fear and superstition, which they call faith. That old fellow's got something to answer for, if he believes what he preaches.'

'Now, now! I shouldn't have given you that last drink,' laughed Peter.

'You know what I'm saying is true,' said Rodney earnestly, hoisting himself from the deep, leather arm-chair and leaning forward. 'You two are Catholics, and enlightened ones, at that, but can you honestly say that, at sometime or other, the tenets of the Catholic faith have not scared you stiff?'

'No, of course not!' Peter said. 'You've been dealing with a type of person who would have hysterics in any case.'

'You know, Rodney, I've always found the greatest comfort in my religion,' said Peggy seriously. 'And, honestly, I've never known fear of a priest ... just the reverse.'

'Well, tell me,' persisted Rodney, 'do you believe in Purgatory, as it is preached? Do you believe that some of the poor devils around these towns are to be made to suffer for a period of time after death for the actions they do, named sins, mostly the result of the squalor in which they live? I've yet to meet a delinquent of another religious body troubled by the same fear. It would appear that Catholics can commit sins, any sins, for which they will be forgiven if they obey the rules: mass every Sunday, and confession and communion at least once a year. But let them break the rules, and then comes the penalty—Purgatory, Hell! Their misery of the present is nothing to what's in store for them. I tell you, Peter, the majority are Catholics through fear.'

'It's a wide question, and neither of us knows much about it, but I admit you are right, up to a point,' said Peter, with urbanity.

'No, he's not!' put in Peggy vehemently.

'Yes, he is,' went on Peter quietly; 'but only up to a point. There are a number of people who attend mass mainly out of fear, and it's all to the good; that very fear is a preventative. For what control have the civil authorities over men like Pat Donovan, say? and Danny McQueen of Jarrow? or Micky Macgregor of Shields? and of Tim Hannigan of the fifteen streets? A priest can manage men like these, where a policeman would be knocked flat for looking at them.... I admit it's the old fear of the supernatural; but if they had no fear of something, or someone, if they thought they would not suffer personally after death for their misdeeds now, can you imagine, Rodney, what life in these few towns would be like? Let us hope that education in the coming generations will erase the necessity for fear.'

'But the number of bad hats is few compared with the number of ordinary people; don't forget that, Peter!' said Rodney. 'And, anyway, I'm not concerned with men like McQueen and Hannigan, I'm concerned mainly with children. The religion is crammed into them, the fear is crammed into them; they don't stand a chance.

'You talk of education erasing fears; do you think it will ever be allowed to? When I proposed seeing the headmistress of the Borough Road school and the priest, because I had been called three times in one week to a child of eight who had had screaming nightmares of the Devil coming to take her to Hell, the mother almost had hysterics too, and said, oh, I mustn't go to the school; it was nothing to do with the school, or the church, for she had had the same spasms when she was young—it was her stomach! Stomach, yes; racked nerves playing on the digestive organs! Doesn't that speak for itself?'

'Christmas Eve,' said Peggy, 'and peace on earth; and you two having a theological discussion.'

'Sorry, Peggy. And you, too, Peter. It is very bad form of me, and at this time too. But you've yourself to blame,' Rodney said, wagging his finger at Peggy.

'Carry on, carry on!' said Peter. 'We'll convert you yet.'

'So that's your game, is it?' said Rodney, getting up. 'Well, I'm off!'

'Sure you won't stay, Rodney? The children would love you to be here in the morning.' Peggy made one last effort, 'Come on, do!'

'Temptress!'' Rodney laughed down at her.

'By the way,' said Peter, 'speaking of the children, don't you buy my bairns more expensive presents than I can afford to give them. You have estranged their affections enough already.'

'Oh yes,' laughed Peggy. 'Do you know, Rodney, we listened to Michael and Cathleen talking? They were on about Santa Claus. Of course, Cathleen is well aware of his identity, but Michael is not quite sure; so he said to her, "What do you think Santa will bring us, Cathleen?" "Oh, I don't know," said Cathleen, "but I do know that Uncle Rodney will bring us something worth while. He's the only one who does!" ... Now what do you think of that?'

'See what you've done? Made them mercenaries,' said Peter. 'And we'll have to watch him, Peggy,' he said to his wife, with mock sternness, 'or he'll be giving them talks on religion next, for they are two very scared children.'

'Shut up!' said Rodney.

'Have one more before you go,' laughed Peter, going to the sideboard.

'No more for me, I'm just right. I've had about as much as I can carry,' protested Rodney, 'and I've got to drive a car.'

'Here, drink that! You're too sober for my liking.'

'All right. But, you see, you are judging me by my legs only.' Rodney raised his glass: 'The very best in life to both of you. And thank you for all your kindness to me.'

Peter looked over his glass, his eyes crinkling with a warmth and affection. 'The boot's on the other foot,' he said.

'See you tomorrow, then,' said Rodney, as he got into his coat.

For a moment the three stood on top of the house steps; the sky was high and ablaze with stars, the light of a pale moon was reflected in the river below them. 'Look!' cried Peggy, 'it's started to snow, just a slightest bit.'

'It won't be much,' said Peter, sniffing the raw air. 'Good night, then, Rodney.'

'Good night. Good night. Happy Christmas.'

They watched him drive away; then turned indoors. 'Oh, I could shoot that woman!' cried Peggy. 'It's the second Christmas she's gone off and left him on his own. Her and her house parties and literary dinners! He's so unhappy, isn't he? Doesn't he say anything?'

'Not a word.'

'He looks as if he were burning up inside, and he's working too hard.'

'Well, he's got one of the biggest practices on the Tyne, and it's growing every day. He'll soon have to have help.'

They stood on the hearthrug, shoulder to shoulder, looking down into the fire. A silence held them. The shabby room, with its Christmas tree and paper-chains, was seeped in peace. 'You don't think he knows what they say about him?' asked Peggy quietly.

'Good gracious no!'

'But that's why all the women went daft over him.'

'Yes, maybe.'

'And you still think there's nothing in it?'

'Certain of it.'

'Does he ever speak of her?'

'Kate, you mean? No, never.'

'But he does make a fuss of the child, doesn't he?'

'So he does of Michael and Cathleen. So am I to understand you've misbehaved yourself?'

'Oh, Peter!'

He laughed, and pulled her to him gently.

'I often wonder, though, how he accounts to himself for his sudden popularity,' mused Peggy.

'I don't know,' said Peter. 'But it's certainly not because he's suspected of being the father of Annie Hannigan. And I shouldn't like to witness his reactions should he ever hear it. Of course, he never will.'

Rodney followed the road of the Don, around by St. Bede's church, then past Bogie Hill, past the fifteen streets and the New Buildings, and along the stretch of the East Jarrow slacks. The tide was high and the lights were dancing on the ships at anchor in the narrow strip of the river Tyne, where it left the docks and meandered before expanding between Jarrow and Howden. Tram cars, on their way to Jarrow, clanked by him, full to the steps, and stray groups of people, loaded, inside and out, shambled on and off the pavement in their walk, all making their way to Jarrow. One man, with the coaldust of the pits still on him, clung to a lamp-post for support, a Christmas tree trailing from his hand into the dirt. Going in Rodney's direction were more orderly groups; Midnight Mass bent to the Borough Road or Tyne Dock church, he thought. It said a lot for Peter's argument ... they had a goal of sorts, something to cleave to; at least it made Christmas mean something.

Conister House loomed up vividly before him. No Christmas tree there, no paper chains, no stockings in the morning. He felt a great reluctance to return, and was tempted to keep to the arrangements of a week ago, before the last row with Stella, and drive straight on to Jesmond; the party would be on until four o'clock at least, and he could drive back tomorrow. But that would mean meeting Herbert Barrington. No, it would be wise to keep away from that gentleman, feeling as he did; and if he were to go, naturally he and Stella would have to share a room ... he thought with bitterness of the room she had prepared for herself across the landing. No, he wouldn't go. As long as he could bear it he wouldn't force himself upon her; he had made up his mind on that score, he told himself, adding whimsically that the mind hadn't much say in it at times. She was a devil, he thought, like some evil temptress, a mythological figure, beckoning, then rebuking with disdain.... He prayed for strength for the next time she should beckon.

He had almost reached the Tyne Dock arches when he passed a lone figure, walking with a free stride, the skirts of her long coat swinging from the hips. She was walking in the shadow of the dock wall, but as she passed in, then out of the weak rays of a street lamp he knew she was Kate Hannigan.

Kate Hannigan, and Christmas Eve! They seemed to be linked together. He didn't often see her, but when he did it seemed to be on a Christmas Eve. He would stop and speak to her. Why not? he questioned himself. Why not? She had not married that fellow, after all. Peter hadn't known why; something had gone wrong, but what? He was curious. Anyway, he hadn't liked the fellow. Of course he would stop and speak to her!

Pulling up the car to the kerb, he waited. He swivelled round in his seat and watched her coming towards him. She spoke first, without a trace of embarrassment: 'Happy Christmas, doctor.'

'Happy Christmas, Kate.'

'Thank you so much for Annie's present. But you really ought not to do it; she is being spoilt.'

'Annie being spoilt! Nonsense; you couldn't spoil Annie. Anyway, I get much more fun out of buying the toys than Annie gets in receiving them. It's a part of me that's never grown up. How are the Tolmaches, Kate?'

'Oh, quite well. Only Mr. Bernard's had sciatica rather badly. But it didn't stop him from going away.'

'Where are you off to at this time of night, Kate, a party?'

'No; Midnight Mass.'

'Oh! Yes, of course. Well, jump in and I'll give you a lift.'

Kate looked up at him, perched above her. His black eyes seemed unnaturally bright. He'd had one or two, she thought, or he'd never have suggested such a thing. Imagine how the tongues would wag if she drove up to church in a motor car, sitting beside the doctor.

'Thank you, doctor,' she said; 'but I've never driven in a motor car; I'm a wee bit afraid. And they make such a noise. Traps are more to my liking.'

'You've never driven in a car?' cried Rodney. 'Oh, come on then, Kate; you must, you simply must.'

He drew up his long legs and stepped down on to the pavement beside her. 'Go on, up you get, Kate!'

'No, doctor, no.' She glanced back uneasily up the road. Dim figures were approaching, likely people from the fifteen streets. Anyway, people who would know them both; and it would not take much to set tongues wagging. Oh, why hadn't he just gone straight on? They'd be on them in a minute! ... She was too wise to argue with a man who had had a few. If she persisted in her refusal he'd only stand talking. So she said, 'I'll go for a short drive, doctor, but not to church.'

'Up the Newcastle road then, Kate!' He helped her in; then swung the starting handle vigorously, and hurried around to his seat.

As the car swung out of the main road and up the narrow, steep incline of the Simonside Bank, Kate gasped. Rodney's dark eyes laughed at her. The moon, gleaming on the frost-covered road, reflected a pale light through the high glass windscreen on to her face. She looked dewy and warm, like a soft summer morning, he thought.

'Like it?' he shouted.

'I don't quite know,' she called back. 'Yes,' she turned her head and smiled at him, 'I think I do.'

'Splendid!'

On they sped; past the Simonside school and the little group of cottages, past the Maze Hall and into the open country; only a mile or so from the docks but seeming, in its rural spaciousness and neatly ploughed fields, to be in another world.

'The country looks different from a car.'

'What's that?' shouted Rodney.

'I said, the country looks different from a car,' called Kate, leaning forward eagerly. 'It looks so beautiful in the moonlight, but a little unreal. I feel I'm taking part in a fairy story,' she laughed gaily.

Suddenly Rodney stopped the car. She looked at him enquiringly.

'Kate, don't go to Midnight Mass!' he brought out, with a rush.

'What!' Kate retreated into her seat.

'Let's drive on. Let's talk and laugh for an hour...will you?'

Something in his voice startled her; she leant back, tight against the leather, but said nothing.

God, he thought, what had made him propose that? She would get it all wrong. Hell! Well, why not? What harm was there in taking her for a drive? His wife would likely be sitting in a corner with Barrington at this moment, promising easy seduction, with her eyes. Damn

Stella! But he must make it clear to this girl that it was a
drive he was proposing, and nothing more.... 'Don't
misunderstand me, Kate,' he said; 'please don't misunderstand me. You see, I was going back to an empty house,
and I don't think anyone should be alone on Christmas
Eve.'... Heaven, he did sound sorry for himself, he
thought. 'And there's another thing,' he went on. 'All
these years I've known you, I've wanted to talk to you,
but there's never been the opportunity up till now.'...
He must be drunk, rattling on like this.... 'You know,
Kate, you've grown from a very young girl into ... well,
to say the least, a self-composed woman, and I've often
wondered how it came about. Don't think me rude, Kate,
please.' He looked closely at her. But her long, dark
lashes lay practically on her cheeks, so he couldn't see the
effect of his words. Lord, what a fool he was! This was
Stella's fault, and Peter's whisky.... What was she thinking? ... He gripped the wheel: 'I'm sorry Kate, if I have
annoyed you. I'll turn the car round at the next bend
and take you back. I suppose you have the impression
that you are riding to Hell with the Devil?'

Kate raised her eyes: 'I could be going there in worse
company.'

'Kate, you're not annoyed with me!' He laughed in
relief. 'Am I to drive on?'

She nodded. 'But I must be back in Tyne Dock by a
quarter past one at the latest, doctor.'

'You'll be there on the dot, Kate.' He got out and did
some more winding.

Kate sat up, as if throwing off a cloak. She watched him
through the windscreen. He looked up, and their eyes
met; they smiled at each other.

On past Jarrow, Hebburn and Pelaw the car chunked
in a soothing rhythm. They sat, silent now, just looking
ahead, relaxed against the seats, feeling knit together in
an exciting warmth.

'Shall I stop on the top of one of the Felling Hills?'
asked Rodney; 'where we can survey the world lying at
our feet, as we talk.'

'Yes, if you wish,' replied Kate.

Presently he drew up on the brow of a hill. Far away,

like a strip of shining steel, lay the river. To the right, the town of Felling, its streets of little houses clinging to the hillside, rested at peace under the moon.

Rodney brought the car off the road on to the grass verge of the open hilltop. 'Put this rug around you,' he said, lifting a heavy blanket from the back seat. 'There!' He leaned back and began to fill his pipe. 'We're all set for our talk, now,' he said, giving her a sidelong smile.

'What do you want to know?'

'Oh, Kate, don't say it like that. It makes me feel I'm being rude and inquisitive.'

'If you were inquisitive, you wouldn't be asking me now, you would know already all there is to know; you can't keep your life private in the fifteen streets.'

'No, I suppose not.... Well, the last time I spoke to you, Kate, you were engaged to be married. Something happened?'

'He wouldn't have Annie,' said Kate; 'he wanted me to leave her at home.'

'Not have Annie?' Rodney's voice was incredulous.

'No. He wanted me to leave her with my mother ... for good. But I couldn't give her up altogether, I couldn't do it. If it wasn't that it would upset my mother, I'd take her away now. But to leave her there, all her young life, while I was with someone ... oh, you can see it was impossible!'

'Of course, Kate. And it's just as well you found out in time, isn't it?'

'Yes, and for him, too; for I wasn't being quite fair to him.'

She did not say where her unfairness lay.

'Couldn't Annie stay with you at the Tolmaches?'

'Yes, they offered to have her years ago.... But it's my mother; she clings to Annie and ... me.'

'Of course.... Yes, of course, I can see that.'

'You know, doctor, if I hadn't had Annie I should never have met the Tolmaches, and I daren't think what life without them would have been.... Annie, you, Dorrie Clarke and Doctor Davidson, all leading me to the Tolmaches.'

'Why give Dorrie Clarke credit for a virtuous deed?'

76

Rodney queried.

'Because had she not hurt her leg you would never have sent out for Doctor Davidson, and had he not come I should never have learned about the Tolmaches. Some other girl would have got the place. He told me of it only to ease my mind; he is what Mr. Bernard calls a psychologist.'

Rodney looked at her in silence for a moment. 'Mr. Bernard gives you lessons, doesn't he?'

'Yes,' said Kate, her voice vibrating with a depth of feeling; 'nearly every day, except holidays, for six years, Mr. Bernard has given me a lesson.' She clasped her hands on top of the rug and stared across the hilltop, through the sparsely falling snow, into the star-laden sky where it came down to meet the river.

Rodney, still staring at her, thought, And she has certainly profited by them. It seems incredible.... 'Yes?' he prompted.

'Well, the first year was very hard work,' Kate went on, 'but I kept at it because I wanted to speak differently.' She cast a swift glance at him, half apologetic. 'Then followed a period during which I didn't want to learn at all. But Mr. Bernard encouraged me, and the desire suddenly came not only to speak differently but to think differently. From that time life changed entirely for me. Nothing can affect me in the same way as it did before, nothing!'

'What does he teach you?'

'Oh, mostly English, and appreciation of literature. He was a lecturer in English at Oxford, you know.'

Rodney nodded, his eyes riveted on her face.

'I'm doing German now, and I've done quite a bit of French. I can read French works—Honoré de Balzac and...' She turned towards him, her blue eyes darkly bright with excitement. 'You are the first one, doctor, I've been able to talk to about it, other than the Tolmaches. Can you imagine what it means to me?'

He didn't answer, but continued to stare at her, his pipe held within a few inches of his mouth.

'To leave the fifteen streets,' she went on, 'and live with those three people, day after day, to listen to them talking, to eat at the same table.... Yes, I eat at the same table. Can you believe that?' Her face was serious and her voice questioning, but still he didn't answer. 'And I know of people like Edmond Gosse, the critic ... well, more than I do of you and Doctor Davidson. Mr. Bernard has promised to take me to the House of Lords some day. He is a friend of Mr. Gosse, who is librarian there. Do you read his articles in *The Sunday Times*?'

Rodney shook his head.

'Then there's Swinburne and Robert Louis Stevenson, and Reade, men I'd never heard of. And I've read everything I can find of Steele and Addison. I've even read Gibbon's *Decline and Fall of the Roman Empire*.' She was excited now, her hands clasped tight. 'Every evening I read aloud to Mr. Bernard; I'm reading Lord Chesterfield's letters now, Mr. Bernard likes their style. But I think Lord Chesterfield would have been a very dull man to live with; he didn't like laughter, did he?'

'I don't know, Kate, I've never read him.'

'Do you know what we are going to do in the New Year?' she asked him eagerly. 'Read Shakespeare, the four of us. We are to take so many parts each. *King Lear* first; there are nice long speeches in that for Mr. Bernard to get his teeth into. Then *The Taming of the Shrew*. I am to speak Katherine's part; I've already read it over and over again.'

'*The Taming of the Shrew*?' cried Rodney. 'Why, Kate, what do you remember? ...

'I say it is the moon.' He made a dramatic gesture through the windscreen.

'I know it is the moon,' answered Kate, her face aglow.

'Nay, then you lie; it is the blessed sun,' said Rodney.

'Then God be bless'd, it is the blessed sun:
But sun it is not when you say it is not,
And the moon changes even as your mind.
What you will have it nam'd, even that it is;
And so, it shall be so for Katherine.'

They turned to each other, laughing like children, their bodies swaying back and forth.

'How splendid of you to be able to quote so pat, Kate! I played Petruchio when I was at college. Oh, that was

78

good! But, Kate,' his voice lost some of its merriment, 'what are you going to do with all this learning? Stay on at the Tolmaches?' He didn't add, as a maid, which was in his mind.

The laughter died out of Kate's face. She looked soberly ahead again. 'That seems to be the trouble. You see, I'm not in the least ambitious. I'm quite content to go on as I am, cooking, and cleaning and learning. Mr. Bernard wants me to take a course in teaching, but I don't want to be a teacher; I want ...' But she couldn't put into words what she wanted. Even as thoughts they were kept firmly in the background of her mind. Impossible to say to him, 'I want a home of my own, as near the Tolmaches as possible, and to see Annie grow there ... and ...' the deep, deep thought ... someone to love and be loved by, someone who would think on the level of the three people she adored, yet would be young and warm and ardent, demanding of her all she had to give, freeing that burning that made her body restless ... the feeling that could only be brought about by marriage; there could be no more Annies. No, no! That fear kept the thoughts in check and quietened the urgent demands of her body....

'What do you want, Kate?' Rodney asked quietly.

'Oh, I don't know,' she said, shaking her head. 'I only know I can't bear the thought of leaving them. They are all set on this teaching business because they think it is for my good, but in their hearts they don't really want me to go: You see, doctor'—she turned towards him again— 'if I left there now, I'd never go back. From a training college I'd naturally go on to a school. One, two, three years ... and any one of them might die at any minute. This seems to be my daily bread, their dying.... And Mr. Bernard, what would he do if he hadn't me to teach? He'd still have his books; but he's taught all his life, and finding someone as ignorant as I was, and eager, and right to hand, was like new life to him.'

'I couldn't imagine you ever being ignorant, Kate.'

'Oh, I was. I am still.'

'I won't argue that point,' said Rodney.

'I have so much to learn,' said Kate, 'and time goes so quickly. Every week now a discussion takes place on what

I must do. I tell them that I have no other ambition but to work for them. And they talk at a great rate and say how silly I am; and Miss Henrietta says I have the slave complex and that she must write to Mrs. Pankhurst about me. Yet I know in their hearts they are glad ... and, oh, how happy that makes me! You can't imagine how it feels to be liked by them; I seem to belong to them, I sing all day!' she ended, on a joyous note.

'Kate,' said Rodney, bending towards her, his knees pressing against the rug covering her, 'where did you get all your wisdom from?' He brought his face close to hers, in the dim light. 'You know so much not culled from books. It's in your eyes, a great kindliness enveloping all you look upon. You would have that wisdom without learning; no wonder they don't want to lose you.'

She made a little inarticulate sound.

'That's why I've always felt drawn to you. We must talk often, Kate; you make me feel the world is a good place to live in.'

She gave a start as though something had leapt within her; her eyes grew larger for a second as she gazed back in the black pools before her. In the silence of the hushed night they heard their own laboured breathing. . . . She spoke suddenly, with a startling crispness, and he was aware of the rebuke in her voice: 'I have no wisdom, doctor; I want to stay there from gratitude to them. They took me in, knowing I had just had an illegitimate child.' She paused, as if to make him recall this fact. 'They treated me with kindness and courtesy from the very first moment I entered their house. If I work for them until I die I'll still be in their debt.'

'You're purposely misunderstanding me, Kate. Don't be alarmed or afraid of me.' He felt for her hands and gripped them, stopping their withdrawal.

'I'm not, doctor.'

'Yes, you are.'

She was silent.

'We could be friends, Kate.' The dark appeal of his eyes made her catch her breath.

'Doctor, that's impossible, and you know it is. I should

never have come with you tonight.' She moved her head restlessly.

He gazed at her averted head, and found himself on the brink of a chasm, so full of warmth and loveliness that the desolation of his life appeared blacker than ever before.... He would persuade her.... But what of Stella?... Well, what of her? He didn't owe her anything. If he were drawn into the ecstasy of beauty that was Kate, what would it mean? Hole in corner? The term struck him like a cold douche; the fastidious part of him reared its head.... No, he had always been against affairs of that sort; hole-in-corner affairs which had aroused his disgust in others, even while sympathising with them. He drew away and settled in his seat again. He was shaking slightly, and his voice betrayed it: 'You're right, Kate; and I'm sorry. But don't let us spoil this hour, it has been so good up till now. Tell me more of yourself; or Annie. Have you any plans for her?' He fumbled at relighting his pipe.

She didn't answer. And when he cast a quick glance at her, she said dully, 'I'd like her to go to a good school.'

'Are you going to send her to a convent?'

'No. You see ...' she hesitated; then went on, 'I'm even afraid to put my thoughts into words. I never have done yet ... but ... well, I want to take her away from the Catholic school.'

'Really, Kate!' Rodney stopped ramming his pipe in surprise. 'Why?'

'You wouldn't understand as you're not a Catholic. It's religion, religion all the time. Learning takes a second place, especially in the elementary schools. And then there's the fear....'

'Fear, Kate?' He seemed to have forgotten the personal issue of a few minutes ago, and was the professional man once again. 'You think that the religion frightens the children, then?'

'Well, not exactly the religion; because if all the priests were like Father White and Father Bailey and all the teachers were like Miss Cail and Miss Holden you couldn't imagine being frightened. But it's the priests like Father O'Malley and teachers like the headmistress

6                                    81

of the Borough Road school who instil fear into you; and I don't want Annie to be afraid as I was.'

'Go on, Kate; tell me how it affected you. I'm very interested, as I've had a few cases of children being afraid of Hell this past month.'

Kate seemed relieved, and begun to talk as if recently the beating of her heart had not threatened to suffocate her: 'That was my main fear, too. After my first confession, at the age of seven, I had the idea that hosts of people in Heaven were watching my every move and would report to God on all my misdeeds, and so I would be sent to Hell. I used to placate them, one after the other—the Virgin Mary, Joseph, St. Anthony, St. Catherine, St. Agnes—and instead of getting relief by going to confession Father O'Malley made it worse, a thousand times worse. After being told I'd end up "in Hell's flames, burning", I had a mightmare. I dreamed that I was thrown into Hell, falling through layer after layer of terrible blackness, with things in it, not seen but felt, until I reached a red, gaping void. For years that dream recurred, and sometimes, even now, it comes back.'

'Are you still afraid?' asked Rodney.

'No, not really; althought at times I am haunted by vague fears for which I have no explanation. Do you know, I have never prayed to God in my life until recently. The Tolmaches, who practise no religion, have really brought me nearer to a knowledge of God than I have ever been before.'

'Not prayed to God!' exclaimed Rodney. 'To whom did you pray, then?'

'The Holy Family, the saints, the martyrs.'

'But what about Jesus, Kate?'

'Jesus? ... Well, Jesus was more frightening than the rest, for he was dead, dead and aweful, so dead that no resurrection could ever bring him to life again. Every Sunday, in church, I sat opposite to him, a life-size Jesus, just taken down from the cross, his limp body trailing to the ground from his mother's arms, his blood realistically red and dripping from his wounds. He was naked but for a loincloth, and all his body had that sickly pallor of death. He was quite dead, and Easter Sunday could do nothing to bring him to life again.'

'Good heavens, Kate,' exclaimed Rodney, 'do you think the statues make the same impression on most children?'

'No,' said Kate. 'Some don't seem to mind. But I know I did, and I don't want Annie to suffer in the same way. So that's why I want to take her away from the school and the Borough Road church. But I'll still send her to a Catholic church, for they don't all have such gruesome statues as in the Borough Road church. But whatever I do it's going to be difficult, because as long as she's at home there's my da—father to contend with.'

'Kate, stick to the decision you have already come to in your mind,' Rodney entreated her. 'Don't let your father or anyone else turn you from it. I should hate to think of Annie's little mind being tortured like that. And if there's anything I can do to help you with Annie, Kate, you know I will; I'm very fond of her.'

'I know that, doctor. You have always been so good to her, and I am very grateful. But it's my father and Father O'Malley I'll have to fight. If only I could take her away; but I can't. I can't hurt my mother, she's suffered so much. Everything is so difficult.'

Rodney sought an answer to a question he was asking himself: 'Why were you going to Midnight Mass, Kate, feeling about things as you do?'

Kate considered a minute: 'Habit, I suppose, and ... yes, because a part of me is attracted by the mass and, I feel, always will be. There is a lot of beauty in the religion, if one were allowed to look at it without its coating of Hell and sin. I have thought a lot about it, lately, and I think more care should be taken over the choice of priests. Quite a number of them lose more Catholics than they convert. But my real reason for going tonight was to keep the peace at home; it makes things easier for my mother.'

'Does she go?'

'No, her legs are so bad. What is really wrong with her legs, doctor?'

'It's dropsy, Kate.'

'Is it very serious?'

'Well, she needs a lot of rest; she should keep her legs

83

up as much as possible.'

Kate sighed, and they were silent for a moment.

Rodney looked at his watch: 'Time's getting on, Kate. Let's get out for a moment and take a breather on the hill, eh?'

She nodded. He got down and came round the car and helped her to alight. As he touched her, back floated the warm, disturbing feeling. He stood near her, on the road, and looked at her face as she gazed up into the sky and inhaled deeply. His throat felt tight, his muscles gathered into knots in his arms, he moistened his lips; her face, pale and lovely, began to draw him, as if over a great distance. He was saying to himself, 'It's no good; I want her, and I'm glad I want her,' when her voice recalled him to himself: 'There's a car coming over the hill,' she said, with the crispness of tone she had used before.

He turned and looked at the oncoming car and sighed heavily. Then, taking her lightly by the elbow, he led her on to the hill.

Two of the occupants of the passing car watched Rodney and Kate, shoulder to shoulder, walk over the sparkling grass. They craned round until the figures disappeared into the shadows and blurr of the hillside.

Mrs. Richards was the first to speak: 'Upon my word! I would never have believed it if I hadn't seen it with my own eyes. At one o'clock in the morning! What do you make of it, Joe?'

Doctor Richards, the look of surprise still on his face, settled himself further into his seat. 'Well, what can you make of it?'

'That was the Hannigan girl, wasn't it?' said Jennie Richards, leaning forwards from the back seat towards her mother. 'The one Miss Tolmache dresses like a duchess.'

It's a question as to who dresses her, Mrs. Richards thought; but she said aloud, primly, 'Whether it was or not, you keep your mouth shut, Jennie.'

'Oh, don't treat me as a child, mother,' said Jennie petulantly. 'Why, it's common knowledge that Doctor Prince is the father of her child! And he certainly makes

84

no secret of it; he takes the kiddie all over the place in his car.'

To the peril of them all, Doctor Richards swung round in his seat, his head nearly colliding with his wife's.

'Look where you're going, Joe!' she cried. 'Do you want to kill us?'

Turning back to the wheel, he asked over his shoulder, 'Where did you hear that?' ,

'I heard Bella talking to cook ... oh, ages ago.... Mary, the Prince's maid told her.'

'Good God!' said Doctor Richards. Mrs. Richards said nothing; she was thinking of two years ago tonight when they had all gone to the pantomime.

# ANNIE

Annie opened her eyes slowly. She was surprised to find she had to open them, for the last thing she could remember was sitting up in bed, feeling very frightened after having shouted at her granda. Her mind cleared of sleep at once, and the frightened feeling returned; but not so badly, for it was morning now and she could hear her grandma moving about downstairs.... Things didn't frighten you so much in the daytime as they did at night, and although she was always afraid of her granda, the feeling became a choking terror in the night when she heard his voice muttering and grumbling at her grandma. She had never before heard her grandma's voice from the other room until last night, and it was this that had made her shout out. Her granda's voice, low and terrible with menace, had come to her through the thin wall, causing the little body to stiffen on the bed; then her grandma's voice, thick and full of something that struck greater terror into Annie's heart, had cried, 'Don't! Oh, don't! I won't! I won't!' It was then she could bear it no longer, and she yelled, 'Leave her alone, granda! Leave her alone!' A terrible silence had followed, and she had sat, paralysed with fear, waiting for the door to open. And now it was morning, and it was Christmas Eve....

A little shiver of ecstasy passed through her, sweeping fear and all thought of last night away. Bringing her knees up, she curled into a ball and put her head under the clothes, a favourite position when she wanted to think something nice.... Tonight she would hang up her stocking, and their Kate would be home today, and at half-past eleven she would see the doctor, and perhaps he'd have time to give her a ride.... She gave a succession of shivers and hugged her knees tighter.

When her grandmother gently turned back the clothes, Annie's green eyes laughed up at her, her lashes curled like a dark smudge under the line of her arched eyebrows, her delicate-tinted skin flushed with her own breath. Her grandmother straightened out the strands of tumbled, silver hair that had escaped from one plait, and arranged, with little stroking movements, the fringe on her forehead: 'Come on, hinny; it's time you were up.'

'It's Christmas Eve, grandma!'

'Yes, hinny, it's Christmas Eve.'

'And Santa Claus will come tonight!'

'He will that, my bairn. But come on, get up now; and hurry.'

No word of last night, but the sight of her grandma with her sleeves down brought it all back to Annie's mind. She didn't expect her grandma to make any reference to it, for it was an unspoken understanding that granda was not mentioned in any way.... Yet with her shouting out like that, she thought perhaps her grandma might have said something; and she couldn't remember seeing her grandma with her sleeves down before. But other strange things had happened like that after her granda had shouted at her grandma; such as the time when she wore a scarf for weeks in the summer; and there was the time, too, when her finger was bad, and she had kept it wrapped up; and when it had mended it was crooked.... She looked searchingly into her grandmother's face, but the pale eyes, with little wrinkled bags beneath them, crinkled at the corners reassuringly.

Annie put her arms around her neck and kissed her: 'Have I to put my clean vest and bloomers on?'

'No, not until tomorrow, hinny. And come on, now, and hurry downstairs and get washed.'

When Annie was told to hurry downstairs and get washed it meant her granda was coming into breakfast at half-past eight from the long shift, and that she must be ready and have had her breakfast and be sitting quietly while he ate, or go out to play, or down the yard.

She washed in the bowl that stood on the backless chair in the two-foot recess between the kitchen door and the cupboard. Her grandma had given her hot water with which to wash, and she would have liked to play about, but she knew that she mustn't. Standing before the fire that held the big black frying-pan with her bacon and fried bread sizzling in it, she put on her vest and bloomers, her one calico-topped petticoat, her flannel one, her blue woollen dress and her white, frilled pinafore. Then she sat down at the table and said her grace.

When she had finished her bacon and had wiped up her dip with a piece of oven-bottom cake, keeping one eye on her grandmother while she did it, knowing that this was one of the things that Kate said she was not to do, and which her grandmother reluctantly enforced, she again said her grace and left the table. The fire looked inviting, and she would have liked to have sat before it on the fender and read one of her story books until it was time to go and meet Kate. But, again remembering last night, she hurriedly got into her thick reefer coat, pulled on to her head a red woollen hat with a pom-pom on the top, picked up her gloves, and kissed her grandmother.

'Keep on the dry parts, hinny,' said Sarah; 'and don't play with the snow, it's too dirty now. You must keep yourself clean for Kate coming, you know.'

Annie nodded and hurried out, down the yard and into the lavatory, just as the back-yard door opened and her granda clumped up the yard. She gave a little sigh, shot the bolt and got on to the seat. And then the safe feeling crept over her, the feeling she always had when she was in here. No one could get at you here; it was quiet, like a little square house, all red and white, and you were tight locked in.

The red bricks of the floor, the whitewashed walls, the white wooden seat extending right across the breadth of the lavatory and filling half its depth, was a place of sanctuary for Annie. There were rarely any bad smells here, for her grandmother kept it fresh with ashes down the hole, and daily scrubbing. The only time Annie got a violent distaste for it was when the men unexpectedly lifted the back hatch to clean it out with their long shovels. Then a revulsion for it would overcome her. She didn't like the scavengers, nor would she follow the cart with her companions, shouting:

'*Cloggy Betty, on the netty*
*On a Sunday morning ...*'

She never looked at the men, they were so filthy; but she felt pity for the bushy-footed horse, and had wild visions of herself unharnessing it and letting it away.

She heard a scramble of feet in the Mullen's yard, next door. Their back-door banged and her own opened, and a plaintive voice chanted up the yard, 'An-nie! ... are-ya-comin' out? ... An-nie! ... Are-ya-comin' out?'

Quickly scrambling out of the lavatory, she joined her friend, and marshalled her with unseeming haste out of the yard into the back lane.

'I didn't know yer granda was in, Annie,' said Rosie Mullen, apologetically; she hadn't asked for an explanation of the hustle; she knew all about Annie's granda, in some ways much more than Annie did, as her parents were outspoken in their comments on their neighbour. Rosie was two years older than Annie, but much shorter. She was a replica of her mother, being dumpy and fat, with small, bright eyes and a round face. Her dark hair stuck out in two-inch plaited points from behind her ears. She looked ugly and quaint and likeable, and Annie had a deep affection for her, for which Rosie was grateful, although she didn't know it; she only knew that Annie Hannigan was her best friend, and if the girls said things about her granda that made Annie cry she punched them in the chest or slapped their faces.

'I've got to take our Nancy out in the pram,' said Rosie, in disgust. 'That'll mean I can't go with you to meet your Kate.' Which would also mean she would miss either some sweets or a ha'penny.

'Oh, well, I haven't got to go till half-past ten, so we can take Nancy round to the shop and have a look in,' said Annie; and, with great intuition, added, 'and I'll keep you half of whatever our Kate gives me.'

Rosie grinned broadly, and, taking hold of Annie's hand, dashed with her into their backyard, seized the big, dilapidated pram, in which a two-year-old child lay sucking a dummy, and pushed it out into the cobbled back lane, down which they hurried, the pram tossing about like a cork on the ocean, past seven back doors with their accompanying coal and oozing lavatory hatches, round the bottom corner, across a piece of waste land where children were already playing among mounds of dirty snow and wet, brown grass, and into the front street of the houses opposite their own. About half way up, one of the houses suddenly changed its pattern; above its window a large, yellow tin placard said, DRINK BROOKBOND'S TEA, and a gay old gentleman, on another piece of tin, asked you to look at him to see how fit he kept on ALLY SLOPER'S SAUCE. The house window itself held tier on tier of bottle of sweets receding away from the gaze of the beholder to dim regions beyond, while, balancing on the front of every shelf, were boxes of hearts-and-crosses, sherbet dips, everlasting stripes, scented cachous and jujubes. In front of the window were large jars of pickled cabbage and pickled onions, and seven-pound jars of loose jam and lemon curd. Among these, at crazy angles, were placed Christmas wares of 'Shops with real scales', dolls in the minutest of gauze chemises, work-boxes, miniature boxing-gloves and tram-conductor sets of hat and ticket puncher. Paper-chains hung in loops from the ceiling, together with huge red and green paper bells, of a honeycomb pattern. From the chains and bells, held by fine threads, dangled swans, balls, dolls, ships and fairies, all in fine glass and painted a variety of colours.

Annie and Rosie pushed the pram against the wall and joined two other children, who were endeavouring to get a first-hand view by hanging on to the high window-sill by their elbows and sticking their toes into the wall. . . . 'Ooh! ain't they luverly?' said Rosie, gazing in rapture at the display.

'I'm getting a great big doll,' said the taller of the two girls in front, jerking her head round.

'Oh, you! You are always saying that, Cissy Luck!' snapped Rosie, without taking her eyes from the chains and their dangling splendour.

'I am, ain't I, Peggy?'

'Yes, she is,' said her companion; 'and she's going to take me into their house to play, ain't you?'

'Yes,' said Cissy, pursing her lips, 'and she's going to play with my doll the morrer.'

There was a questioning silence while the two girls turned from the window and confronted Annie and Rosie. When no further remarks regarding the integrity of her statements were forthcoming, Cissy said to Annie, 'Whatcher getting in yer stockin'?'

Annie, whose eyes, like Rosie's, were fixed upon the magic array behind the glass, answered abstractedly, 'Oh, I don't know yet, not until Santa Claus comes; I've sent him a letter.'

Cissy and Peggy exchanged sidelong, incredulous glances. Then, suddenly throwing their arms around each other, they shrieked with laughter.

'You gone barmy?' asked Rosie, looking at them stolidly.

Annie smiled, feeling that she was the source of their enjoyment, but not knowing why.

'She says ... she sent 'im a letter,' spluttered Cissy into her friend's neck.

'Well, what about it?' demanded Rosie, her square jaw thrust out. 'Ain't nowt funny about that.'

The other two suddenly turned on her, their faces aggressive with knowledge; 'She's a silly bitch! There ain't no Santa Claus; it's yer ma and da,' said Cissy.

Rosie blinked rapidly; she knew this to be the truth, but, glancing at Annie, something in her friend's face caused her to deny this statement hotly: 'You shut yer mouth up! There's a picture of Santa up there,' she pointed into the window. Then, grinning broadly at Annie, she said, 'That must be a picture of Cissy Luck's da!' This sudden piece of wit sent her off into loud guffaws, to which Annie joined her high-pitched laugh.

Cissy's face grew dark, her eyes narrowed, and her loose, lower lip pouted. She took a step forward, not towards Rosie but towards Annie.... This Annie Hannigan, with her thick lashes and fair hair, her big top coat and her woolly hat with the red pom-pom, who was she anyway? She wanted to destroy her, punch her face, kick

91

her, hear her yell; but there was Rosie Mullen, you had to be careful with Rosie Mullen! 'What you laughin' at?' she demanded of Annie. 'Laughin' about my da! You're the one to laugh, you are! You ain't got no da, like Santa Claus nor nobody else, so there! Me ma said so.'

The eyes of the four children darted from one to the other, following this startling announcement. Annie's face showed utter bewilderment. She made a mute appeal to Rosie, but Rosie was for once tongue-tied and hid her embarrassment by a sudden and violent rocking of her pram, to the delight of the youngest Mullen.

Annie's voice did not sound convincing to herself, when she heard it, for there were dreadful new fears attacking her, and, rising to the surface of her mind, hazy and troublesome impressions that weren't new: 'I have got a da, you know I have. I've got a da and a ma....'

'Don't be daft!' cut in Cissy. 'That's your grandma and your granda; we've all got grandmas and grandas. But you've got to have a ma and a da too, and you ain't got any.'

They stared at each other in silence; then Annie's head dropped slowly forward. A terrible emptiness was creeping over her, and a longing to fly away and never see Cissy Luck or anyone else ever again, to hide for ever and ever. But where could she go? The new fears were growing bigger every minute, like the dream she had in the night of the lion going to swallow her up. The fears were like that.

Peggy put her arms round Cissy and whispered into her ear, and Cissy, after listening intently, seemed to grow with new power. Her next announcement brought Annie's head up with a jerk: 'Your Kate's your ma, so she is,' she cried.

Denial sprang to Annie's lips, but was checked by another fear, a fear that stripped Kate of wonder and made her into a ma. Her world was suddenly topsy-turvy; she must get away, fly from everyone. 'I've got to go ... I must go ... I'm going to the lavatory,' she stammered at Rosie. 'But I'll come back.' And, turning, she flew down the street, around the corner, up the back lane and burst into the yard and into the lavatory. When she had shot the bolt she didn't sit down, but stood with her back to the wall, her hands behind her, her bottom pressing her palms into the rough-edged bricks until she could feel the points through her woollen gloves.... They said she hadn't a da; what could she do? Where was her da, then? Should she go in and ask her grandma about it? No. Some instinct told her that it would hurt her grandma. Then, could she ask Kate? ... She dropped her head and stared at her shoes. A queer sense of shame, inexplicable, filled the lavatory, flowing over into the yard, the house and all the world of her knowledge. There was no place it did not penetrate. Great tears rolled down her cheeks, dropping heedlessly from her chin.... She had no da; was that why her granda didn't like her, and never called her Annie, but ... that one, or that funny name that sounded like ... bedstead?

But you must have a da; Jesus had given everybody das; you couldn't be borned unless you had a da.... And if Kate was her ma.... But her mind switched away from Kate; Kate was mixed up with something so painful that it hurt.... Where was her da? ... She remembered Alec. No, he wasn't her da. He had been going to marry Kate, and she was glad he hadn't. No, he couldn't be her da ... Well, who was?

She began to pray: 'Oh, please Jesus, tell me who my da is.' Raising her head, she looked up as if the answer would be found in the air above her, and she licked her tears, savouring their saltiness as she waited. But no answer came.... It must be right, then, what they'd said, she wasn't like other girls. What could she do? Nothing! Nothing!

In fresh despair she turned to the wall and buried her face in her hands. Through long practice, she cried quietly, and when, eventually, she stopped, she sat on the edge of the lavatory seat wondering what she could do about this dreadful shame which had come upon her; for she had no doubt but that it was a shame. Then the solution came; like a streak of dazzling light it flashed into her mind, bringing with it the remedy. Although it would be only 'making on' it would be wonderful, for she'd have a da. Though her choice was already made she felt she must arrive at it by a process of elimination.... She was going to 'pick' a da for herself! None of the other girls could do that, could they? Now, who did she know? There was Mr. Mullen, next door; he was kind and nice ... but he swore awful. No, he wouldn't do; and besides he was a da eight times already. Then there was Mr. Todd, the coalman; he always heaped her buckets so full she could scarcely carry them into the yard ... but he spat, didn't he? Of course, it was with sitting in the middle of the coal-cart all day that made him do it ... but still, he spat! Then there was Patrick Delahunty, the big Irishman who had come to lodge up the street; he always stopped and spoke to her, and he sometimes gave her and Rosie a penny. Yes, he was nice, but ... !

Then there was the doctor! She shivered, and joining her hands together, pressed them between her knees. She turned her head and gazed at the wall, a hot feeling of shyness sweeping over her because of the tremendous thing she was about to do. She sat lost in contemplation of the wonder of this new existence wherein the doctor was to be her da; so lost that had she heard Tim's heavy boots coming down the yard they had ceased to be a warning to her for flight. Only when he tried to open the door and, finding it locked, shook it with such violence as to nearly wrench it off its hinges did she start up, withdraw the bolt and, pushing open the door, sidle out.

A muttered curse and a quick movement from Tim lent wings to her legs. She was out of the yard and into the back lane in a flash. She looked about her like a startled hare.... Had he been going to hit her? He put his hand to his belt ... the leather belt with the big steel buckle which was part of her regular nightmare. Sometimes the buckle became a face, the face of her granda.... She blinked her eyes and shook her head, as if this would dismiss it from her mind. It did; and she thought again of the beautiful, new 'make-on' game.... And it wasn't all 'make-on', was it? she asked herself, for the doctor was a real person, the reallest person on earth and she loved him ... better than God! Eeh! what had she said? Well, she did love him, as much as God. Wasn't it lovely to feel like this, all shivery and jumpy inside, because he was her da? And it was her secret, just hers; she wouldn't tell anyone. But what about Rosie! Surely she could tell Rosie.

While walking slowly down the back lane and into the next street she debated in her mind whether Rosie should be let into this secret. She couldn't quite understand why she was hesitating about telling Rosie, for Rosie was her friend, and she told her everything. But, somehow, she had the same feeling about it as she had with her grandma when they didn't talk about the things granda did.

The sight of Rosie leaving the pram to chase Cissy Luck and thump her in the back decided her. Rosie was shouting: 'Take that, you cheeky bitch ... and that! You're as soft as clarts ... and your ma's as soft as clarts, and your da's as soft as clarts!'

Annie dashed up to her and, taking her face between her hands, a gesture which always warmed Rosie, whispered, bending a little so that their noses nearly touched, 'I have got a da!'

Rosie drew back: 'What! Who?'

Annie pulled her forward again, 'The doctor!'

'The doctor?'

'Mm-m.'

Rosie again withdrew herself to a short distance from where she could look steadily at Annie.... Annie didn't tell lies, but, the doctor her da! Well, of course ... yes, that explained everything—the rides in his car, the sweets and fruit, right in the middle of the week, and then those great big presents at Christmas.... Of course; he must be her da. Why hadn't she thought of it before? ... But then, he wasn't married to Kate. Well, that was a thing she couldn't understand, but definitely he was Annie's da ... only das brought you things.

'It's a "make-on" secret,' again whispered Annie.

But Rosie didn't hear this last confidence, or else she was conveniently deaf, not meaning her next course of action to be restricted.

Turning from Annie, she advanced halfway across the road again and addressed the now snivelling Cissy and her comforter, Peggy, on the opposite pavement: 'Think yer clever, doncher?' she yelled. 'Well, she has got a da, see! And a better one than yours. Her da's the doctor, if you want to know ... there!.' she said, jerking her head violently in their direction. Then, turning her back, she lifted up her clothes and thrust out her bottom at them, and, leaving them with this final insult, she grabbed the handle of the pram at one end, assigning the other to Annie, and led a triumphant march at a smart pace down the street.

It was just on ten-thirty, and Annie waited near the police-house, as she called the small dock police office that stood at the side of the big dock gates. She watched the men pass in and out of the docks with great interest. The policeman on duty had spoken to her, saying, 'You waiting for your ma again?' She remembered now he had called Kate her ma before today ... so he had known. Everybody had known, except her.... She nodded at him, shyly.

The tram from Westoe came rolling down the 'dock bank', and, when it stopped, Kate alighted and the conductor lifted her suitcase on to the pavement.

Annie paused a moment before running to her, savouring a feeling akin to that experienced earlier in the morning ... this was her ma; and Annie realised for the first time that she was different from everyone around her ... none of the women wore a beautiful green coat and a big green hat and a fur with a lot of tails ... the fur must be new, she hadn't seen it before ... and none of them stood like Kate did, or walked like her; she stood very straight and, when she walked, her skirts danced. The women she saw every day wore dark, drab clothes, and stood hunched up, like the group which was waiting for the Jarrow tram now and had turned their eyes, like the eyes of a wolf pack, on her.

As Kate looked about her, Annie ran forward, and, as she heard herself say 'Hello, Kate', as Kate bent to kiss her, she knew, with great certainty, that she'd never be able to call her anything else; it would always be 'Kate', never 'ma'.

Kate looked her over quickly, tenderly. She touched

her cheek with the back of her hand before picking up the suitcase and crossing the road to the tram terminus. 'Have you been waiting long, dear?' she asked.

'No,' said Annie; 'and I've been talking to the policeman.'

'Grandma all right?' asked Kate.

Annie hesitated, thinking of the rolled-down sleeves. 'Ye...s. Yes, I think so. She's going to bake, she's making me a yule doo.'

Kate glanced down at her, swiftly, and sighed. Annie thought it was because the case was so heavy: 'Let me help, I'll take one side,' she suggested.

'No, of course not,' said Kate. 'Here we are, anyway, and there's the tram coming.'

They stood for a few minutes while the tram disgorged its passengers, some giving Kate a brief nod of acknowledgement and a long stare, others calling cheerily, 'Hallo there, Kate! Happy Christmas.' Annie noted it was the men who were nicer.

Kate pulled Annie's arm through hers as they sat together on the long wooden seat, while opposite sat a row of women. All the women seemed to have sat on the opposite side of the tram, Annie noticed; perhaps they wanted to look at Kate's fur; yes, that was it, for they were all staring at Kate; but Kate didn't seem to notice, for she was talking about Christmas and ... What was she saying? ... She was going to take her up to Newcastle in the train this afternoon? And they would go to the big bazaar where Santa Claus lived!

She pressed herself against Kate, against the green coat and the tails of the fur. There was a faint smell, warm and lovely. Her mind could offer no name for it; it wasn't scent, for Connie Fawcett, who was Kate's cousin and had been hers up till today but had now become in some way disconnected with this new relationship, she used scent. When Connie came from High Jarrow to see her grandma, her grandma always waffed her apron around the kitchen after she had gone to get rid of the smell; but you wouldn't want to get rid of this smell.

'Come on, dreamer,' said Kate softly, 'we're nearly there.'

Annie looked about her in surprise: yes, so they were. There was the first of the fifteen streets.

The tram stopped just before the first street. 'The stops've been altered,' explained the conductor; 'we only stop at each end of the fifteen streets now.'

Kate made a wry face at Annie; the case was heavy and she'd have to carry it past the breadth of eight streets before coming to her own.... Still, it wasn't like walking past the streets in the late afternoon or evening when each corner had its special clique of loafers.

As she rested at the corner of the second street she noticed a woman running from the far end towards her; she carried her hat in her hand, from which a broken feather dangled, a coil of her hair was hanging on her shoulder, and Kate noticed, as she drew nearer, that the front of her coat was covered with soft filth, and that angry tears were running down her face.

'Why,' exclaimed Kate, 'what on earth's the matter, Jessie?'

The woman stopped and leant against the wall, gasping: 'It's them bitches, Kate. They did this to me,' she said, holding out her hat with one hand and pointing to her coat with the other. 'I'll have the law on them, see if I don't. They won't get off with it, I'll make them pay, every one of them. Dirty swine!'

Kate looked at her pityingly as she made this idle threat.... Poor Jessie! ... Had she really gone to school with this woman? Played with her? Knelt beside her at mass? It seemed impossible; she looked old and haggard now ... spent. Could she be only two years older than herself?

'I was only goin' to see me ma, Kate, that's all, it bein' Christmas Eve an' all. Ooh ... h! I wish I was dead.' Her head dropped to her chest, and she moved it from side to side in a gesture of despair that wrung Kate's heart.

Kate knew what Jessie's life had been. After a youth spent working in a laundry, ten hours a day, and the rest of her waking life at street corners or in dark recesses of shop doors, Jessie had married one of the boys from the fifteen streets, who, in the neighbours' opinion was much too good for her; which must have been God's opinion

98

also, said the God-fearing members of the community, when, just a year later, he was killed in the pit. Jessie had a friend who lived next door and who was very kind to her during her trouble, to the extent of allowing her husband to do odd jobs for her. It was later brought to the friend's notice by kind neighbours that it seemed funny that her husband and Jessie had to go up to Newcastle on the same day, and that as soon as she went out to do her shopping her man was in with Jessie when he was supposed to be getting his sleep ready for the night shift. The result of this exposure had been a promise from the husband to have nothing further to do with Jessie. But he had counted without Jessie, for she had found someone at last who could satisfy her physically, and she could no more leave him alone than she could stop herself wanting him. However, she moved to Shields to make things easier, and nothing the wife could do about it could loosen Jessie's hold on her husband; until nature took a hand. Aided, no doubt, by the wife's feverish desire to keep her man, it presented her with a child after eight years of marriage.

The baby was an enemy against whom Jessie was powerless, and the visits of its father became less and less, until they ceased altogether. Desperate, Jessie came to the fifteen streets, where she hadn't been for two years, supposedly to see her mother. This morning's visit was her third within a week, and some of the neighbours, seeing which way the wind was blowing, became self-constituted avengers, determined to protect the reformed husband against this shameless woman.

Most of this story was known to Kate, and the right or the wrong of it passed her by. She only knew that she felt a great pity for her one-time schoolmate. 'Why don't you get right away, Jessie? Go into service somewhere; you'll forget all about this. There are good places to be had ... look at me. Why don't you try it?' she urged.

Jessie began to sob helplessly: 'You fell on your feet, Kate; there ain't many places like yours. And you've got your bairn, I've got nothing.... Anyway, I only want him,' she added, with finality.

A gasp at her side brought Kate's attention from Jessie

to Annie; she was staring wide-eyed at Jessie, and the tears were raining down her cheeks. Kate was about to tell Annie to run home when they heard shouts coming from up the main road, and there, pouring from the street next to her own, was a group of women, who were gesticulating and pointing towards them. There was no doubt in Kate's mind that they were bent on further destruction. 'Get away, Jessie, as quickly as you can! Look, there's a tram coming; you'll just get it!'

'I can't go on the tram like this, Kate,' gasped Jessie, desperately; 'I'll walk.'

'You must get the tram,' said Kate. 'The way they are feeling, some of them would likely follow you to the docks. Surely you know them by now.'

A stone hurtled past them, and Kate pulled Annie close to her. It decided Jessie. Sobbing afresh, she took to her heels and ran, boarding the tram just as the women came up with Kate, frustration and hate predominant in all their faces. They paused a moment, breathless, watching the tram roll away.

'Yer wanter give that'un a wide berth,' said one of them, turning to Kate, 'she's a real wrong 'un.'

'I'm surprised you speak to her, filthy bitch that she is,' said another, hitching up her enormous breasts with her forearms. 'She's shameless, bloody well shameless. If I'd got me hands into her hair instead of grabbing that hat I'd have let her see, the——!'

Kate looked at the last speaker coldly, an anger that was only stirred by injustice rising in her.... How dare this woman whom she had known from childhood, and who had always shocked her with her obscenities, in spite of having been brought up under the specialised language of Tim! How dare she, who delighted in exchanging the filth of her mind with any man so interested, appoint herself judge of another woman! She was feared, and consequently fawned upon by most of her associates; she was Kate's idea of corruption; there was no tempering of judgement here, Mrs. Luck was bad! Her mind was a sewer; she could defile by a look. She had eleven children alive, which made Kate shudder at the productive power of evil....

Kate's distaste and anger showed clearly in her face as she looked at the little crowd before her, and it wasn't lost on them. There was a moment of hostile silence as they stared back at her and the child, pressed close to her side. A moment ago they had felt protective towards her, warning against the contamination of Jessie ... but now, with her looking at them like that, and her dressed up to the knocker like a goddam queen or somesuch ... their attitude changed ... and if all the tales were true she was a damn sight as bad as that whore just gone.

'I don't think it's for you to judge Jessie Daley, it behoves us all to mind our own business,' said Kate scornfully.

They gasped, speechless with surprise at her daring, and listened, fascinated by her tone, for Kate was unconsciously speaking to them much as Miss Tolmache would have done. 'You'll never right wrongs by the methods you are using. Can't you see you'll only make matters worse? A little kindness from one of you would have had much more effect than all your horseplay ... but then, of course,' Kate's eyes swept them with disdain, 'you wouldn't have enjoyed it so much.'

As she stooped to pick up her case there was a murmur of, 'By damn, who the hell does she thing she is? ... We're coming to something now, ain't we?' but nothing really audible until she had passed through the midst of them, with Annie clinging to her hand.

She had walked a few yards ahead when the first voice reached her, which she recognised as Dorrie Clarke's: 'Birds of a feather, lasses!' Dorrie yelled. 'Only this one picks on professional blokes; they can pay more; look at her clothes. What did I tell you?'

Kate jerked to a halt as if a bullet had struck her in the back. She had no time to think before Mrs. Luck screamed words that seemed to freeze her blood; all the hard-won beauty in her life was darkened from this moment, never to fully return to its previous brightness; her real misfortunes seemed to date from the moment Mrs. Luck shouted: 'It's coming to something ... by God it is! Who jer think yer talking to ... brazen hussy! No wonder yer bairn brags in the street that the doctor is her da. She gets her barefaceness from the right one, you bloody upstart you!'

All the terror Annie had known in her short life paled before this new terror. As she lifted her eyes to Kate's her heart seemed to leap from her body by way of her mouth, for she saw there something that chilled her and turned her stomach over as never Tim's look had done. Kate's face was white, and her blue eyes black and deep and full of that something that made Annie want to hide her face. But she had to go on looking up into Kate's eyes for they wouldn't let her's go. Slowly Kate turned her face away, and with it her body, and she was facing the women again.

The women were all quiet now, some a little awed at the length Nell Luck had gone, and growing uneasy.... Why couldn't Nell keep her mouth shut? This Kate Hannigan wasn't Jessie Daley. Besides, having the doctor for a fancy man she was in with the toffs. Best keep clear of them, money was power; and most of the houses around here were owned by the Westoe toffs. You could be put on the street and never know the reason why.... Well, why didn't she say something instead of standing there like that? She certainly was putting up a good bluff; but it had taken the wind out of her sails, she looked like a corpse, but not a frightened one ... no, nothing frightened about her, she wouldn't run.... Ah, she was going through, and without a word too!

They watched her turn and walk away, the child walking behind her, tearing the thumb of her glove with her teeth. No one spoke. They were suddenly deflated; even Mrs. Luck voiced no thought, merely rolling her folded arms tighter in her shawl. It was as if they were fed by one artery, so general appeared their sense of defeat. All at once they seemed to remember they were busy women and were wasting time. They dispersed in twos and threes, Dorrie Clarke and Mrs. Luck together. 'Well, you showed the bitch,' said Dorrie.

Mrs. Luck straightened her shoulders: 'Yes, I showed the bitch.'

'Nice way to spend a Christmas Eve! Who started this bloody business, anyway?' said one of the two remaining women.

'I think it was Dorrie.'

'Aye, it would be. But, if my Sam gets to know I've been mixed up in this he'll bash me face in!'

'Did you see Kate Hannigan's face, Mary? D'yer think there could have been a mistake? ... About the doctor, I mean. She looked so surprised.'

'No, there's no mistake; he's her fancy man, all right. But she was a damn fool to let the bairn know.'

When Sarah opened the door to Kate, the glad smile of welcome died out of her face. 'My God, hinny ... what's happened? What's the matter? Are you ill?'

Kate said nothing, but walked past her. Annie followed, the thumb of her glove now a mass of tangled wool. Sarah closed the door and hurried after them into the kitchen, crying, 'Kate, hinny, tell me what's happened.'

Kate sat down heavily on a chair by the side of the table and leaned her head on her hand. Annie stood in the dark recess which housed the wash-bowl; her eyes gleamed out of the dimness in mute appeal to her grandmother, but when Sarah put the same question to her, 'What's happened, hinny?' she only dug her fingers into her lower lip and remained silent.

Kate looked up at her mother.... 'She's been telling people the doctor is her da.... They're all saying he's my ... that I'm ...'

There was a strangled silence in the kitchen.

'No, Kate!' Sarah's voice was horrified and incredulous.

'Yes,' said Kate dully. 'They were baiting Jessie Daley; I told them they should mind their own business, and they turned on me. It was Mrs. Luck and her crowd. If they think that, others do ... everybody must....'

'Dear God,' said Sarah, 'what'll happen if he hears? ... Oh, and him such a nice man too.... But how can they say that, Kate? You didn't know him, did you?'

To the question behind the question Kate replied, 'No, ma, I didn't know him; I never saw him before he came upstairs when she was born.'

'Oh, what made her say such a thing?' Sarah looked at

Annie. 'What made you say it, hinny?'

Annie simply stared back, her eyes becoming wider, threatening to slip beyond the boundary of her face.

'Come here,' said Kate quietly.

Annie came slowly forward, and the look on her face broke the ice in Kate's heart. 'Don't be frightened,' she said, 'you won't get into trouble.... Only tell me, what made you say it? Has anyone ever said it to you?'

Annie shook her head.

'You just made it up?'

Annie nodded quickly.

'But you knew it was a lie, didn't you, and it was wrong?'

'They said . . .' whispered Annie.

'Yes?' prompted Kate.

'Well ... they said I hadn't got a da at all, and I wanted a da, and I just made on the doctor was my da. And I told Rosie, and she told Cissy Luck.... Oh, Kate, I was only making-on!'

Looking at her child, Kate realised the hurt and loneliness that must have preceded this game of 'making-on'. She was suddenly overwhelmed with the pity of it. She had done everything in her power to make up to Annie for the lack of a father, but it would seem nothing one could do would ever fill that gap. 'How long have you pretended he was ... your da?'

'Just this morning, round at the shop.'

'You've never said it before?'

'No, never, Kate. I made it up in the lavatory.'

Kate looked at Sarah. 'It isn't something fresh they have just got hold of, ma. They must have thought this ... for a long time; I could see it in their faces. But, oh, the irony of it, that she should play into their hands by picking on him.' Great tears welled up into her eyes; she dropped her head suddenly on to her arms and sobbed.

Sarah stood mute, mechanically rolling and unrolling the corner of her apron. She had never seen Kate cry since she was a child ... not even when she came home that time did she cry! And now the sound of her sobbing was more than she could bear. 'Don't, hinny, don't,' she pleaded; 'he can't know, and nobody would dare say anything to him; and you know it's all lies. Oh'—she turned to Annie—'why did you say such a thing?... What made you?'

Kate put her hand out blindly and drew Annie's shivering body to her. 'Don't blame her, ma; please. She's not to blame.' She sat up and dried her face with her handkerchief, and unpinned her hat and put it on the table. Then, taking Annie's two hands in hers, she drew her close to her knees: 'Dear,' she began, 'now listen carefully to what I am going to say...'

Annie listened, but the softness of Kate's voice and the love and understanding in her eyes in no way eased the blow when it came. 'You are not to ride in the doctor's car any more, and you are not to wait for him at the corner ... you understand? You must keep out of his way.... If you can't avoid him, then you must tell him ... well, tell him you are going a message, or you've got to hurry home. But you mustn't wait about for him. Now promise me you'll do as I tell you.'

No amount of blinking would keep the scalding tears from falling, or quick swallowing dislodge the lump that was choking her; nothing that could ever happen could be as bad as this.... Not to see the doctor again, not to sit beside him on the beautiful leather seat in the front of the car and see him laughing down at her, and to watch his long brown hands coming forward to lift her down, and the thrill as he whirled her though the air ... or not to stand at the corner and see him wave to her, when he couldn't stop ... not to do any of these things, never, never again....

'Answer me, dear.'

Annie tried to speak, but couldn't. Kate suddenly pulled her to her breast and held her close: 'There, there, my dear, don't cry like that. Stop now!'

Sarah, too, had her apron to her eyes when the front-door knocker banged once. In answer to Kate's startled glance, she said, 'It's all right, hinny, it'll be the insurance man, that's his knock.'

'You won't ask him in?' said Kate.

'No, hinny.'

Sarah took some coppers from a cup in the corner of

the cupboard and a book out of the chiffonier, and went through the front-room.

'Come on, dear,' said Kate to Annie, 'dry your eyes. We'll still go to Newcastle and . . .' She got no further, the blood slowly mounting to her face as she heard the voice at the front-door speaking to her mother. . . . Surely she wouldn't let him in. . . . He was in, in the front-room. She pushed Annie, who was staring, as if petrified, towards the door, to one side, and in the matter of seconds she made and reversed a decision . . . to escape upstairs; no, to see him and finish this thing once and for all. As the strands of the web are like steel bands to the fly so she felt the fine-woven strands of circumstance holding her to this fate, of which she would be free, for she saw nothing but disaster for all concerned and the fulfilling of the prophecies of the women of the fifteen streets. . . . She would put an end to it and stop their evil tongues, and still for ever the desire that was eating into her. In that minute she realised how this could be accomplished. The decision surprised her, for she had scorned it before today. But she saw it now as the only way out of this enveloping tangle. She felt it was inevitable; these things had to happen; life was planned; do all you could, learn, try to be different, you were brought back to the path that was set for you the day you were born. . . . And, if you happened to have made a mistake as she had done, you were dragged back. But anything was better than following the dictates of her heart. . . . Goodbye to Mr. Bernard, and Mr. Rex, and Miss Tolmache . . . but, oh, goodbye to Mr. Bernard and evenings of strange delight! . . . Why should she be called upon to do this? Why had he come into her life, when he could have no part in it? And now she had to give up all she valued because of him. Hostility welled up in her, but died as she met his eyes as he stood in the doorway, looking at her. . . . Why must he look at her like that? He had no right to do it. . . . She felt suddenly weak and sick. . . . Oh, God, why had he come? He, too, playing into their hands.

'Hullo, there, Kate,' he said. 'Happy Christmas.'

'Hallo, doctor,' she answered quietly.

He walked to the table and put down a long box he

had under his arm, ignoring Annie as he did so, although he could see her standing close to the wall in the dim corner of the kitchen. He also ignored the fact, but for a different reason, that the three of them had been crying and that the atmosphere was strained. 'A certain young lady had an appointment with me at eleven-thirty this morning, Kate,' he said, 'but she failed to put in an appearance, although she knew I had been to see Santa Claus last night, and that I would have a message for her, if not a present, from him. ... This is the first time this young lady has let me down; I thought she must be ill.'

A strangled sob came from the corner. He looked towards Annie and back to Kate again. 'Is anything wrong, Kate?'

Kate didn't answer him but turned to Annie: 'Go upstairs, dear,' she said.

Annie, her eyes lingering on Rodney, stood as if she hadn't heard. 'Annie!' said Kate again, sharply.

Annie turned away and made a dash for the stair door, fumbled blindly with the latch, then ran upstairs. They heard her footsteps overhead before speaking, and then it was Rodney again who asked. 'What is wrong with her, Kate?'

'She is getting out of hand; I'm afraid she's being spoilt.'

He laughed. 'You're always saying she's being spoilt. It's nonsense, you couldn't spoil Annie ... no more than you could spoil ...' He had been going to add 'you', but withheld it and let his eyes speak for him.

'She needs control,' went on Kate hastily; her hands were joined together, the knuckles showing white. 'She can't get used to the idea of having ... a father!'

Rodney's exclamation of 'A father!' covered Sarah's gasp of amazement.

'Yes, she doesn't like the idea of me getting married.' There, it was out; it was quite simple really, just a few words and everything was altered.

Sarah dropped quietly into Tim's chair. Rodney stared across the width of the table at Kate. Why was it, he thought, that her face always swam towards him; no matter what the distance, it seemed to bridge it until he felt it near his own, warming him with its radiance. She seemed more beautiful than ever today because she looked sad. It was only a week since he had seen her. He had tried to keep away from the Tolmaches' after his attendance on old Rex was no longer necessary, but it had been so easy to drop in to tea, once in a while, knowing that she'd be there. Only the once in a while had become a regular habit. Last week she had presided over tea. Sitting proudly beside Miss Tolmache, she had joined in the general conversation, and he had seen her in a new light, quite at ease, laughing and talking generally. She never wore uniform, but a grey dress with a white collar which gave her a Quakerish air. He had felt she was glad he had seen her thus, and had noted the pride with which old Bernard always watched her, and the tenderness in her eyes when she looked at old Bernard or cleverly turned some remark, purposely set by him to be parried.... And now, what was she saying?

Kate thought, he's not listening to me ... he's got to listen: 'Doctor, I think it would be better if you gave Annie no more presents.' She swallowed hard and forced herself to meet his eyes. 'It has been most kind of you, and I am grateful.... But now ... well, Patrick thinks.... well, we won't be quite in the position to buy her these kind of things.' She pointed to the box on the table. 'Patrick says ...'

'Yes, Patrick says,' said Rodney in a cold voice; 'go on.' His mind raced ... what has made her do this? ... Something has happened.... Who is this Patrick?

Sarah looked from one to the other.... Oh, what was this? ... What was this? Why didn't Kate speak? Why were they standing looking at one another like that? ... And it couldn't be true about Patrick Delahunty! Only last week she had laughed the idea to scorn. He had haunted the house for days, asking about her and when she was coming home. And look how often she had had to tell him Kate had gone back to Westoe, when she'd been sitting upstairs all the time. He'd been after her for a year now, and she wouldn't even look at him ... her Kate and Pat Delahunty! ... He was a nice enough fellow ... but not for her Kate. Oh no!

'You were saying you were going to be married,' said Rodney, his words falling like tinkling ice; 'and Patrick says. . . . What does Patrick say?'

His eyes were black and hard and were boring into her. A quiver passed over Kate's face. She couldn't carry it through, she couldn't, she couldn't. Why must he . . . ? It wasn't fair. And, oh, he looked so hurt! She dropped her head.

In the months to come she was to ask herself what they would have done had not Father O'Malley walked in the back-door at that moment accompanied by her cousin Connie from Jarrow. The strident voice and loud, sense-less laughter of Connie as she bid everyone 'A merry Christmas' might have slackened the tension if Father O'Malley had been the loving, trusting Christian that his cloth proclaimed. But he prided himself that he knew human nature and the baseness therein, and between Kate Hannigan and this doctor, whom he had grown to hate, having been forced to listen to his views across the table of the boardroom in the workhouse, he sensed baseness like a hungry dog.

If Sarah could have put into clear thought her in-tuitive knowledge of the priest she would have been astounded and not a little frightened, and he, if he could have read her mind, would have credited her with possess-ing supernatural gifts. 'Happy Christmas, Connie,' said Sarah to her niece; 'and to you, Father. It's well you've come at this minute, you're just in time to hear the news. Kate here . . . well . . . she's going to be married.'

'Married! Oh, Kate!' yelled Connie.

'And who are you going to marry, Kate?' asked the priest, in a tone of polite enquiry.

Kate regarded him steadily. From now on he would think he had a tight hand on her life. . . . 'Patrick Dela-hunty,' she replied quietly.

The pin-points of the priest's eyes widened through his glasses: 'Patrick Delahunty . . . well, well! I'm surprised at your common sense. . . . A good, steady-going, God-fearing man; you've done well for yourself.'

Kate's head went up, a look flashing from her eyes, which the priest read only too well.

'I've never known him miss mass,' he went on; 'nor the altar rails on a Sunday morning for the three years he's been over here. He'll be a great influence on Annie....'

'Oh, are you going, doctor?' said Sarah. 'I'll show you out.'

'That's quite all right, Mrs. Hannigan,' said Rodney. 'Good morning.' He inclined his head towards Connie, where she stood, strangely quiet since she had heard the name of the man Kate was going to marry. 'Good morning,' he said to her, and, looking at neither Kate nor the priest, he went out through the front-room.

Father O'Malley watched Kate's gaze follow him.... Patrick Delahunty, he thought; there's something funny here. Why, I was talking to him at nine o'clock this morning and he said nothing to me.... His mind suddenly switched to the doctor.... That man's dangerous, I'm never mistaken; and this one, she's ripe for the Devil; and she's too strong for Pat, she'll have an influence on him. Well, God's will be done!

# THE PATH IS MAPPED OUT

Sitting before the kitchen fire, at three o'clock in the afternoon, Kate reviewed the happenings of the past year, with not a little wonder at the change time and the simple personality of a man had wrought in her; her mind, compared with the turmoil it had been in a year ago today, was at peace. In a fortnight's time, when she was to marry Pat, her life would change completely. No longer did she dread the idea; in fact, there were times when she actually looked forward to it, for, once married, she would be safe; there would be no more 'wondering' at what might happen, no more mistrusting herself; married to Pat, she intended her sole aim would be to make him a good wife.... Last Christmas Eve, when she had sent for him and told him she would marry him and that she had already told her mother and Father O'Malley, he had asked no reason for her lightning change of front, but had simply taken her two hands in his and pressed her palms against his face, and, in his soft Irish voice, had said, 'It's a miracle, He has answered my prayers. If you ever live to regret this day, Kate, may my death soon follow.'

She had been amused at what she termed his theatrical speech, but was to remember it vividly within the next few hours. Gentleness had been his keynote; he was big and lumbering, but not uncouth; he had thick brown hair and a ruddy complexion, and his temper and love of peace denied his nationality. That he loved her with a deep abiding love she knew, and she felt sure in her heart that ... left alone ... she would be happy and would find peace with him. The phrase 'left alone' was with her less now than at the beginning of the year; contrary to her

usual procedure of facing up to things she had never dis-
sected the phrase, had never asked herself what she meant
by being 'left alone'.

Looking back now, she thought how grossly she must
have exaggerated the emotions of last Christmas Eve, and
on other occasions too, and how near she had become to
making a fool of herself by turning kindly interest into
something that even now made her feel hot inside. She
excused herself with the thought that the evil-tongued
women had unbalanced her and that, for a moment, she
had seen things through their eyes. But she had silenced
their tongues, she felt, and felt truly that she had them
guessing and that they did not know what to make of the
turn of events.

She had seen the doctor only twice during the past
year, both occasions being during the past month when
he was visiting her mother. His visits to the Tolmaches
had seemed to coincide with her days off. When they had
met in the kitchen he had been so ordinary and nice that
she had thought to herself: How dreadful it is that one
exaggerates things so much; the second time Pat had
been with her, and she had chided herself for willing him
to like Pat. But apparently he had found this quite easy,
for within a short while they were talking, even laughing,
together. He had wished them both every happiness.
One awkward moment alone had occurred, when the
doctor had asked Pat if, later, he would be allowed to pay
court to his stepdaughter once in a while. Pat had
laughed heartily at a joke he couldn't see, and Kate,
looking at the doctor's face, had seen nothing but kindly
interest and, perhaps, a little amusement. Pat had been
loud in his praises of the doctor: 'There's a real gentleman, and a man, Kate. . . . If it wasn't that I love Ireland
I'd want to be an Englishman like himself.' Dear, simple
Pat.

Yes, the year had turned out much better than she had
expected. Her hardest task had been to tell the Tolmaches. They had covered their regret at their coming
loss by taking an active interest in the preparations for
her wedding. Miss Tolmache was providing all the linen,
Mr. Rex had bought them a carpet and Mr. Bernard

had given her a cheque for ten pounds. The unfailing kindness of these people was sometimes more than Kate could bear. That her marriage was not to cut her off entirely from them, she owed to Pat's understanding; for it was he who had suggested she should go to them at least two afternoons a week, and even to keep up her reading with Mr. Bernard if she wished. Seeing with what bands of prejudice the women around her were tied to their houses, welded by the men's domination, she felt this augured good for their future together.

Their house was all ready for them; it was in the quiet corner of Simonside, only a mile from the fifteen streets but as distant as heaven from earth. It had four rooms and a garden, back and front. When Kate thought of the garden she thought of Annie; there she would grow and blossom, away from these filthy back lanes and streets. She had been worried about Annie, after the business of last Christmas Eve; she had lost the sparkle and eagerness of childhood and a sadness had settled on her. Remembering her own short memory at Annie's age, Kate felt there must be another cause other than that of not seeing the doctor for this continued staleness. Pat, through time, had won her round to laughter again, for he loved her already as his own. But still Sarah's reports of her were that she sat too long looking at nothing. Well, thought Kate, once she was married it wouldn't matter; she could let her see the doctor occasionally, if this were really the reason for her unusual behaviour. But not so much as before. No, that wouldn't do, she had been far too fond of him; but just now and again wouldn't do any harm.

She was feeling that everything would settle in its groove. What a fool she had been to worry so much.... Her mind flashed back to last Christmas Eve.... What would have happened had the priest and Connie not come in when they did.... Now, she told herself, you've been through all that before. Stop dramatising things! Whatever happened was only in your imagination....

She looked at her mother lying dozing on the saddle.... How old she looked, and ill. If only she could take her with them, away from this house and him. Her ankles overflowed over her slippers, the swelling seemed to get worse every week. Kate wished she were staying over Christmas, she would have been able to make her rest. But the Tolmaches had decided that, at last, they were too old for hotels. With the war being on, they had said, the hotel would likely be overcrowded and noisy anyway, and it would be nice to have Kate spend her last Christmas with them. So she was returning tonight; it was no hardship, she could never have too much of their company ... only she knew how much her mother looked forward to this week alone with her ... and then there was Annie.

As Sarah lay, she kept muttering to herself. It sounded, to Kate, like a single word, a name being repeated, but it was unintelligible. She's tired and worn out, thought Kate. I'll let her sleep as long as possible, there'll be no one coming in before tea-time, unless Connie comes.... The thought of her cousin aroused a slight uneasiness in Kate's mind. Why had she ceased calling these past two months? Her mother, who had grumbled that she was never off the door-step, was now wondering why her visits had stopped altogether. Perhaps, thought Kate, it's because I demurred about going to Peter's wedding.... She and Pat had been invited to her cousin Peter's wedding, and when in an effort to evade what she knew would be a drinking bout, she had said she thought she would be unable to get off that week-end, Connie had caused quite a scene and accused her of thinking herself to be a cut above them all now. So she had gone, and sat in the packed front-room, watching whisky and beer being drunk in such quantities as to ensure that everyone was having a real good time. Her refusal to touch anything had only made Connie more firm in her belief that 'Kate was looking down her nose at them all'. It was in his endeavour to turn Connie's spleen from her that Pat had laughingly drunk all Connie had pressed on him, and, not being used to it in quantity, for as he was wont to say he could 'take it or leave it', he was soon quite befuddled, if not actually drunk. At four o'clock in the morning it was impossible for him to attempt the three miles walk home. There he had sat, smiling broadly at everyone and powerless to use his legs. Kate told herself she was glad she had seen him in drink and witnessed his reactions to it, and she was amazed, and not a little pleased, that he hadn't followed the usual course of his countrymen and become fighting mad.

The house had been full with the family alone, there being ten of them in the four rooms, so, when it was decided that they couldn't possibly go home until Pat had sobered up, Kate found herself sharing one of the two beds in the back room, lying between two of her young cousins. Pat, amid screams of laughter, had been assigned to a cupboard which ran under the stairs. Apparently this had often been used as a spare bedspace and a straw mattress had been made to fit it. Kate had rebuked herself for feeling disgust of her cousins, for, after all, she had told herself, they were her people, and had it not been for the Tolmaches she would have found them, if not likeable, at least amusing, but the only impression they left on her was disgust. After the wedding Pat seemingly thought as she did, for he blamed them for having made him drunk and spoke bitterly of drink, swearing he had tasted his last.

She had laughed at him, and although she was glad he intended to drink no more she thought he had taken the effect of his lapse too seriously, for in the weeks that followed he was at times openly hostile towards the Fawcetts as a whole, and Connie in particular, going so far as to walk out of the kitchen whenever she came in.

Kate could find no reason for this. Had he made a spectacle of himself when drunk she could have understood his attitude. Sometimes she thought that Connie did not like the idea of her marrying.... She was five years Kate's senior and anything but attractive, being inclined to fat and, as her own father was won't to say, 'wore too much on her hat and not enough on her chest'.

Kate, in the quiet peacefulness of the kitchen and the knowledge of the home that was soon to be hers, in the love that Pat showered on her, and in the deep friendship and kindness ... yes, and love of the Tolmaches, felt it in her heart to be sorry for her cousin and her vain, and all too obvious, attempts to attract the opposite sex.

Resuming the smocking on a frock for Annie, that she

had laid aside when she had begun her reverie, Kate's thoughts wandered lovingly around her daughter and her future. She'd still have to be brought up a Catholic, but not at the Borough Road school, on that she was determined; and, although it would mean a two- or three-mile walk there, and perhaps back, every Sunday, she would take her to either Shields or Tyne Dock church; St. David's in the Borough Road and Father O'Malley would see them no more.

A cry from her mother suddenly startled her; Sarah was sitting upright on the saddle, calling out a name, 'Stephen! Stephen!'

'Ma!' cried Kate, shaking her gently. 'Wake up! Wake up, dear!'

'Oh!' whispered Sarah, opening her eyes. 'Oh, hinny, Stephen's here.'

'You're dreaming, ma. There, lie down.' Kate pressed her gently back.

Sarah lay for some minutes staring up at her daughter. There was a look on her face that was new to Kate, a youthful, happy look; but, even as she watched, it died away and Sarah sighed.

'Yes, lass, I've been dreaming.'

'You were calling someone named Stephen. Who's Stephen? We don't know anyone by that name, do we?'

'Did I shout that name out?'

'Yes, you've been muttering for some time.'

'Dear God! Dear God!' The look of fear that was almost habitual returned to Sarah's eyes. 'It's because I've been thinking lately ... been wondering what I should do. I've been thinking, hinny, that I'm not long for the top.'

'Oh, ma, don't talk like that! Your legs will get better, you only need rest. . . . Please don't say that. Things will be different next year, I'll be able to come and help you. Oh, ma!' Kate stroked her mother's thin, grey hair, and her eyes looked anxious.

Sarah lay for some minutes in silence. Then she said quietly, 'Is anyone in? . . . Annie, or anyone?'

'No, dear. Annie's gone to the matinée with Rosie. There'll be no one in till five o'clock ... I hope,' she added.

'Then,' said Sarah, 'I've got something to tell you, lass.... I never meant to tell you, or anyone, I meant it to go to the grave with me.... But somehow, lately, the thought has come to me that you've the right to know.... You're sure there's no one about?'

'No, dear.'

'Then close the front-room door, lass, and slip the bolt in the back, and bring up your chair.'

Somewhat mystified, Kate complied. Taking her mother's hand in hers she waited for her to speak.

'I don't know where to begin, hinny.' Sarah's voice had the catch of tears in it. She gazed up at Kate, taking in the warm beauty of this child of hers, wondering vaguely how she could have been born of her. She licked her lips with the old, nervous habit. 'I think I'd better tell you straight out, if it's got to be said.... Tim isn't your father, Kate!' Anxiously, she watched for some startling change in the face of her daughter.

The pressure of Kate's hand on her mother's remained the same as a moment before.... She was conscious only of thinking, I hope Annie doesn't get wet, it is raining so hard. She heard the fire drop, and with it some of the glow faded from the kitchen.... The gas would soon have to be lit.... Her mother was looking up, searchingly, into her face. Kate knew she should say something ... but what? She hadn't words with which to describe this new surge of happiness, what this revelation meant to her. For as long as she could remember she had hated the thought of Tim Hannigan being her father. But it had been something she was powerless to alter, like being blind or deformed. The very sight of him always made her recoil, and an early fear of becoming like him had not wholly vanished. But now! Oh, now! This blessed, blessed relief....

'Hinny,' said Sarah anxiously, 'you don't mind, do you?'

'Oh, ma!' Kate suddenly laid her face against her mother's.

Sarah put her hand on her hair. 'There, lass ... there! Well, it's out.... But, hinny'—she pressed Kate away

from her—'you'll never tell a soul until I'm gone?...
promise!'

Kate promised, but at the same time the desire was in
her to tell the world. For to know that Tim Hannigan
had no part in her being, that her cousins in Jarrow were
not really her cousins, was so uplifting to her spirit that
she had the quaint urge to sing and dance ... really frolic
around the kitchen. She remembered short spasms of
happiness she had experienced as a child; they had come
unbidden, unannounced, called from some central pool
of delight that supplied all children, at some time or
another, whether they had cause for happiness or not....
At these times her desire had been to run, to feel her feet
just flicking the earth.... And now this was the same feeling.

To her mother's surprise she suddenly stood up, flung
her arms above her head, and pivoted rapidly two or
three times, her full skirt billowing against the kitchen
table. Then she flung herself on her knees by the couch
and buried her head on her mother's shoulder. They
stayed thus, in silence, for some minutes.

After a while Kate began to think more steadily about
the matter; questions tumbled into her mind, and she sat
up on the chair again, and held her mother's hands once
more....

'Does he know, ma?' she asked.

'Yes, and no,' said Sarah; 'he's always been suspicious.
When you were born you were so like your father that he
tried to make me admit it.... But once I had done that, I
was afraid of what he might do to you. So I've always
denied it strongly.'

'Who was my father?'

'He was an artist, lass.'

'An artist!' Kate's face lit up.

'Yes, hinny.... He painted pictures of slums and docks
and people like the blind beggar who used to sit under
the arches, never anything pretty. He came to the back
door there one stifling night in July and said someone
had told him we'd a room to spare.... Would we let him
have it? Just for a few weeks? I asked him in; Tim was
eating his tea, and I felt he was going to say no. But then

he looked him up and down, and I could see he didn't think much of him; for he was rather short and slim and his hair was going grey at the temples, although he wasn't forty. And when he offered to pay thirty shillings a week, that settled the matter, for thirty shillings a week was a fortune.'

'How long did he stay? ... And did he know about me?' asked Kate, eagerly.

'He stayed three months.... No, he didn't know about you ... but he wanted me to go away with him.'

'Oh, why didn't you, ma?'

'I had married Tim, hinny, for better or worse.... Anyway, I hadn't the courage then. Had it been a few years later, God knows what I might have done. But then it was too late.... It was too late eighteen months after.'

'Why? Did you hear from him?'

'I never heard from him after he left, but I had an address to go to if ever I wanted him. But he died.... I saw it one morning in the paper, half a page was taken up with his paintings, and his picture was there too ... but I daren't even keep that.'

'Oh, ma.' Kate stroked her mother's hand. 'Why didn't you tell him about me?'

'Because he would have come back, and there'd 'av been murder; Tim and him had grown to hate each other in a very short time.'

'Did he love you, ma?'

'He said he did.'

Kate looked at her mother's grey hair, the weary eyes with the wrinkled bags beneath, the tremulous mouth, the nervous, twitching tongue; how old she looked! ... It was hard to imagine her young and attractive, with an artist in love with her. But she must have been pretty once. And anyway, there was her disposition; he would have been attracted by that alone, thought Kate, for she was so sweet, so gentle, asking nothing, and giving all.

'I love you, too,' said Kate suddenly, bending above her, her eyes large and dark with tenderness.

Sarah blinked rapidly and shook her head, evidently embarrassed.... Kate came out with the oddest things, putting into words thoughts that she would never dream of voicing, even if she felt them deeply.... She supposed it was living with the Tolmaches that had made Kate like that, and yet it was good to hear her say what she had.... How many years was it since she had heard someone say they loved her? Nearly twenty-six!

They both started as the back door was shaken with considerable violence. Their eyes flashed the same message.... It can't be him, he isn't finished till five o'clock.

When Kate withdrew the bolt and saw Pat standing there, she sighed with relief. But the laughing comment she was about to make died on her lips as she noticed the expression on his face. 'Why, Pat, what's happened? Don't stand there like that, come in.'

But from the first sight of her his eagerness to get into the house was gone. He stared at her as if storing up for all time all his eyes could take in.

'Have you had an accident? ... Do please come in, and don't stand there!' she repeated. 'What on earth is the matter, anyway?'

He passed her and took a few steps backwards into the kitchen, never letting his gaze drop from her face.

Kate closed the door, thinking, Something, Something dreadful's happened.... Oh, and I was so happy.... Why must it always be like this?

'Sit down,' she said quietly, 'till I light the gas. I thought you were working right through when you didn't call in at dinner-time.'

The gas lit, she pulled down the blind and turned to him. His eyes held a stricken look. She put her hand out in compassion and touched his arm, and found herself pulled into his embrace so fiercely and crushed so hard against him that her breath caught in a gasp and there was a surging in her ears. His arms, like steel bands, moved about her, pressing her, crushing her into him, and when his hand came behind her head and his mouth covered hers, in such a way as she had never experienced before, she thought dimly.... Don't struggle, he's ill.

Sarah, her legs dangling over the edge of the saddle, looked on in dumb amazement. She was well acquainted with trouble, and she knew it was once more in the kitchen, but the form it was taking was unusual.... He's in a way, poor lad, he's in a way, she kept repeating to herself. And oh, if he would only stop carrying on like that!

When Kate, after what seemed an eternity, felt Pat release her lips and the tenderness she was used to creep back into his touch, she gently pressed him away and sank down into a chair. She was breathless and a little afraid.

As he still did not speak, but stood looking so strangely at Kate, Sarah said quietly, 'What is it, lad? Tell us what's happened.'

After a silence that was painful in its length, he turned slowly to Sarah. He looked suddenly childish and forlorn. 'It's Connie Fawcett, ma! She's done this.'

'Connie!' Kate and Sarah exclaimed together. Then, 'What's Connie got to do with us, Pat?' Kate asked; while a rising fear told her that Connie, at this moment, had everything to do with them.

'Oh, me darling. Oh, me Kate.' Pat's long frame doubled up and he was on his knees in front of her, with his head in her lap and his arms around her once more.

Kate looked helplessly over his bowed head at her mother. Sarah, pink with embarrassment, for she had never witnessed anything like this, murmured, 'Oh dear! Oh dear!'

'Look, Pat,' Kate said, taking his head between her hands and raising it. 'You must tell me what has happened. What has Connie done that you should go on like this? I must know,' she said firmly.

His eyes roamed over her face, and he moaned aloud. 'Yes, you must know.' He lumbered to his feet. 'And I've got to tell you! I've been telling meself that for hours as I walked the streets. I've been saying ... I've got to tell her! ... Holy Mary, I've got to tell her.... Well, I'll tell you; but I can't look at you and say what's got to be said.... Don't go, ma,' he added, as Sarah got up; 'it's best you should hear this, too.' He turned and looked into the fire, and began to talk.

Kate and Sarah stared at his broad back and at his outstretched hands, clasping and unclasping the brass rod under the mantelpiece, and listened as he went back to the night of Peter Fawcett's wedding.

The pain in Kate's chest was like a tight band, constricting her breathing; her eyes and throat burned.... She saw the cupboard under the stairs and the straw mattress. She saw Pat, roused from a drunken sleep, open his arms to a woman whom in his stupor he imagined to be her.... It was over and done with, there was no going back ... and the probable consequences, that had only too truly come about, had sobered him, and he had threatened to strangle her.... The weeks had passed, and he had tried to forget it and what she might do. And then, last night, her father had come to him, together with Father O'Malley, and Father O'Malley had made him swear to marry Connie. He had made him give his word for the sake of the child.

'Do you hear, Kate?' Pat said, turning to her, tears streaming down his cheeks. 'I had to swear that I would marry her. But, as Jesus is my judge, I hate the very name of her. This also I swore, and on the altar, unknown to Father O'Malley, that she'd have me name but nothing else. I made sure of that this morning, for I joined up.'

'If you ever live to regret this day, Kate, may my death soon follow....' His words of a year ago came back to her, and she had a horrifying glimpse into the future.... As on a screen flung up before her mind's eye she saw his mangled body half buried in mud, unrecognisable but for the crucifix he always wore round his neck. She felt hot and sick; the kitchen receded. Her mother was standing close to Pat, begging him to do something.... 'Forget your promise,' she was saying ... as if he could; Father O'Malley knew how to seal an Irishman's oath.... They floated away from her, and she felt herself falling gently into thankful blackness.

She came to herself breathing air that stung and pricked and made her gasp; and she realised she was sniffing smelling-salts, and wondered vaguely from where they had come ... she hadn't any, there wasn't any need, for she rarely had a headache and she had never fainted before.... This feeling of lying in between two worlds was pleasant, you didn't think here, not about new fathers or lost husbands, or anything. If one could just go on and on like this.... She felt her head lifted and a glass put to her lips. She was comfortable and at rest in the crook of an arm, until a burning liquid ran down her throat. As she coughed, her mind flashed back once more into the throes of pain. Her eyes opened and she looked up into the doctor's face. She felt the tweed of his great-coat against her neck and cheek, and his gay, woollen scarf dangled like a ladder on to her chest. His black eyes looked down into hers, and he smiled at her as he laid her head back on the saddle.

'That's what is meant by a doctor being on the spot, Kate,' he said. 'You faint, and I knock at the door.'

She neither answered nor smiled, but closed her eyes again. Her mother said, 'Is she all right, doctor?' And Rodney answered, 'Yes, she'll be all right; just let her rest.'

There was quiet in the kitchen. Kate felt the three of them looking down on her. Then a sob from Pat rent the silence, and she heard a thud as he turned away and flung himself into a chair, and the beat of his fist on the table.

She listened to Rodney's voice, low and questioning, and she listened to Pat's muffled replies. Then, from soothing tones to one of utter incredulity, Rodney's voice changed to low, bitter cadences: 'He can't do it, Pat! ... Why, man, don't be a fool! ... Come on, pull yourself together!'

There was a movement of the chair as Pat writhed in agony.

'See here, Pat! You don't mean to tell me you are go-ing to let that damn priest wreck your life, and, what is much more important to you, Kate's? ... You can't let him do it! He hasn't the power to make you marry any-one you don't want to; he has only the power you give him, through your fear of him.'

Kate thought, You don't understand ... You're wasting your breath; you've got to be a Catholic before you can understand....

'Pat ... go to him now; tell him you'll support the child; tell him that you were tricked into it.... Look, Pat, I'll stand by you in this.... You won't be without friends;

let her take you to court.'

'You're a grand fellow.' There was the utterness of finality in Pat's few words; and they conveyed to Rodney the hopelessness of his appeal.... But it mustn't be hopeless! Pat must marry Kate; he had got to marry her! She must be made safe, put out of reach.... He didn't want that internal war over again, it had been hell. He had seen the danger signal last Christmas Eve.... She must get married; there must be some barrier put between them.... He started talking again, and no one answered him.

The back-door latch clicked, and Kate opened her eyes. And when she heard her mother's surprised voice say, 'Father!' she thought, No, no, it can't be! This is too much.... Her mother continued. 'We don't often see you.' And, realising it was Father Bailey, she relaxed.

'I've been to your lodgings, Pat; I've been looking all over for you.'

'Have you, Father?' said Pat, in a dead voice.

'I wanted you to know how sorry I am about all this, Pat.'

'I know it.' There was a soothing quality in Pat's words, as if he intended to lessen the pain of the priest's embarrassment.

'Sir, do you consider this is right?' Rodney addressed the priest without using the usual prefix. 'To trap a man, half demented with trouble, into marrying a woman he hates ... ?'

Father Bailey, looking at Rodney sadly, broke in, 'We all have our own ideas of what is right and wrong, doctor. When a wrong is done someone always suffers, it's inevitable. And when it's the ones we know and respect it appears like injustice, and we see the enforcing of right as cruelty or wickedness. But,' he added wistfully, 'a lot, of course, depends on how it is enforced.'

'What right has Father O'Malley or any man for that matter, to wield the power of fear to make another follow the course that he deems right? ... Surely you would admit that such coercion is diabolical?' Rodney faced the priest, his beard stuck out in anger.

'I would admit that coercion by fear is diabolical,'

answered Father Bailey calmly. 'But then, we have both to explain to each other what we mean by fear and by coercion. I think we view the former from different standpoints. It's a question I'd like to talk over with you some time, doctor, for it makes for lengthy discussion. And now, if you will excuse me . . .' He turned once again to Pat: 'Would you care to walk part of the way home with me, Pat?'

Pat nodded dumbly, then made to go towards the saddle for some final word with Kate. But he changed his mind, and, with a violent shake of his head, he stumbled out of the back-door.

The priest went to Kate and bent over her: 'You're not well, Kate. I can understand that; but try not to worry,' he said. 'I will see you later and have a talk. . . . God is good, and the path is all mapped out for us; He knows exactly where we are going.' He patted her shoulder, then followed Pat, and there was silence in the kitchen once more.

The path is all mapped out for us! Kate shuddered. Why struggle? Why try? . . . The path is all mapped out. . . . It always had been; she had tried to take a side road last Christmas Eve. She had seen herself as good and noble, and the spasms of happiness that had been hers this past year she had accepted as payment for her goodness. . . . Pat, the buffer, had gone, and with him the cloak she had wrapped around her real feelings. She had not dramatised anything; she knew, as she felt Rodney standing over her, that it had not been her imagination which had played her false; she had played herself false and had clung to Pat, as a drowning man to a straw.

What lay before her now? . . . A struggle, or a giving up? . . . A delightful giving up . . . and involving what? . . . Scandal? Well, she had been scandalised when she was innocent. But the other person . . . what would scandal bring to him? . . . Disaster, finally! She sensed this more than she knew it, glimpsing the lengths to which his feelings would carry him. . . . And what of her mother and of Annie? . . . and of the other Annies who might come? . . . No, she must fight it! But could she? . . . The path is all mapped out!

She suddenly began to laugh, and once more found herself in the shelter of Rodney's arm.

'Don't do that, Kate!' he said sternly. 'Come now!'

As she saw his free hand come up to touch her cheek, she burst out, 'Did you hear what he said? ... The path is all mapped out!'

'Stop it, Kate! Do you hear?'

She laughed the louder.

'If you don't stop it I'll have to slap you!'

'The path is all mapped out!'

He laid her back and struck her twice on the face, two ringing slaps which made her head reel.

She stopped and lay still, then the slow tears brimmed her eyes and rolled down her cheeks. Her breath caught in her throat and she sobbed painfully and bitterly.

Rodney stared down at her, and gritted his teeth. Then, swiftly falling to one knee, he gathered her into his arms. His face pressed into her hair, he held her, and she clung to him in the paroxysm of her weeping.

Sarah leant against the kitchen table, listening in amazement to the endearments dropping from his lips; her hands, gripping each other, were pressed into her chest. She stared at them, her eyes fixed with anxiety and fear, praying, 'Don't let her do it.... Oh, Mary, Mother of God, don't let her do it!'

# THE BELT

Rodney opened the gate which led from the lane, and walked up between the frost-painted shrubs of the lower garden and across the glassy lawn of the upper to the house. How different it all looked after only ten weeks! Different, but as formal; absence could do nothing to soften its formality, either inside or out. The difference lay, he thought, in his seeing it after a complete break; for nine years he had merely felt it, without seeing it.

Mary opened the door to him: 'Why, sir, we weren't expecting you. The mistress is in Newcastle; she went right after lunch, and she won't be back till tea-time.'

'That's all right, Mary. I'll have a bath and something to eat in the meantime.... How are you?'

'Oh, fine, sir.'

Mary watched him as he walked up the stairs.... Coo! he didn't arf look funny without his beard ... barelike! But the khaki suited him all right. Well, that would mean another one for dinner tonight.... But cook wouldn't mind; fair daft about him, she was ... be dashing upstairs as soon as she knew, seeing her ladyship wasn't in.... I wonder if she'll be pleased! The thought brought an inward smirk.... See, what did I tell you! she said to herself, as cook hurried up the stairs as fast as her lack of breath allowed.

Rodney called 'Come in!' to the knock on his door. 'Hallo, cook, it's good to see you!' he said.

'Oh, sir, and it's good to see you.... I am glad you're home for Christmas, sir.'

'So am I, cook, and I'm as hungry as a hunter. Can you do anything about it?'

'I'll soon fix that.... Do you like the life, sir?' she asked.

'Oh, it's all right, cook; you get a bit bored at times, you know; nothing much to do ... likely to be more next year!'

She nodded. Yes, when we went over the water there would be more, not arf there would. But she would see he had a good Christmas, for her part, anyway; might be his last, you never could tell. He wouldn't like it when he knew there was a high falutin dinner tonight, with that band of conchies! What else were they, with all their palavering and reading parties, when poor lads were roughing it in the trenches and being knocked off like flies? ... 'Well, I'm glad you're home, sir,' she said. 'And I'll have a meal ready as soon as you are; say half an hour?'

'Fine!' He grinned engagingly at her. 'I've missed your cooking.'

'Go on, sir!' she said, smiling back at him.... Ah, it was nice to have him home; he was human, he was.... 'I'll get Mary to light a fire, this room's like ice,' she said.

'Thanks, cook.'

'Look, sir, there's a good fire in the mistress's room. Why don't you dress in there after your bath, sir, till this warms up?'

'All right, cook; don't you worry, I'll pick the warmest spot. Trust me.'

Mrs. Summers went out, leaving him strangely comforted, with the new sensation of being fussed over.

As he lay in his bath, luxuriating in the pine-scented warmth, he wondered what he would do with his seven days.... Seven days with nothing to do! No bodies to examine, no feet to inspect. He'd see old Peter and Peggy a lot, that'd be good, and do a few shows in Newcastle ... with Stella? No, he didn't think so. What was the good of putting on a front when things stood as they did; he had made his last and final effort a long time ago. What time does to one! he thought; it seems impossible to believe she can hurt me no more and that she hasn't an atom of power over me. I've been a fool all my life where she's concerned, but now I'm free.... What had really brought it about? he asked himself. Kate? No, I was waking up long before Kate entered my mind. I suppose I saw her shallowness and devilry, for she is a devil. Oh, God, what it was to feel free of all desire of her! ... He lashed the water with his feet for a moment; then became still, thinking of Kate.... But was he free? Wasn't he chained to Kate with stronger chains than ever Stella had welded? Yes, he supposed he was. But with what a difference!

He thought back to last Christmas Eve, when he had given up fighting and held Kate in his arms, for the one and only time. He had known then that, had the mother not been there and they could have talked, she would have been his.... She was his; he was convinced of that; as irrevocably as if they had been joined together by that damned, fear-inspiring priest. He had wanted her more than he had ever wanted Stella, the ache for her had persisted from the night he had taken her for the drive two years ago. But he also felt for her something he had never felt for Stella; a certain protectiveness, coupled with a deep admiration for the fight she had made to emancipate herself from the fifteen streets ... he had wanted only Stella's body, her mind had irritated him.

When he had left Kate, on the sound of Tim Hannigan's steps in the back-yard, he already knew what he intended doing.... He would take a little house, perhaps a cottage, outside Newcastle, and install her there, with Annie. No one need know, and if they did what would it matter? He could laugh at all their social codes which cloaked such rampant immorality. He would be hurting no one, the only hurt to Stella would be to her pride.... Over the holidays he had been excited and on edge. When he had called and found that Kate was not on her usual Christmas holidays, but was back at the Tolmaches, he had gone straight there, feeling he had but to see her to hold her in his arms again. His heart had pounded against his ribs at the first glimpse of her; she had looked pale and tired, with a sadness darkening her eyes. He had tried to catch her eye, so that a mingled glance would join them together once again; but within a few minutes of his arrival she had left the room without looking at him. The brothers and sister had discussed the recent happenings with concern, being as troubled and worried as if she were their own. His conscience had pricked him when, using Sarah as an excuse, he had asked if he might go and speak to her about her mother, as he had found her in a really bad state and was afraid she would have to go into hospital. This, he comforted himself, was the truth, but he had hated the idea of making use of it and of deceiving these kind and trusting old people. He had felt sure that, frail as Bernard Tolmache was, he'd have been quite capable of kicking him out had he known the real reason for his desire to see Kate.

When he had opened the green baize door of the kitchen and had seen her sitting by the table, her head resting on her hands, a deep and protective tenderness had been born in him. Swiftly he had taken her hands in his and had drawn her to her feet; but no further, for when his arms would have gone round her she had whispered tensely, 'No, no!'

'Kate, darling,' he had pleaded, holding her hands tightly against his breast, 'you know it's no good, don't you? We have both fought for so long. It's useless.... Oh, Kate, my dear....'

'Please!' she had protested.

But he had gone on, in low, urgent tones: 'You know I am sorry about Pat. There was no one more eager than I that you should marry him; for I was afraid of this very thing happening.... I love you, my dear ... I worship you. Can't you see that? You can ... you've always known it. Oh, Kate, I need you so.... Don't be afraid.'

She strained away from him, and turned her face to one side: 'Mrs. Prince!' The words had seemed wrenched from her.

'Kate, I can explain.... Look at me! I must explain all that; when can I see you? You need not worry about ... Mrs. Prince.... She ... we ... I can't explain here, there's so much to say. When can I see you, Kate?'

'Doctor, I can't ... I mustn't! Don't ask me.'

'Don't say doctor; Rodney, Kate.'

Kate had shaken her head desperately: 'It can't be!'

'You love me, Kate. Look at me.... You do, don't you?'

She had remained silent as he forced her to meet his eyes. 'Even if you won't say it, I know you do; nothing can alter that.' They had stood tense, their eyes holding, hers dark with misery.

On hearing the drawing-room door open he had released her hands and whispered urgently, 'I will write you.' Then, with as much calmness as he could command, he had gone on and told her about her mother, while she had stood looking blankly down at the table.

He had written to her, making an appointment, but she had neither answered the letter nor kept the appointment. Desperate, he had written again and yet again, with the same result. It had been Sarah who had provided the opportunity for seeing her alone, for he had had to send her into hospital; he had taken the task on himself of informing Kate and taking her, by car, to the workhouse. Her genuine anxiety for her mother had silenced any appeal he had intended making. He had driven her and Annie back to the Tolmaches that night, after having met them near the docks; Kate had protested strongly when he had proposed coming to the house to collect them. Annie's delight in being near him and riding in the car again had been touching.

During the following weeks he had seen quite a lot of Kate, but never alone; there had always been Annie or the Tolmaches.

Sarah came out of the hospital and Annie had returned reluctantly home, and things took up their normal course again, at least on the surface. It was when he had decided that he could wait no longer, and that he must see her to explain his case, that he received the letter. He had opened it at breakfast, with Stella sitting opposite him.... It had started, 'Dear Doctor,' and had ended abruptly, 'Kate Hannigan'. It had told him in concise terms that he had a wife and a career to think about, she had her mother and Annie; her mother was still ill and, she knew, was worried about her; she must give her no cause for worry; finally, she loved the Tolmaches, and it would distress her greatly if she had to leave them entirely; but this she would have to do and seek work elsewhere unless he could see her point of view.

No word of love, just an ultimatum; yet he was sure that she was his, as if every line had proclaimed it. Why was it, he had asked himself at that moment, that he, a man of strong passions, as he knew himself to be, should be incapable of having but one woman in his life? ... First, and from boyhood, it had been Stella. He had married Stella when the torch of his passion was at its height, and she had quenched it swiftly and surely. He had been unable to do anything about it, for as long as he had loved Stella he had been incapable of taking from another woman what she had withheld. Now Stella was like the remains of a burn; the scar she had left would always be visible to him, but it didn't hurt any more.... And Kate, this was something different, something higher than any feeling he had had for his wife, which, he knew now, had been all physical. But Kate had bound him as surely as ever Stella had, and he couldn't seek relief from her either. Nor did he want to, in spite of her ultimatum.

He had looked across the table at Stella, so beautifully calm and insolently sure of herself. Divorce had crossed his mind ... non-consummation of conjugal rights.... Yes, he could get it on those grounds; but would he? No, he knew he would never do it.... But she could divorce him.... Would she, if he gave her cause? Not unless it would suit her purpose; and she would have to want it very much, for she was as vain as a peacock, and the very fact of his wanting another woman would make her fight. The whole position had seemed impossible.

An easing, at least, of the situation had pointed itself out after days of mental strife. True, there were feelings of patriotism in the gesture, but it was more as a means of escape that he had enlisted.

Rodney got out of the bath, and was towelling himself vigorously when Mary's voice, following a knock, came through the bathroom door: 'Doctor Swinburn's downstairs, sir; would you like to see him?'

'Why, yes!' Rodney called back. 'Tell him to wait a second; I'll be right down.'

Swinburn had been his locum at one time, then, under pressure of work, he had taken him on as assistant. Now he was in charge and, thought Rodney, thinking himself no end of a fellow, I bet. He had found traits in Swinburn's character which had become evident only through time, and which he did not like; a certain meanness and lack of sympathy and an eye to the main chance were among them. Getting into a dressing-gown he went downstairs and found him in the study.

Doctor Swinburn, a lean young man of middle height, with dark-brown eyes and fair, crinkly hair, a sensual mouth, and a nose that could only be described as pinched, greeted Rodney effusively. They shook hands, and he offered Rodney a cigarette, and lit it for him. 'You're looking fit,' he said; 'although seeing you without your beard is a bit of a shock.'

'It was a bit of a shock to me at first,' laughed Rodney. 'I'm used to it now. Only it's this continual shaving that gets me down.'

'You'll have to let it grow before you come back on the job, or the ladies won't like it,' chuckled Swinburn.

Rodney frowned inwardly. That was the kind of chat that made him annoyed with Swinburn. 'How's everything?' he asked.

'Up to the eyes,' said Swinburn. 'Half the calls are damned unnecessary ... such as Lady Cuthbert Harris. I had a time with her after you left; she wouldn't believe you had gone, wouldn't have me near her; she demanded to know where you were every time I saw her, and said that you must come as you were the only one who understood her. Still I persevered, as one call on her equals a day's work around the docks. But it is hard going. I spend my visits answering questions about you, and tell her you send enquiries about her by every letter....'

'You've no right to say that!' broke in Rodney, somewhat sharply. 'That woman's got enough ideas in her head already.'

'Well, what can I say? We don't want to lose her.'

'We certainly shall if it depends on me visiting her, for I've intended passing her on to you for some time. I never could stand the woman.'

'What will you do when you get the socks? She's knitting some for you,' laughed Swinburn.

'Good God!' exclaimed Rodney.

'Still, it's people like her who keep the practice going,' said Swinburn smugly. 'You know, your books are in a heck of a mess. Some of these dockites haven't paid for as long as six years; I've been rounding them up.'

'I don't want them rounded up,' said Rodney stiffly. 'Some of them can't eat, let alone pay doctor's bills.'

Fool! thought Swinburn.... Can't eat, indeed! No, but they can drink.... Still, keep on the right side of him.... 'Well, just as you say,' he said. 'But it's a devil of a lot of money you're out. I was only thinking for your good.'

'That's very kind of you, but don't press any of them.'

Swinburn looked at him with ill-concealed resentment.... All right for him, with his damned private income; he can afford to talk big. Wonder how much that Hannigan girl has to do with his kindness to the poor? he asked himself. There's never smoke without fire; damn funny rumours going around about her kid.

'You know about old Tolmache dying, I suppose?' he asked Rodney, scrutinising his face for any confirmation of the rumours his words might evoke.

'No,' said Rodney. 'Which one? And when did it happen?' The very mention of the Tolmaches had brought a quickening of his pulse, but he showed nothing of it in his query, his tone implying professional interest only.

'A fortnight ago; the elder one, Rex. And the other two seem to have gone all to pieces lately, since they lost their girl.'

'Lost their girl?'

Swinburn noticed that although Prince's face didn't alter he pressed the cigarette he was holding to his mouth quite flat between his finger and thumb. 'Yes, she went home to look after her mother. It was either that or the workhouse.... I had to put it to her quite plainly. The mother couldn't be left alone, with just neighbours popping in, she needs constant attention. I told her her mother couldn't last long, and if she went into the workhouse it would be to die. So she left the Tolmaches and went home.'

Staring at Swinburn with an expressionless face, Rodney thought, God, I thought he meant she was dead! But

Kate, back in the fifteen streets! All day, every day, living practically in that kitchen, cut off from the Tolmaches and all they stood for.... For a moment he experienced the pain that the wrench must have been to her. Sarah might linger on for months ... years even ... with care and attention. And Kate getting older, living alone.... For he knew the Tolmaches had spoiled her for ever for the fifteen streets and the companionship that community had to offer. Mentally she'd be alone, and he could do nothing. Gone even was the chance of seeing her on this leave; he couldn't go to the fifteen streets, she would only be disconcerted, knowing that it would upset her mother.

He's not giving much away, said Swinburn to himself, but he didn't squash that cigarette for nothing. 'Well,' he remarked, getting up, 'I must be on the move again. I just called in to see if I could do anything for Mrs. Prince.' His eyes flicked away and he turned towards the door; and Rodney thought, Good Lord, him too.

Rodney felt a sudden pity for Swinburn, for it seemed such a frightful waste for anyone to lavish affection on Stella; it was like falling in love with the statue of de Milo. 'I'll tell her you called,' he said, 'I'll be seeing you again; I'll look in at the surgery at the beginning of the week.'

'You'll see me tonight,' said Swinburn, continuing towards the front-door, 'I'm coming to dinner.... See you later, then, goodbye.'

Rodney returned upstairs. So there was a dinner tonight: Barrington; Tollyer, her publisher; that modern poet chap, with his hair on his shoulders; and Swinburn. For two pins he'd make a dash and get a train home.... Then there'd be the question: Where was Stella? and 'It's just as I expected' looks from Frank. There was nothing for it but to stick it out.

He found his room struck cold, after the warmth of his bath and the room downstairs. The fire was alight, but as yet giving off no heat. So he took a change of underwear and a suit out of the wardrobe and went into the room across the landing.

Stella's room ... her own, of which he had no part, the

room she had made for herself after their final break. Funny, he thought, I haven't been in this room half a dozen times in three years. As he dressed he looked around; it expressed her perfectly, everything ice-blue and gold, all except the old walnut bureau that stood in the deep shadow of the recess. The sight of that simple piece of furniture brought back to his mind the day they had bought it ... that had been one of their happy days, when Stella had given way to the excitement and thrill of furnishing a house. The bureau was one of the few pieces left of those they had had chosen together; all the others had been gradually replaced. He thought of the young man who had sold the bureau to them; he had sensed their excitement and added to it by betting them they would never find the secret drawer. Rodney had soon found the button which would release the spring, but he had kept the knowledge to himself, leaving to Stella the pleasure of discovery.

Looking down on the bureau now he felt a sudden sadness. Gone for ever was the wonder of life that had seemed to be opening for him when they had bought it. Gently pulling open the right-hand side drawer, he felt in the roof for the button. Pressing it, he watched the narrow top of the desk slowly rise, exposing two sets of two drawers, divided by a miniature cupboard, and he felt again the romance of the workmanship and ingenuity. He opened one of the tiny drawers and pressed another button. The door of the cupboard swung open, revealing an exquisitely panelled recess in satinwood.... He could almost hear Stella's squeal of delight on that bygone day ... such a faraway day, for now she apparently used the desk only as a receptacle for broken pieces of jewellery.... Inside the cupboard was a square box, filling most of the space. He took it out and idly examined it. The lid was in a beautiful mosaic pattern of mother-of-pearl. Just as idly he lifted the lid; then stood staring down at the collection of tubes within. Two were full, but the majority empty and tightly rolled up. After reading the writing on one of the tubes, which was in both French and English, he stood staring fixedly at the box for some time. Then he opened the cylindrical box which was partly covered by the tubes.

Slowly the blood drained from his face. Like one in a trance, he closed the secret drawer and, taking the mother-of-pearl box, he returned to his room.

His discovery had given him the biggest shock of his life, and, for the moment, he was quite incapable of thinking; he could only feel. As he stood looking down into the frozen garden, some atom of respect that he still retained for his wife cried out ... Don't let this be! She couldn't have done it.... But, then, she had done it, and with what success!

He stared again at the box, and all that it implied rushed into his mind, searing it as with a hot iron. Right from the beginning, from the night of their marriage she must have practised this. From where had she obtained such knowledge? she was barely twenty at the time. She had deliberately killed ... yes, that was the word ... she had killed every chance of giving him a child from the word go, and he had never for a second suspected it. How could he? So gentle, so fragile, so ... virginal a creature. She had fooled him, oh, so easily! How she must have been laughing all these years!

He could see her now, with that pathetic air, when he had spoken of children. So hurt had she looked that at times it had wrung his heart, feeling that she suffered the miss as greatly as he.... Explained now, also was the freezing attitude which could leave him distraught and the rages which his spontaneous love-making would bring about ... there were the times when she had been unprepared. And all these years he had been duped by that delicate, gentle creature! Of how many sons had she deprived him? Had she withheld herself after having given him one son, how different life would have been! ... His son. His mind conjured up a boy of nearly fourteen, bursting with vitality, eyes bright with the eagerness of life. He would be home for the holidays now, turning the house upside down, thumping up the stairs calling ... 'Father! ... where are you, father?'

Rodney listened. The cry of 'Father! father!' re-echoed from his mind through the stillness of the house. He shuddered violently and ground his teeth. Waves of hatred swept through him.... Where was she? If he could only get his hands on her!

Recognising the strength of his emotion, a fear took its place and he realised he must not see her yet, but must get out of the house and try to walk this off, giving himself time to let the blow settle and rest among the many hurts she had dealt him. For he knew that, should he encounter her now, he would kill her as surely as she had killed his sons.

He locked the box in his suitcase, and put on his greatcoat and went downstairs. Mrs. Summers hurried out of the kitchen: 'It's all ready, sir. I hope you enjoy...' She stopped, taking in his outdoor apparel and, most of all, the change in him from half an hour ago. He looked ill, as if he had had a shock.... But there'd been nobody in the house except Doctor Swinburn. Ah! perhaps that was it! He had found out about him and the missis. Although, what with them separate rooms an' all, you wouldn't have thought he'd have minded like this. But there was nowt so funny as men; just look at her Sep.

'I'm sorry, cook, I've got to go out.' His hands fumbled with his hat.

'That's all right, sir, that's all right,' she said gently. 'Perhaps you'll feel like it when you come back.'

'Yes. I may feel more like it when I return.'

She watched him leave. The straightness had gone out of his back, he seemed humped, somehow. She returned to her kitchen and sat down; and suddenly began to cry, without knowing the reason.

It had been three o'clock when Rodney had left the house. He had walked right through Shields to the sea. But there were soldiers everywhere, mostly near the sea, which he was wont to seek as a balm. He had walked back through the town, choosing the back streets and alleys like someone trying to escape, through Tyne Dock and East Jarrow, and on to the Davidsons. He had turned his mind from the fifteen streets as he passed them in the darkness of the early evening; Kate must not come into this pit of hate which no walking or reasonable thinking seemed to erase.

Peter and Peggy and the two children were having late

138

tea when he walked in on them. In the enthusiasm of shaking hands and exclamations of delight at seeing him, they did not, for the moment, take in his weariness and the drawn, strained look about his eyes. He smiled on the children, but hardly spoke. Michael and Cathleen clambered about him, shouting. 'Where's your beard, Uncle Rodney?' until Peggy ordered them to finish their tea.

Having packed them off to the kitchen to Anna, she turned to Rodney: 'Sure you won't have something to eat, Rodney?' she asked looking hard at him.

He shook his head.

'Well, have a cup of tea then,' she pleaded.

'All right, a cup of tea then,' he said.

While he drank the tea Peggy and Peter exchanged bewildered glances. 'Anything wrong, Rodney?' asked Peter.

'No, no,' Rodney replied, twisting his mouth into a smile.

'How are you finding the new life?' Peggy enquired.

'Oh, all right, Peggy.'

'Glad you went?' Peter questioned.

'Yes.... Yes, I'm glad I went.'

The almost monosyllabic answers, so unlike Rodney, both puzzled and alarmed them. They sat talking to him, covering up his silences. When he suddenly got to his feet they rose with him, deeply concerned. 'I'll have to go; I'm not very good company tonight. See you both soon.'

Peter set him to the door: 'What is it, Rodney?' he asked. 'Surely you can tell me.'

'Yes, I could tell you, Peter.... Oh, I don't know,' he said, running his hands through his hair. 'I feel so boiled up with hate that I.... Have you ever thought of killing a woman, Peter?'

Peter stared at him: 'You're not going home tonight, man,' he said quietly, putting his hand on Rodney's arm; 'you're staying here.'

'It's no use, Peter.... I've got to go. I've got to see her; I'll not rest until I do. And there's a dam' dinner on!'

'What has she done?'

'She's ...' But he was unable to put into words what his wife had done to him. 'I'll tell you another time,' he said and was gone.

'What do you think I'd better do, Peggy?' asked Peter, some minutes later.

'Follow him,' she answered.

'But she has one of her dinners on,' he said, pointing to the clock. 'It's half-past seven now, they'll just be sitting down.... He can't do anything with people there.'

'Never mind; you go. You can always pretend you haven't seen him, and say you heard he was home and called.... He'll understand.'

'He's walking. I'll give him time to get there, and then I'll take the car,' said Peter.

The company had just finished dinner and settled themselves in the drawing-room, Stella, three other women and four men. The women, who were all unusually plain, were not the wives of the men, but were very pleased to be there in any capacity. The men were very glad to be there too; for what could be more pleasant than to eat one of Stella's dinners, and then to sit and look at her for a whole evening. For each of the men she had a peculiar charm. She spelt romance, and romance always beckoned. That the beckoning was becoming an irritation, Herbert Barrington was forced to admit to himself; he was heartily tired of promises. Only once had he experienced anything with Stella that could be given the name of an affair. And then it had been very disappointing, petering out to nothing, leaving him without the stimulus of his urge for her; quite a dead thing, yet full of live irritation.... She had promised it would be better next time, but there had never been a next time. And now there was Swinburn, and she still kept him dangling on ... promising ... and he was unable to free himself.

He was thinking of all she had told him about her husband, and not for the first time a vague mistrust of what she had said entered his mind, when Rodney himself walked in. He watched Stella's eyes dart to him, and he knew her well enough to know she was uneasy behind her polished smile. He rose with the other men and joined his greeting to theirs. It wasn't until the ladies were introduced that Barrington realised that Rodney

140

had neither spoken nor smiled, but had merely acknowledged the introductions by a nod.

They all sat down again, Rodney taking a seat opposite Stella. A strange silence, which no one seemed to have the power to break, fell on the room. He's heard about Swinburn, Stella thought, and as usual is acting like a fool ... she had heard from Mary of their meeting earlier in the day and of his rejected meal.... He looks ghastly. But she felt the thrill of power rise in her with the knowledge that she could still make him feel like this. For lately she had been piqued by his indifference.... She had got what she wanted, a life free from what she called his sexual pesterings, but it had turned out to be less satisfying than she had thought. Well, by the look of things, she could alter it at any time. She smiled, and addressed him, for the benefit of the company, as if they had met but a short while ago, instead of nearly three months: 'We didn't wait dinner for you, dear; I didn't know what time you would get back.'

He made no answer, but sat looking at her, his face set.

Her poise began to slip away, she felt uneasy.... He hadn't taken his eyes from her for a second. What was everyone thinking?... She turned to Herbert ... you could always rely on him to keep the tone of the party just right.... 'Will you begin reading, Herbert?' she asked sweetly.

But Herbert was being awkward too. 'You begin,' he said. 'Let us hear some of the latest prose poems.'

'Yes!' chorused the ladies, glad to hear the sound of their own voices, for since the husband had come in things had become decidedly strained.

Without further ado, Stella took up a slim volume from the table at her hand, settled herself in her chair, gave one quick glance at the company, and commenced to read:

> Let the beauty linger in my soul
> Of a rose just bursting into bloom,
> Of a bird in flight,
> Of the moon, new born into the night,
> Reflecting on a sea of gentle ripples.

*Let the beauty linger in my soul*
*Of a winter morn draped in patterned frost,*
*Of air like wine,*
*Of sunlit snow on limbs of trees,*
*Of black, brown trunks bare to the winds that*
*    sweep the woods.*
*Of drifts of crisp brown leaves,*
*Swept, now here, now there, with the breeze.*

*Let the beauty linger in my soul*
*Of firelight in a darkened room,*
*Of kindly words,*
*Of lovers' laughter coming through the night,*
*Until, at last, I know no greater peace nor ease*
*But to remember these.*

The company was startled and shocked by a harsh
sound; Rodney, his head leaning against the high back of
the chair, was laughing. He stopped abruptly and bent
towards Stella: 'I like that; so full of feeling; so much
understanding of the simple things of life, especially that
part: Of lovers' laughter coming through the night.'

Stella stared at him, anger and fear fighting each other
in her face. The women looked distinctly shocked, and
the men indignant. Swinburn stood up and impulsively
took a step towards her. Barrington, watching him,
thought, I would have done that at one time, and wondered why he did not do so now. His mind was suddenly
distracted from the scene before him by steps on the
gravel outside the french window. He was sitting close to
the heavy velvet curtains, and when the sharp rap came
on the window he started, as did the rest of those in the
room; thankfully, it would seem, as the tension was unbearable.

They all turned towards the window, and Stella, gladly
clutching at this distraction, said: 'Someone's knocking;
who on earth can it be? See who it is, Herbert; but do be
careful of the lights.'

Barrington stepped within the closed curtains and
opened the window: 'Who is it?' he asked.

'I want Doctor Swinburn. I've been to his house, and

they said he was here. I couldn't find the door, then I saw a bit of light,' the childish voice floated into the room.

'You'd better come in,' said Barrington, 'or the light will show.'

When Annie stepped through the velvet curtain she brought a sense of unreality with her. Everyone, including Rodney, sat or stood perfectly still, looking at her as she stared from one to the other, blinking in the strong light.

'Christ!' said the poet to himself. 'What a picture!' He looked at her hair, springing away from the crown of her head and floating down to her waist in sheer silver lines, at the deep fringe which curved inwards just above her dark eyebrows, and at her slanting green eyes, set in skin so delicate as to appear artificial.... Here was beauty!

Annie's frightened eyes searched the faces before her, looking for Doctor Swinburn's. They passed over a face that seemed familiar; then darted back to it: 'Oh!' she cried, and ran towards Rodney at the same time as he stepped towards her. 'Oh, doctor!' She flung her arms around his waist, and pressed her cheek hard against his waistcoat. Rodney stroked her hair and held her close, oblivious of the incredulous eyes upon them.

'What is it, Annie?' he asked. 'What's wrong?'

'It's Kate,' said Annie, recalling the urgency of her errand and gazing up into his face. 'My granda hit her with the belt. He hit her and hit her, and the sharp prong stuck in her neck. And it won't stop bleeding, the blood's all over the place. Oh, come quickly!'

For one startled moment Rodney looked down on her face, then turned and hurried out of the room. Annie followed him into the hall, keeping close on his heels. He was getting into his coat when Swinburn and Stella came out of the drawing-room.

'You're not going!' said Swinburn. 'Surely I'm the person to deal with this.'

'Have you gone mad, Rodney?' asked Stella, with deathly calm. 'What will people say? And how dare you place me in the position of having to explain your behaviour to my guests! I think you are out of your mind ... I'm sure you are,' she finished.

Without a word Rodney buttoned his coat; then slipped into the cloakroom off the hall and filled a small case with necessities from a medicine cupboard. When he returned he said to Swinburn, with studied politeness, 'I would like a word with my wife, if you don't mind.'

Swinburn, with compressed lips, went into the drawing-room.

Before Rodney could speak Stella said under her breath, 'What is this girl to you? How dare you insult me ... for a maid, a common servant! ... You shan't do it, do you hear? I'll have her hounded out of the town.'

'Will Barrington and Swinburn go with her?' Rodney asked calmly, as he picked up his hat and took Annie's hand. He felt quite calm now.

It was years since he had uttered a prayer; but when Annie had stepped into the room, she had appeared like an angel sent to stay his hand and calm his mind; and her arms, as they went around him, seemed to extinguish that blaze of hate which had urged him on to Stella's destruction; and he had offered up a silent prayer to a God in whom he had not believed.

Rage flashing from her eyes, Stella gazed at him. That she should be overlooked, in any capacity, for a maid was unthinkable. She turned her furious glance on the child ... that's why he had always liked this child; the mother was his mistress.... But for how long? Not so long ... it couldn't have been. He had been all hers until three years ago, she knew that. Well, he would be hers again.... Suddenly she wanted him back, wanted him as she had never done before. His charm, which had been dead to her, sprang to life again, and she saw him as he must appear to other women.

The anger died out of her, and she seemed to melt to a clinging softness before his eyes.

'Darling, don't go,' she pleaded. 'Or if you must, hurry back.' She touched his arm.

Rodney looked from her changed face to the hand on his arm, and laughed softly.

'Wait,' he said to Annie; 'I won't be a minute.'

Then to Stella: 'I have something for you. You'd better have it now, as I don't know when I'll be back.'

She watched him take the stairs two at a time, and return, hurrying still, with a box in his hands. She was looking at his face, thinking: No common slut will get the better of me, so she did not see his gift until he had placed it in her hands.

Slowly the blood drained from her face as she saw the familiar mother-of-pearl box. She raised her eyes to his, and for a moment they stood looking at each other. And in that time she knew he was gone from her for ever, and a destructive hate was let loose in her.

He left her without a word.

When they were outside, Rodney gripped Annie's hand.

'Can you run?' he asked. 'We'll catch a tram; it's no use me tinkering with the car, it hasn't been used for weeks. Come, keep tight hold of me.'

They ran down the garden and out into the lane.

'What happened?' he asked, as they ran.

'My granda said I had to go back to the Borough Road school,' panted Annie, 'and Kate said she wouldn't send me. He's been on about it ever since Kate came home.... Oh, doctor, will she die? the blood was all over the place.'

Rodney gripped her hand tighter and increased his pace.

They were nearing the end of the lane when they almost ran into a figure.

Rodney gave an exclamation.

'That you, Rodney?' asked a familiar voice.

'Yes, Peter,' said Rodney, surprised. 'What are you doing here?'

'What are you running for?' asked Peter anxiously. 'Are you all right? ... What's happened?'

The reason for Peter's presence flashed on Rodney, and he put out his hand and gripped Peter's arm.

'Nothing's happened, Peter. But thanks for coming, all the same.... Have you got your car here? Something's wrong with Kate; old Hannigan has been beating her. Annie here came up to the house for Swinburn, and, incidentally, brought me to reason again.... Will you run us up to the fifteen streets?'

Peter did not question why Swinburn wasn't seeing to

10

the case, nor why Rodney should be so concerned about Kate Hannigan. Enough that he was himself again.

When they reached the end of the fifteen streets, he dropped them, not offering to accompany Rodney to see what the trouble was. Although he didn't believe for one moment that Rodney was the father of Annie, there was something here he could not understand, but something into which, he felt, it was not his business to probe.

So he left them, saying, 'Come up tomorrow, Rodney ... come to dinner.... Mind, don't forget ours is at one o'clock,' he added, laughing.

'I will,' said Rodney. 'Many thanks, Peter.'

And, taking Annie's hand again, he hurried off.


It was Mr. Mullen who opened the door to them, peering at them in the dim light.

'Oh,' he said, 'it's you! You've been quicker than I thought.'

Then, on closer inspection, 'Begod, if it isn't Doctor Prince, himself! ... Well, I didn't expect to see you, doctor; I thought you'd be across the water by now. But I'm glad to see you, all the same.... Mind how you go,' he admonished; 'this place is in a hell of a mess.'

Rodney looked at the kitchen aghast. The table was end up near the window, the floor was strewn with broken crockery, Lord Roberts had been ruthlessly torn from his frame, and from his horse, which, with his black bodyguard, was now lying on top of a pile of brasses in the far corner of the room. The mantelpiece, which the brasses had adorned, was bare; the chiffonier door was splintered, as if a foot had gone through it; and the wall near the staircase was spattered with blood.

'Yes; just look at it!' said Mr. Mullen. 'He should be put bloody well inside. I wanted to go for the bobbies. But would Sarah hear of it? No! Didn't want the disgrace of fetching the bobbies. But I told her that if anything happens to that lass, there'll be more than a bit of disgrace ... he'll swing! ... 'Bout time too, I say; bloody maniac!'

'Where is he?' asked Rodney.

'Oh, he's cleared out. He always does after a bout like

this. You won't see him for days; goes to his sister's in Jarrow, I think. Hope he breaks his bloody neck in getting there. That's my prayer.... Can you see your way?' he asked, as Rodney went up the stairs, and added: 'You stay here with me, Annie, and we'll see if we can get this place straight.'

Sarah, sitting beside Kate's bed, gave a start as Rodney entered the room, and her fingers went uncertainly to her mouth, and Mrs. Mullen, looking up from the fire she was tending, exclaimed in surprise: 'Why, doctor!'

Rodney gave her a nod and bent over Kate, whose face was ashen except where it was spattered with blood. A towel, pressed to her neck, was red and wet.

He stripped off his coat.

'Come,' he said to Sarah gently. 'You must go to bed; you shouldn't be up, you know.' Whatever had to be done, he couldn't do it with her sitting looking at him, with that pained and frightened expression.

'Will she die?' asked Sarah, letting him help her to rise.

'Not if I can help it ... you know that,' he added softly.

She turned to him at the door, looking up into his face: 'You'll not hurt my Kate?' she pleaded.... 'Oh, doctor, don't hurt her.'

'I'll never hurt Kate,' he answered, after a moment. 'You can rest assured.'

She sighed and turned away as if satisfied. Mrs. Mullen, taking her arm, put her own construction on the conversation. 'Of course he won't hurt her, Sarah. You know that. If anyone can put her right, it will be the doctor.'

'Pray God you're right,' murmured Rodney, as he set about examining Kate.

She lay quite still, her eyes closed. When he lifted up an eyelid he saw she was conscious, but she gave no sign of recognition.

He took the towel gently away from her neck and examined the wound, his eyes narrowing as he did so. What an escape! Another fraction and it would have been a jugular vein. As it was she had lost a lot of blood.

She was still in her clothes—what was left of them. Her blouse was torn in shreds, disclosing the weals on her breast and shoulders. The flesh was torn in places, and was now beginning to discolour. His jaw stiffened, even as his heart melted with pity.

'Can you help me, Mrs. Mullen?' he asked, as she came back into the room.

'I'll do whatever I can, doctor,' she answered.

'That's good. Then just follow what I say and we'll get along fine.... First get me some boiling water, and then we'll start.'

'You've missed your vocation, Mrs. Mullen,' said Rodney, some time later. 'You should have been a nurse.'

Her homely face flushed at his praise.

'Never had no chance of being anything like that, in my time,' she said.... 'Will I try to get her clothes off, doctor?' she added.

'No, her corsets are loose, so that's all right.'

'I'll sit up with her,' said Mrs. Mullen. 'I'll just go and settle them next door, and I'll come back. She'd better not be left, had she?'

Rodney turned from washing his hands and picked up the towel and dried them carefully.

'No, she can't be left,' he said; 'but I'll be staying, Mrs. Mullen.'

For a moment she looked her surprise.

Then: 'Very well, doctor,' she said. 'I'll get you some wood up to keep this fire going.'

It was none of her business. She had heard rumours, which she hadn't believed for a minute; but now ... well, he was a fine chap. But he was married and Kate was a Catholic, and these things didn't ought to be. Still, she had a family of her own, and God knew what some of them would come to. Look at her Michael, for instance, going after Betty Farrow, and her a rank Nonconformist. You see, you couldn't tell what'd befall your bairns. And with Kate being so bonny and that, it was harder for her. Well, she'd keep her mouth shut. Nobody would know owt from her....

'I'll bring you up a bite to eat, later on,' she said, and went out.

It was close on two o'clock when Rodney heard the carol singers. At first their voices were distant and thin. They were some streets away, he thought, and he hoped they would come no nearer and disturb Kate.

She was sleeping peacefully, after having had a light draught, and the deathly pallor had gone from her face. He felt he had been sitting there for an eternity; he felt no weariness nor any discomfort from the straight-backed chair. Had the choice lain with him of being whisked away to any place on earth at that moment, he would have elected to stay exactly where he was.

The room had changed since he had last seen it; the floor was now covered with linoleum, a chintz frill camouflaged the wash-hand stand, and a number of books stood upon a chest of drawers. These additions, together with the innovation of a gas mantle, had transformed the appearance of the room from that of stark poverty, which he remembered, and gave it an air of homeliness.

Kate had neither spoken to him nor looked at him, but he knew she was aware of his presence. He sat close to the bed, feeling more at peace than he had been for years.

The carol singers, suddenly giving voice a few doors away, made him start. Strong male and female voices rose to the heavens, crying:

'God rest you merry, gentlemen,
Let nothing you dismay . . .'

He clicked his tongue with impatience, and was about to rise when Kate said, in a small voice, 'It's all right; I like to hear them.'

'I thought you were still sleeping,' Rodney said softly. 'Kate, look at me. How are you feeling?'

She opened her eyes slowly and looked up at him, as he bent above her, and her answer surprised him.

'At peace,' she said.

They stared at each other, in silence. Then she murmured, 'Do you believe in prayers being answered?'

Before Rodney could reply, she went on, 'No, you don't. You don't believe in God, do you?'

'Don't talk, my dear,' he said soothingly, his fingers on her pulse.

'I must talk. Don't stop me. If I don't speak now, I never shall.... Rodney,' she whispered his name for the first time.

He caught her hand and carried the palm to his mouth.

'Oh, my love!'

'I prayed to see you before you went to France, and my prayers have been answered.'

'Beloved!'

The dropping of her defences was so unexpected that he felt light headed. He sat down and pulled his chair nearer to her, and traced his lips over her fingers: 'Oh, Kate!'

'Nothing can be changed,' she whispered, 'only I wanted you to know before you went that I ... I ...'

'Say it, my darling.'

He remained still, her hand pressed to his mouth, waiting.

'I love you.'

Making a little sound like a sigh he laid his face on the pillow beside hers. His cheek couldn't touch her because of the padding around her neck. But she turned her head slightly, and they lay looking at each other in silence.

When she would have spoken he put his fingers on her lips: 'Not now, my beloved. Not now. Go to sleep.'

He gently stroked her hair, and the delight of touching it was overwhelming. 'You can talk tomorrow and tell me all the things I long to hear.... It's all right,' he assured her as a flicker of apprehension came into her eyes, 'nothing is changed; I know that.... Sufficient to hear you say you love me. Sufficient for life, my dear.'

As she dropped off to sleep again, he thought of the strangeness of the past twelve hours; most of all, that she had to be beaten almost to death for her prayer to be answered, and that through her suffering he had been saved from himself.

# FRANCE

'No, Annie; you're not going. And don't ask again.'

Kate went on kneading lumps of dough into loaves and putting them into tins.

'There's hardly any coal left, Kate. And Rosie and Florrie and Jimmy got a sackful of lovely cinders yesterday, nearly six bucketfuls. . . .'

'I've told you you're not going!' Kate turned sharply on Annie as the back door opened. 'And don't ask again.'

'And why not, may I ask?' queried Mrs. Mullen, coming in. 'It's going to do her no harm, Kate, going getting a few cinders.'

Kate sighed. 'She's not going, Mrs. Mullen.'

' 'Tisn't any disgrace, Kate. They like it; it's a sort of game to them. And when they sit round the fire at night, it's their fire.'

'It's no use talking . . . she's not going.'

'You make me sick, Kate, so you do. You can't bring her up in cotton wool, not round these doors you can't. . . . And you can't burn the candle at both ends, either.'

Kate gave her a sharp glance.

'Ah!' went on Mrs. Mullen; 'thinks nobody knows; but you can't sneak out of the house at midnight and come back in the small hours of the mornin', without anybody hearing you. You weren't back at three this mornin', for I listened for you. . . . Now, don't you think it's better to let the child go and pick in the daylight than you to sit on the tip among a lot of men in the dead of the night?'

Kate arranged the loaf tins along the fender and covered them with a cloth.

'They are mostly women who are there, the few men are old,' she said.

'It's a disgrace that you should go at all,' said Mrs. Mullen.

'But not that Annie should go?' questioned Kate sharply.

'No, that's different; she's only a bairn. Anyway, why doesn't that big lazy hulk do some picking? He's not working half his time. What's up with him?' Mrs. Mullen felt she knew, without asking, what was up with Tim Hannigan. He was puzzled, as she was herself. He, of course, would know about Kate and the doctor being thick, and wondered why, consequently, money wasn't more plentiful. She wondered herself. She couldn't, somehow, understand it. It was usual to be in funds, under the circumstances, but Kate certainly wasn't. Hannigan, she thought, was suspecting Kate of withholding her money from the house, and was playing up, making his bad leg an excuse for staying off work.

'Leave the house without a fire for a few days, he'll soon get a sack on his back then,' she finished.

'There's my mother's fire to be kept going, and bread to bake, and food to cook. I'd rather freeze than ask him ... you know that.'

'Aye, lass, I know,' said Mrs. Mullen flatly. She patted Kate's arm. 'It's a hell of a life.... What makes me mad,' she suddenly started, 'is that lot o'er there,' she indicated the houses opposite, 'getting pit coal for practically nowt and selling it for tuppence and tuppence ha'penny a pail, and not a roundie in it. The lot I got yesterday was all slack. Daylight robbers!'

Three faces suddenly appeared at the kitchen window. 'Is Annie coming?'

Mrs. Mullen opened the door: 'No, she's not. Get yerselves away.'

'Aw ... w!' They stood, shapeless bundles of old coats and scarves, each carrying a bucket and a raker, and Rosie with an empty sack slung over her back. 'Aw ... w! Why not?'

'She's got chilblains,' said Mrs. Mullen. 'Off you go now, and get a nice lot. And if we get a good fire going we'll have panhacklety tonight and ask Santa Claus to come and have a tuck in.'

'Ooh! Panhacklety and Santa Claus!' the younger ones cried, banging their buckets together.

They went off down the yard, yelling, 'At the cross, at the cross, where the Kaiser lost his horse and the eagle on his hat flew away....' But Rosie followed more slowly, turning to the window to look at Annie, standing wistfully there.

'You're a fool, you know, but I suppose you know your own business best.'

Mrs. Mullen opened the stair door: 'Anything you want taking up?' she asked.

'No thanks,' said Kate. 'She's had her wash and her breakfast. And, Mrs. Mullen ... you won't mention the tip?'

'Now what d'you take me for, a numbskull?' Mrs. Mullen gave a toss of her head and went upstairs.

Kate turned to Annie: 'Look out and see if the postman's coming,' she said, glancing at the clock.

It was a quarter to ten. Surely he hadn't been.... He'd be late, it was Christmas Eve. Oh, there must be a letter this morning; he couldn't have gone to France without letting her know ... if he were still in England, he would have written.... Over a week now and no letter; when every other day had brought a letter from him. What was wrong?

Annie returned: 'I can't see him, Kate.... Do you want me to go any messages?' she asked.

'Yes, you'd better go and get some things.' Kate sat down and wrote out a list of groceries, pausing as she did so to consider whether the money would run to all she was putting down. She thought of the case of groceries which had come every Christmas from the Tolmaches and she experienced again that deep sense of personal loss for the very dear people who had provided them. It seemed impossible to believe that she would visit the house in Westoe no more, that the three people who had given her new life now lay, side by side, in the earth.

The brother and sister had seemed to wither away after Rex had died and Kate had left them. They had died in the previous summer within a month of each other, Bernard going first. In his will Bernard had left Kate twenty-five pounds of the hundred which was the total amount of his estate besides his books. Their generosity had amazed Kate afresh when she had learned that they had been living on annuities, not over large for their wants, either. Yet there had always been an outfit every year from Miss Tolmache, and clothes for Annie, expensive books from Mr. Bernard, and sly boxes of chocolates and a pound or two from Mr. Rex. Oh, Kate thought, were there ever such people born, as they!

She remembered her last talk with Mr. Bernard: 'Take happiness, Kate,' he had said, holding her hands. 'It's all that matters. To be happy and to make another supremely so is the reason for being. In all my life of thinking and pondering I have come to know this as an essential truth. I learned it a little late, more's the pity, but you, Kate, can build your life on it. . . .'

She wondered if he had known. She thought he had . . . dear, beloved Mr. Bernard.

'Will I get the taties from the shop, Kate, or will I fetch them from the docks?'

'Potatoes, Annie!'

'Potatoes . . . I'm sorry, I forgot.'

'Get them from the shop; they are too heavy to carry from the docks. Here's the list, and that's a ha'penny for your tram back. And don't stop if a man should speak to you, unless you know him; you understand?'

'Yes, Kate.'

'Go on then.'

'Here's the postie, Kate,' Annie called from the front door. . . . 'Postman, I mean,' she added.

'All right, dear, I'm coming. Go along.'

Kate waited tensely at the door for the postman's approach.

'Two for you,' he said, as he put them into her hand.

She looked down at their open flaps . . . Christmas cards!

Oh, Rodney, what is it? What's happened? . . . The anxiety was like a heavy weight bearing her down.

She returned to the kitchen and stood looking round her; the feeling of being hemmed in, chained for life within these four walls, returned. That was how she had felt when she had first left the Tolmaches, but Rodney, from last Christmas Eve, had lifted her spiritually out of this house and these streets.

The sufferings she had experienced that night had almost broken her spirit. The humiliation of cowering under the merciless flailing of the belt had affected her more than the physical pain, bringing with it a desire for death.... And then he had come. From the moment he entered the room she knew that he alone could give her the desire to live, and she would fight against him no more.

After a week he had gone, leaving her still in bed, dazed with a strange happiness that demanded nothing but the knowledge that they loved each other. And then his letters had come, sometimes every day, at least every other day. They were like beams of clear light shining through the muck of her surroundings.

Only once had they met since ... a few stolen hours taken from a broken journey when on his way to a remote corner of Scotland. He had wired her to meet him in Newcastle, and they had sat for most of the time in a restaurant, strangely tongue-tied, offering each other food which they neither wanted not could eat. Her love on that day, as now, was no dazed thing, content with words as it had been earlier in the year. Her body had cried out to give him all that she knew he desired but for which he would never now ask. His love had taken on a tender quality that seemed foreign to the desire that emanated from him. It puzzled her and made her impatient. If only he would take her by force, would give her no time to be afraid or to reason, no time to think of the future, the time that would come for looking back, and around her at the living consequence of their union ... this was what she dreaded, another child, who would perhaps say to her, as Annie had said, 'They said I hadn't a da.' Later, Annie might forgive her for having, in the ignorance of youth, created her, but would be ashamed of her for having knowingly created another.... Her mind had repeated, 'She's right,' but her heart had cried, 'Nothing matters'.

Mrs. Mullen came down the stairs and into the kitchen, breaking in on her thoughts.

'She's a bit brighter this morning, Kate.'

'Yes, she seems to have had a good night.'

Kate changed the loaf tins around on the fender.

'Well, I suppose I'll have to go and make a start,' Mrs. Mullen sighed. 'It isn't a bit like Christmas this year. I've no heart to do anything. What with the war and our Michael I don't know where I am.... I just can't get over him. He's never missed mass or benediction for years until lately. Our Peter used to scoff him and say he should be a priest, and now he wants to marry a Nonconformist.'

'She's a nice girl,' said Kate. 'I can quite understand him wanting to marry her.'

'There are plenty of nice Catholic girls, and you know, Kate, there's no good ever comes of a mixed marriage.'

'No, I don't,' said Kate sharply. 'I suppose it is better if they are both of the same religion, but if they love each other that's all that matters.'

'Love! Kate, you talk like a child.' Mrs. Mullen was scornful. 'I'm surprised at you. When you start getting bairns around your feet there's not much time for love. It's quite hard enough when you're both of the same creed; but what's going to happen when he wants them to go to mass and she's bent on sending them to chapel?'

'If they care for each other they'll work that out.'

'I wish Father O'Malley thought like that.'

'Oh, Father O'Malley!' said Kate bitterly. 'He'll do more harm than good.... Father O'Malley!'

'Aye, I've thought that meself, but I daren't say it. It was like hell let loose when he collared our Michael last week. Mike hadn't been to mass and had been keeping out of his way, and there he was, waiting for him when he came in to tea.... The things he said! But it only seemed to make Michael worse. And then later his da started on him....'

'But why?' put in Kate. 'Neither you nor Mr. Mullen go to mass, do you?'

'No. But we've always seen to it that the bairns go.'

'But why should you make them do something that you don't do yourselves, because you either can't be bothered or you no longer believe in it? If you went with them it would be different, and then Mr. Mullen might be justified in going for Michael.... Oh, what's the good of talking?' Kate ended.

'Aye ... what's the good of talking? You're a new generation, and you've got new ideas. You're cleverer than us, you can talk it all out.... But still, in the long run, I can't see it's making you any happier. Well, I'll get away in,' she added. 'And by the way'—she turned from the door—'don't you think it's time you got out for a blow? It's weeks since you've been across the doors ... except at night,' she added slyly. 'If you feel like taking Annie around the shops this afternoon I'll pop in and see to Sarah.'

Kate smiled. 'Thanks, Mrs. Mullen, it's very good of you. I'll see and let you know.'

Left alone, she thought: I can't go before four o'clock, I must see if there's a letter then.... Could anything have happened to him? She wouldn't know if there had ... she wouldn't hear of it until everyone else did.

She took his last letter from inside her blouse, where it lay close to her flesh, pricking her with each movement, a constant reminder of him. Sitting by the fire, she read it again, and it brought him near, into the room....

Beloved,

Let me kiss you. There! I feel better. I am sitting looking at you; your eyes are deep blue pools and they are playing their old tricks on me.... My darling, it seems years since I really looked into them, but I have hopes that it won't be long now. Things are moving at last. In what direction I can't say, but undoubtedly they are moving; and not before time.

It is only the constant thought of you that has kept me sane these past months in this God-forsaken hole. Imagine, three times thinking that I should see you within a few days, and then leave to be cancelled! I felt I should go mad. Everyone is so fed up, and would welcome orders for France. I long for orders for anywhere so long as I can break my journey at Newcastle.... Do you love me, Kate? ... Let me hear you say it. Write it, darling; you don't write it enough, some of your letters are constrained...

Constrained! Kate gazed into the fire. If he were only here now she wouldn't be constrained, overboard would go every fear.... Let there be a child! Let there be two, three!

She thrust the letter into her bosom and began to walk up and down the kitchen.... The years she had wasted in fooling herself! Empty, empty years. Why had she let anything stop them from coming together? His wife, who was nothing to him, her mother, Annie, her religion ... yes, even her religion, which said this beautiful thing was wrong, this feeling of life that he infused into her by his very presence was sin. How could anything so fine be bad?... She couldn't give herself where she didn't love.... Yet they would say it was. Oh, if he were only here.... Rodney! Rodney!

Annie came in, loaded down with her basket of groceries. She had an orange in her hand.

'Look, Kate!' she said. 'Mrs. Clarke gave me this.'

'Dorrie Clarke?' Kate stared at her, apprehension in her eyes. 'What did she say to you? Did she ask you any questions?'

'She only asked me how I was getting on, and said I was getting a big girl. And she asked about grandma, and said she must come and see her.'

'Don't speak to Mrs. Clarke unless you must,' said Kate. 'And never tell her anything about me or ... anyone else. If she asks, say you don't know.'

'I wouldn't tell her anything, Kate,' said Annie, who still carried the memory of a certain Christmas Eve vividly in her mind. 'I didn't want to take the orange, but she made me.'

'All right, dear. Only be careful, she's not a nice woman.'

'Some of the shops are decorated,' said Annie. 'They must be lovely right down Shields,' she added wistfully.

Kate tweaked her nose: 'All right, I'll take you down later.'

'Ooh, Kate!' Annie put her arms around Kate's waist.

They clung closely for a minute.

'There, now,' said Kate. 'Go up with grandma for a while, she must be lonely. Tell her I'll be up as soon as I get the bread in the oven.'

At half-past three Kate and Annie were dressed, ready to go out. They stood beside Sarah's bed.

'Sure you'll be all right, ma?' asked Kate, giving a final pat to the pillows. 'You won't be lonely?'

'No, lass, no. I'm glad you're going out for an hour. You're in too much; you're getting pale and thin.'

She put up her hand and stroked her daughter's cheek. Kate bent and kissed her.

'We won't be long, we'll be back about six. I've set the tea, and there's some fish cooking in the oven.'

'Don't you hurry yourself, it'll be all right. Maggie'll be up, she'll see to the tea.'

' 'Bye, grandma.' Annie kissed the blue lips. 'I'll tell you all about it when I get back ... about all I see in the shops.'

Sarah smiled and watched them go out. She lay thinking, her eyes fixed on the bedrail.... This dying took a long time. But she didn't went to go just yet ... if only she could outlast Tim, so Kate wouldn't be left alone with him, even for a day. She knew the impossibility of her wish. Apart from his leg, which troubled him at times, he was as strong as a horse. She began to pray, but dropped off into a doze, which filled most of her days.

Standing at the front door, Kate said, 'We'll wait a few minutes for the postman.'

'There he is,' cried Annie, 'coming round the corner.'

'It's getting colder,' said the postman. 'Shouldn't wonder if we don't see more snow.... There's nothing for you, they're piling up for tomorrow, I expect.' He laughed and passed on.

Something must have happened ... but what? What? To know the worst that possibly could happen would be better than the sickening weight of this anxiety.

She walked into Tyne Dock, with only a small part of her mind listening to Annie's gay chatter ... 'Would you, Kate?' Annie was asking.

'Would I what, dear?' Kate brought her attention back to her child.

'Would you come into the Borough Road church and see the crib? Rosie says it's lovely.'

'You want to see it?' asked Kate.

'Oh yes,' Annie said. 'Rosie says they've got real straw and a real cave and two new shepherds this year.'

'All right. We'll go before we get the tram for Shields.'

They took a short cut to the Borough Road church, and knelt on the stone steps of the Lady Altar and gazed at the crib, with its infant child and kneeling Mary and Joseph. The flickering candles seemed to endow the group with life.

Annie's lips moved as she said her rosary, and her face was wrapped with the wonder of it all. But Kate knelt stiffly, uttering no prayer.

It was nearly a year since she had said a prayer of any kind, and she asked herself, would her prayers for him be answered? If she believed all she had been taught then the answer was no. For God gave you only the things which were good for your soul; such as poverty and pain! And, unless you made friends with these, life was impossible for her and her kind. Rodney would be considered anything but good for her.

But in spite of her reasoning her heart suddenly cried, 'Oh! Mary, Mother of God, don't let anything happen to him. Please, please keep him safe. Do what you like to me, for I know I deserve it, I know I am proud and vain of my knowledge, thinking I am above my own people, and I criticise my religion ... but only keep him safe, and I will try to be better. I will do anything, anything....'

She suddenly stopped her wild plea, the bargaining side of prayer, which her reason had come to abhor, made her ashamed ... never praying unless one wanted something. She stood up and turned to the main altar....

'Thy will be done,' she said, and felt better.

She sat in a pew opposite the statue she had described to Rodney on that faraway night, sitting in the car on the top of the Felling hills, and, when Annie, face radiant with mystical happiness, came to her, she drew her close and, pointing to the statue, whispered, 'Tell me, dear. Do you like that statue, or does it frighten you?'

Surprised, Annie looked at her. 'The statue of Our Lord frighten me?' she whispered back. 'No, Kate. But it nearly always makes me want to cry. Then I think, He was only like that for three days; 'cos He came Himself again on Easter Sunday, didn't He?'

Kate nodded, and realised that Annie would never be afraid of the things that had frightened her ... except Tim. Christ had certainly risen for Annie.

'Which school do you like the better, the Borough Road or the one you are at now?' Kate asked, as they walked to the tram.

'Oh, the one I'm at now! It's a lovely school. But I don't like their church; I went in with one of the girls when there was a service on. I didn't like it a bit; God didn't seem to be there.... Oh, I love our church; don't you, Kate?'

Kate was not obliged to answer, for they boarded a tram. But she thought, some temperaments make good Catholics, others bad. Mine is in the latter category. But Annie will be a Catholic all her life, and I must never say or do anything which might spoil her faith. It is so beautiful and clean now, and, unlike mine was, without fear. If I have other children, will I bring them up as Catholics?... The question, involving so much not touching on religion, was unanswerable.

Her thoughts returned to Annie and her shining faith, and she knew that it would have hurt and puzzled her had she been told she had committed a sin through attending a service in a non-Catholic church. But it would not have really touched her faith, for she was one of those lucky people, born to believe without questioning. Kate wished she had been born that way too.

Her neck would carry a mark for life as a result of her stand in sending Annie to a protestant school, but her conscience, which had troubled her at times, was suddenly easy. She felt she had deprived Annie of nothing; the Catholic religion, she thought, would always be Annie's choice, and she had given her the best education possible under the circumstances.

It was dark when they returned home, and bitterly cold, with thin snowflakes lazily dropping here and there. Mrs. Mullen was waiting for them at her own front door.

'Where've you been?' she demanded.

'What's the matter? Is mother worse?' Kate asked anxiously.

'No,' said Mrs. Mullen, pulling Kate into the doorway. 'You, Annie,' she went on, to Kate's amazement, 'go on round the back way and sit with your grandma. And if your granda asks where Kate is tell him she's gone for ... groceries, or meat ... or anything. Go on now ... don't stand there gaping ... go on!'

Perplexed, Annie did as she had been told.

'Doctor Prince has been,' said Mrs. Mullen.

'What!' Life whirled through Kate's veins; her head reeled with its force.

'Listen.... There's not much time. He came about fifteen minutes after you had gone. Now he told me to tel you that he's leaving Tyne Dock station at a quarter to seven ... he's for across the water ... but he'll be at the station just after six.'

'For France,' Kate said dully, the new life ebbing away at the thought.

'Yes. Now get yourself off, it's twenty to six now. You'll be there by six if you hurry.... Here, give me your basket.'

Kate turned without a word and ran down the street.

There was no tram in sight, so, lifting her skirts, she raced along the road, her heart crying, 'Rodney! Rodney!' with each flying step.... Two hours wasted, and he going to France! ... She heard a tram coming, and stopped it. When she got to Tyne Dock she took another to the station, arriving there just on six o'clock.

Rushing up the steep, narrow slope of the booking-hall, she found her way momentarily obstructed by a tall fur-clad woman, with a chauffeur in attendance. The latter, she noticed, had a club-foot, and for a second she wondered how one faced life under such a handicap. How one's thoughts flew off at a tangent, especially at times of greatest stress.

Rodney was not in the booking-hall, but she assured herself he would come, it was just six o'clock. She would get a platform ticket ... the respite would steady her.

She was turning away from the booking let when the chauffeur with the club-foot spoke to the clerk. His question startled her, and she stared at him. For he had asked, quietly, 'Has Captain Prince ... you know, Doctor Prince passed through here recently?'

The irritated clerk snapped, 'How should I know? Think I write down the names of everyone who buys a ticket? ... Damn silly question to ask.'

Kate looked at the woman in the fur coat, and was more perplexed still when she heard the chauffeur say to her, 'He left half an hour ago, my lady. He caught the five-thirty to Newcastle.'

He seemed to hover over the woman, and, when she said, 'We'll go to Newcastle,' he answered, 'Very well, my lady.'

As they walked away Kate noticed that, although he did not touch her, he seemed to lead her down the long slope.

A car started up in the darkness beyond, and Kate guessed they had gone.... Who was she? Not Mrs. Prince ... His mother then? No, she was too young.... And why had the chauffeur lied?

She stood, perplexed at the situation, staring out into the night, until a tall, lean, khaki-clad figure came striding towards her from out of the blackness.

Her heart leaped, and she seemed to grow taller within herself. Then he was there, close to her. Their hands met, and gripped. His dark eyes glowed into hers. They stood for a second, caught up in ecstatic silence, then, turning without speaking, they showed their tickets and passed through the barrier. By mutual consent they made their way to the far end of the platform, which was totally deserted.... And they were in each other's arms, without having spoken a word.

Their lips clinging, their bodies endeavouring to merge, they swayed as they stood, holding this moment, willing it to go on for ever.

When at last he released her she leant against him, limp and trembling. His lips continued to move over her face, kissing her eyes and her brow, murmuring words which gave her an inward glow. Presently she said, 'Darling, is it France?'

'Yes,' he whispered, still caressing her.

'Oh, why was I out?'

'Yes, why were you?' he asked. 'The bottom seemed to drop out of everything when I found you weren't there.... Didn't you receive my letter, dear?'

'I've had none for a week.'

'What! But I've posted you two this week; the last one three days ago telling you about this move. I really expected to be here yesterday, but everything's been in such a devil of a mix-up.'

'It's the Christmas post,' said Kate; 'they must have been held up.... Oh, darling, I've been so worried!'

'Have you, my love?... In a way, it makes my heart glad to know that.... Let me look at you. Come here,' he said, drawing her into the weak gleam of a gas jet. 'How do you do it?' he cupped her face tenderly in his hands. 'You are more beautiful each time I see you.... Oh'—he drew her into his embrace again—'how am I going to let you go? Oh, Kate!... darling! darling! I love you ... Oh, God!'

They clung to each other desperately, hungrily.

Then, in a little while, she asked, tentatively, 'Must you go tonight?'

'Yes,' he answered bitterly. 'We are to leave Newcastle just after eight.... Christmas Eve, too! The men are in a devil of a way.... We should all have had leave, but they've tried to tell the men that the unexpected seven days they got last Christmas was really embarkation leave, and that we should have been in France months ago. There's been a frightful bungle somewhere. The few who managed dying mothers and wives got twenty-four hours! I had my business to set in order.... Which reminds me, darling. Come, sit down here; if I hold you I can't talk sensibly, and there is something I want to say to you.... Oh, wait....' He again drew her to him. 'You're too sweet, you're too ... Oh, I can't bear it! ...'

The dark desolate station vanished, together with the cold and the falling snow.

'Oh, dearest; I'm sorry; I'm quite mad. You're like a heady wine.... Come, sit down!'

They sat close together on the station seat. Her eyes moved over his face as he spoke, and her heart cried out, 'Don't go tonight. Don't! Don't! ... I'm mad, too.'

'It's about money, dearest,' he was saying. 'If anything happens to me, you'll be all right; I've seen to that. But it's money for you to carry on with that I want to talk about. I'm going to make you an allowance, through my bank.... I wanted to write to you about it, but it's so difficult to put these things into a letter. I've wondered how on earth you've managed this last year.'

Money! He was offering her money! An allowance.... Money would buy coal and food, and extras for her mother, and clothes for Annie, who was growing so quickly that her things had to be lengthened and she had to cut down her own for her. Her own stock of clothes was rapidly diminishing. Soon there would be none to re-make, which had worried her. But now, an allowance! The dreadful, soul-destroying burden of poverty would be lifted.... No! What was she thinking? She couldn't take money from him.... Money! That was the term in which the women of the fifteen streets thought; you gave so much and you got so much! ... This was the only lovely thing in her life. She couldn't, she wouldn't bring it down to the level of their thinking.

'Please! Please, Rodney, I can't! Don't talk about it.'

'Why not, darling?'

'I can't explain. Only don't, please!'

'Don't be silly; you must! I have more money than I know what to do with; a great-uncle died some years ago, leaving me shares in a steel works. And now, with the war, the money's simply piling up.... So, darling, you must let me do this.'

'No, Rodney. No! Oh, don't let us waste these precious minutes talking about it.... You see, it's because I don't want to spoil this ... our ... , oh, I can't explain.... Darling, don't you see?'

'No I don't. I only know that you must be in need of money and that you're being silly. I'll send it to you whether you give me leave or not.'

'No, don't do that. . . . Promise me you won't do that! How could I explain from where the money was coming? My mother . . . everyone would think that I . . .' She shrugged. 'Well, what does it really matter what they think? It's what I think that matters. No, Rodney; whatever our relationship, I'll never be able to take money from you.'

'That's utterly ridiculous! . . . Dearest'—he held her hands tight against his breast—'I want to buy you things . . . clothes, furs . . .'

'Furs!' Kate broke in. 'Oh, Rodney, I forgot to tell you. Someone . . . a lady, was enquiring for you in the booking-hall, just before you came. Talking of furs reminded me.'

'Enquiring for me?' Rodney's mind flew to Stella. He hadn't seen her, she'd been out when he arrived; she was, he understood from Mary, on various committees. No letters had passed between them during the months he had been away, so it was hardly likely she had come to see him off. 'What was she like?' he asked.

'Tall and pale, with very large eyes. She had a chauffeur with her . . . he had a club-foot.'

'Good God!' Rodney exclaimed. 'That woman! to come to the station enquiring for me!'

'You know her?' Kate asked.

'Know her! She's a nightmare! She's Lady Cuthbert Harris.'

He went on to tell Kate briefly about her.

'Why did the chauffeur lie, I wonder?' said Kate.

'Oh, Henderson knows how to manage her, and he's devoted to her, poor fellow. She's a dreadful woman, really. I should like to know, though, how she knew I was leaving here at this time. . . .' He suddenly thought of Swinburn, who, besides the Davidsons, was the only other person who had known. But why should he tell her? What was his motive? Devilment, perhaps. It would need thinking about later. There would be time enough for that. . . . But now:

'Don't let's talk about her. Look'—he pointed to his illuminated watch—'we've only fifteen minutes, my dear, and I've so much to say.'

'Shall I come to Newcastle with you?' Kate asked eagerly.

He paused for a moment.

'You know I would like nothing better. But Peter and Peggy Davidson are meeting the train at Jarrow. They were determined to see me off ... I could hardly say no; they have been such wonderful friends to me. But if you wouldn't mind ... come, darling. They guess about you, anyway, I think.'

Kate shook her head: 'I won't come ... I'd better not.'

For some seconds they sat quietly, peering at each other in the dimness, each aware of the other's sadness.

'You'll write often?' Rodney asked.

She nodded dumbly.

'Oh, I want to ask you such a lot of silly things ... such as, that you won't look at another fellow, or ever forget me.'

'You don't need to ask me,' she said.

'But you're so lovely, and good. I'm afraid. Oh, I'm afraid.... Put your arms tight round my neck and kiss me,' he suddenly demanded.

She laughed softly, and, as her lips touched his, he held himself still, not touching her.... Then, 'That's what I'll remember always,' he said.

Putting his arms about her and holding her tenderly, he asked, 'What made you suddenly decide to marry Pat Delahunty, Kate, that Christmas Eve? I've always wanted to ask you, but kept putting it off, thinking you would tell me. It was something to do with me, wasn't it?'

'You know Pat's dead?' she asked.

'Yes, I know, and I was really sorry. I liked him, in spite of him loving you.'

'I sometimes think his death was my fault.'

'Nonsense! He would have been called up in any case.... But why were you going to marry him?'

'To escape you ... and because they were saying that I ... was your mistress, and you were the father of Annie.'

'Kate! No!' He sprang up and drew her with him: 'No!' he repeated.

'Yes....' A goods train puffed by them and they stood silent during its passage, Rodney gazing at Kate with knitted brows.

'Oh, darling.... And you've had to put up with all this! No wonder you were afraid. Poor, poor dear.... But what could have given them that idea?'

'I don't know; I can't tell ... only that you made a fuss of Annie.'

Gently drawing her to him, he said, 'If only I had been Annie's father ... I've always loved her. You see, I could love her when I couldn't allow myself to love you ... I sometimes used to imagine I was her father. How funny! When they must have been thinking that, saying that, and watching me. What a queer world! And now they'll be saying, "What did I tell you! It's been going on for years." Oh, if only it had! Kate, I've such a lot to make up to you; life has been so hard for you.'

'Not half as hard as for some. I've had the Tolmaches ... now I've you.'

'Oh, my love, you're so brave.'

'How much longer have we?' she asked.

'For ever.... Don't let's look,' he said, holding her close.

Presently, taking two small packages from his pocket, he exclaimed, 'I almost forgot: here's your Christmas box, and Annie's. They're all I could get in the time. Now don't open them until you reach home.'

She stood looking down at them. 'Oh, Rodney; and I've nothing to give you, not a thing.'

'Don't talk nonsense.'

'You know,' she smiled at him, 'if there were time I'd resent being told I talk nonsense, that I'm ridiculous and that I'm silly. You have a very arrogant manner, Doctor Prince!'

'Oh, darling; do I sound arrogant?'

'You do.'

'Well then, do as I say, and I'll be like a lamb when I get my own way.... Let me arrange about the money.'

She put her hand over his mouth: 'Seriously, dear, don't talk about it ... the time is flying. Oh!' she exclaimed, 'I have something ... but don't laugh.' Opening her handbag she took out a tiny, flat tin box which once had an enamelled picture on its lid ... 'It's my rosary. I've had it since I was a child. Will you take it? I'm still superstitious about it; I haven't done much praying lately, but I feel I must carry it with me. And, if you have it, it will still be with me.'

He held the tiny rosary in his fingers: 'Thanks, my dear. It will never leave me, because it is yours.'

Then he smiled: 'The only thing we want now is Father O'Malley's blessing ... what?'

A gale of laughter assailed them; they rocked helplessly with it.

'Well, we've travelled some distance when we can laugh at the old fellow.... What do you say, darling?'

Kate didn't answer. Suddenly he felt her face wet.... 'Oh, my dear, don't ... don't!' he begged. 'Look, only three more minutes. Come, smile. I want to remember you smiling and those eyes playing their tricks with me.... Tell me you'll never forget me, darling. Say it.'

'I'll never forget you.... Oh, Rodney, take care!'

He dried her face gently with his handkerchief. 'Good heavens, you'll be in much more danger than I shall be, stuck miles behind the lines!'

She turned swiftly: 'Here's the train! Oh, it can't be! It's early, but it won't stop a minute. Oh, my darling! ... Oh, you can't go! I have so much to say ... I love you, I love you.'

They held together as the train slowed down. Doors opened. Rodney dragged himself away, his face stiff and showing grey in the dim light from the carriages.

'Keep on loving me, dearest, always. There'll never be anyone but you. Goodbye, my love.'

He got into the carriage, the door closed and the train moved, and she was left on the platform, alone. It was as if it had been a dream and he had never really been there.

As the red light disappeared into the tunnel, she moved away, thinking, I never thanked him for the presents ... such footling thoughts!

She walked all the way home in a maze of numbed pain, she was back where she was an hour ago, with anxiety lying heavy on her.

When she entered the kitchen Tim was sitting before

the fire, his leg resting on a chair. The fire was blazing up the chimney, glowing bright with coal. She went straight upstairs, anger, for the moment, blotting out her anxiety.... That would be the last of the coal, which she had been keeping to light the fires with.... There was nothing she could do about it, nothing she could say... no word ever passed between them now.

Passing Sarah's door, she called softly, 'I'll be in in a minute, ma, when I've taken my things off.'

She sat on her bed and opened the little parcel Rodney had given her for Annie. It was a silver bangle, hung with tiny charms. Then she opened her own.... She lifted out the gold wristlet watch. The face was small and exquisite, the strap of flat plaited gold. She put it on her wrist and held up her hand, but she could barely see it for the swimming of her eyes.... How beautiful! how beautiful! But when could she wear it? In a few hours, Christmas Eve or no Christmas Eve, she'd be sitting on the tip.

Tears began to choke her.... Rodney! Rodney! Why must life be like this?... She lay across the bed, sobbing, pressing the patched quilt against her mouth to still the sound....

Oh, Rodney, Rodney, come back!

## THE FIELDCARD

Annie and Rosie stood one on each side of the clothes-basket as Kate put the things in: first, the sheets and pillow cases and towels, then the tablecloths, then the shirts and pants, the petticoats and pinafores, and, lastly, three silk blouses. She covered the whole with a cloth. 'Be careful how you carry them,' she said.

'How much have I got to say they are?' asked Annie.

'Three shillings.'

Rosie looked from one to the other. She wished Kate would smile or laugh like she used to, then Annie would be different. But whatever Kate did Annie seemed to do. Perhaps Kate'd stopped laughing because she had to take in washing, 'cos old Tim wouldn't work. Her da said old Tim was a lazy swine who should be hung, drawn and quartered. Sometimes he said that he wanted kicking from here to Hell and back again, for that was too good a place for him to stay.... Oh, by heck, he was glad old Tim wasn't her granda!

'Hurry back,' said Kate to Annie; 'I want you to stay with grandma, I've got to go into Shields.'

Annie and Rosie picked up the basket and went out. The ground was hard with frozen snow and they walked warily, the basket swinging between them.

'Where's this lot going?' Rosie asked.

'To Mrs. Beckett's at Simonside.'

'Coo! She's the one that gives you cake and sometimes a ha'penny, isn't she?'

'Yes, sometimes,' said Annie.

'By, it's a long way though! Let's count our steps from here to Simonside bank, eh? It'll make the time go.'

'I can manage the basket myself if you don't want to come.'

'Lord, what's up with you?' demanded Rosie, her small eyes snapping. 'Who said I didn't want to come? What's the matter with you, anyway? You've got a face like the back of a tram smash.'

Annie did not answer.

'Aw ... w! Come on, Annie,' Rosie coaxed. 'Let's have a singsong, eh. Let's sing "Sam! Sam!" Come on.'

Breaking into a surprisingly strong, contralto voice she sang:

> 'Sam! Sam! The dirty man,
> Washed himself in the frying-pan,
> Combed his hair with a donkey's tail,
> Scratched his belly with his big toenail.'

'Look,' she encouraged the still silent Annie, 'I'll sing "Sam! Sam!" and you sing "the dirty man". Then I'll sing, "Washed himself in the frying-pan," eh?'

'I don't want to,' said Annie. She had no liking for 'Sam! Sam!' at any time, but today he was revolting. Not wishing to hurt Rosie's feelings, however, she added, 'But you sing, I like to hear you. Sing "Venite adoremus" or the "O Salutaria."'

'Oh, all right:

> 'Venite adoremus, venite adoremus,
> Venite adore ... emus ...'

Her voice rang out into the frosty air with power, causing passersby to smile at her. She smiled back, still singing.

As Rosie sang, Annie thought, If only the letters would come again; then Kate would be different. But they wouldn't come again, not now. For weeks there had been no letters. They had stopped when her pretty postcards, with the roses and mandolins worked in silk on them, had stopped.... The cards had come from the doctor ... the letters too had come from the doctor. She didn't know how she knew this, but she did. The doctor had been missing a long time ... weeks. People said that when you were missing you were as good as dead.... Kate didn't laugh any more, she hardly spoke. She said, 'Do this,' or, 'Don't do that.' But Annie thought Kate wouldn't have cared if she hadn't done this ... or did do that. The only thing she wouldn't let her do was to go on the tip. But they bought less coal than ever now, because her granda sat with his leg on the chair most of the time. And, when he did go to work, he nearly always came home drunk. She had noticed, too, that he had taken to standing near Kate. Not to hit her, but just standing near looking at her, with his hand moving up and down his trouser leg. To see him thus had filled her with a nameless horror.... Last night he had said, 'Go to the shop and get me half an ounce of baccy,' and Kate had come out of the house with her and stood at the back-door until she came back.

But if only the letter would come again everything would be all right, she felt sure. Because there had always been her granda, and Kate had been taking in washing for a long time, but she had always seemed happy.... But now she got tired when she was doing the washing, and sometimes stood, leaning her head against the wall. And also she seemed openly afraid of her granda; not that he'd hit her, but ... well .... Annie shook her head in perplexity, the term 'Bad things' coming into her mind ... Oh, she wished her granda was dead ... or missing!

Annie was recalled to Rosie's entertainment by a shake of the basket.

'I don't believe you've been listening to a thing.'

'Oh yes I have.'

'Well, I've a new one,' said Rosie. 'Now listen.'

She performed her next number in two voices; one as near Father O'Malley's as she could contrive, and the other a squeaky treble:

'Pray, Father, I've killed the cat.
Ah, my child, you'll suffer for that!
But, pray, Father, it was a Protestant cat.
Oh! Then, my child, doesn't matter about that.

173

'Isn't it funny?' Rosie looked at Annie, hoping for a laugh, at least a broad grin. But when she was confronted with a weak smile, she said to herself, 'Oh, ta pot!'

When they returned to the fifteen streets Rosie left Annie with the empty basket, in disgust.... No ha'penny, no piece of cake! Annie hadn't even got the money for the washing; the woman was out and it had to be left next door.... Annie had been worse company coming back than going.

Annie put the basket in the washhouse and went reluctantly into the house.

'What! you didn't get the money?' said Kate, when Annie had told her the woman wasn't in. She sat down heavily on a chair and slowly tapped her fingers on the table; Annie sat on the carpet and looked into the fire.

I won't ask him, Kate thought. I'll do anything, anything rather than ask him. She knew she was afraid, and she did not seem to have the strength to fight against her fear.

Whatever money Tim had contributed to the household he had been in the habit of throwing on the bed to Sarah, but these past two weeks he had stopped this procedure and when Sarah had asked him for the money he had replied, 'What'ja want it for?... Who's keeping house?' and had gone and stood near Kate, handing her the money without a word, but with his eyes playing over her.

She had taken it in amazement, and, seeing his look, a new fear of him had come into being, making her sick with shame and terror.

Then, last week, he had waited for her to ask for the money, and when she hadn't he had gone out and drunk it. He was waiting again, and she hadn't a penny in the house!

She went upstairs to her room and, opening the bottom drawer of the chest, she took out a small box. The wristlet watch was all she had of Rodney beside his letters. She had hung on to it these months past, pawning everything belonging to herself except what she stood up in ... and now it would have to go.

She touched it tenderly with her fingers.... Rodney,

Rodney, you're not dead, are you?... You can't be dead. You mustn't die.

Abruptly, she turned and took her coat and hat from the back of the door and went out of the room. If she began to think again she would be unable to go on, something would snap. And there was her mother and Annie to see to.

She put the box resolutely into the pocket of her coat, and went into Sarah's room.

'I'm going down to Shields, ma. I won't be long. Annie's downstairs, I'll send her up.'

Sarah nodded, speaking no word. Speech seemed to have dried up in her; the thing that was in the house now, stalking her Kate, had paralysed every emotion but fear. It stared out of her eyes continually; it was ever in her twitching tongue and plucking fingers.

When Kate had gone Annie went upstairs and sat near the window. Her grandma was asleep. She looked at the houses opposite with the grubby lace curtains and the rail of a brass bedstead showing between them. She looked up into the sky and down into the backyard with its sheet of grey ice strewn with cinders. Everything was grey and dull; there seemed nothing to smile or laugh about any more; nothing made you feel nice inside; there was a deadness in her and all around. Why had things changed so suddenly? Her grandma had been ill a long time, her granda had always been a bad man, Kate had always had to work, the houses opposite had never been different from what they were now. All these things had been happening when the doctor was alive, and she hadn't noticed them very much.... But now he was dead they all seemed to matter.

She unplaited and replaited her hair. He used to like her hair, saying it was 'Fairy Queen's hair'. She examined it. The silver had turned to a pale gold. Sometimes she thought it was funny hair, no one else seemed to have hair this colour. She looked at the bracelet he had sent her last Christmas. She was twirling it round her wrist when the door opened, startling her. Dorrie Clarke, in a bonnet and bead cape, her face red and bloated, tiptoed ponderously in.

175

'Couldn't make anyone hear,' she whispered, 'so I popped up.... How is she?' She went and stood near the bed, looking down on Sarah.

'She's asleep,' said Annie.

'Ah, so she is! I'll sit meself here for a while till she wakes.'

Dorrie Clarke seated herself on a chair by the bed. Annie stood looking at her, stiff with apprehension.

'Growin', aren't you?' said Dorrie.

'Yes,' Annie said.

'Kate out?'

'Yes.' Annie thought, she knows Kate's out, or she wouldn't be here.

I'll not be able to do much with that young bitch watching me, Dorrie told herself. And I'll never have as good a chance as this again.

'Would you run a message, hinny?' she asked. 'Me leg's bothering me. Yer granny isn't the only one with bad legs, you know. Look, run round to the shop and get me a quarter stone of taties and twopennorth o' pot stuff. And there's a penny for yerself.'

Annie hesitated.

'Go on, hinny,' urged Dorrie. 'It won't take you a minute.... Surely you don't mind going to the shop for me. You, with good legs on yer, and me, in the state I am.'

Annie took the money and the bag and hurried out.

'That bitch is as cute as a box o' monkeys,' Dorrie muttered to herself.

She listened until she heard the back door close, then she glanced down at Sarah.... Not long for the top, she's not. No trouble from her.... Now!

Hurrying out as softly as a cat, she made her way to Kate's room.... Not much place to hide owt here.... She made straight for the chest of drawers, and went through them. In the bottom one she found what she wanted.... By God, there weren't 'alf some of them, too. Bundles of them, done up in ribbons.... Well, well! Split yer sides, yer could.

She extracted a letter here and there, taking six in all, and she was back, sitting beside Sarah, within a few minutes.

The idea had first entered her mind some months ago, but when he had been reported missing there was no sense in doing it. But now ... well, things were just as they were before, but she wasn't letting on.

Mary Dixon's brother had given her the idea. He was a postman, and he had remarked, 'That Kate Hannigan's bloke out in France does some writing; she stands on the doorstep waiting for letters every post ... and she gets them. He must have nowt else to do.' And when Mary Dixon got her the job, mornings, at the doctor's, after their cook had left, she began to hear things, and see quite a bit, too. It was then the use to which some of the letters could be put had entered her mind.

It was another score she held against him, that she had to go out charing and cooking, and her a midwife. For never a case had she had in years, and all through him ... and now she was working at his house! What would he say to that, if he knew? Her time would be short, she guessed. Well, he wouldn't know; he was nicely set for a long time yet. God blast him and keep him there!

She liked his wife no better than she did him ... snotty bitch! And she was having a nice titty-fal-lal with the other doctor, wasn't she now. And another bloke in the offing, Mary said. Thinking this over, it had occurred to Dorrie that her mistress might find her husband's letters to another woman useful, should things become too hot for her with her couple of fancy men. And she would likely stump up a pretty penny to get them ... by God, yes! She would stump up, if she had anything to do with it.

Ah! She sighed contentedly; she'd waited a long time to get even with him ... but God was good.

She was sitting placidly on the chair, her hands folded in her lap, when Annie returned.

'That's a good lass. Now I'll have to go, I'm afraid. ... Yer granny hasn't woken up so I won't disturb her. Tell her I just popped in.'

As she went out, Annie thought, Oh, Kate will be vexed. But what could I do? I don't know whether to tell her or not.

It was late in the afternoon, and Kate was cleaning the brasses when Annie said, 'Dorrie Clarke came to see grandma this morning, when you were out.'

'What!' Kate turned on her.

'I couldn't help it ... I couldn't stop her; she came into the bedroom without knocking.'

'You should have said ... oh, you couldn't, I suppose.' She put the candlestick down slowly on the table. 'How long did she stay?' she asked flatly.

'Not long, about five minutes ... or ten.'

'What did she say?'

'Not much. Just how was grandma ... and she said her legs were bad, too. She asked me...' Annie stopped. Should she tell Kate that she had gone a message for Dorrie Clarke and left her in the house with her grandma? No, she wouldn't; perhaps it would make her more vexed.

Kate looked at her sharply. 'Well, what did she ask you?'

'Only about grandma.'

'Nothing else?'

'No.'

Kate stood a moment looking out of the kitchen window.... What did it matter, anyway? Dorrie Clarke could do no more harm.

Saying to Annie, 'Will you finish these for me?' she washed her hands and went upstairs.

In her own room, she sat on the foot of the bed and leant her head wearily on the brass rail. She felt suddenly tired, not the exhausting tiredness that the end of each day brought to her body, but a tiredness that seemed to drain the very spirit from her.... Why, oh why had she to go through all this? One thing after another piling up ... no respite.... The fact of Dorrie Clarke being in the house had created another dread. But what, she asked herself, need she fear from Dorrie Clarke now? If he were still alive there might be cause to worry. She gripped the bedrail.... But he wasn't dead ... he wasn't! Oh God, don't let him be dead! she prayed. I'll do anything, anything. Jesus, save him! Do what you like with me, only don't let him die.

The old bargaining was in her prayer. She recognised it, but was too weary to scorn it. She slumped down, her hands dropping into her lap.

Was God paying her out for all her questioning, for all her probing? she wondered. No; God, as she saw Him now, wasn't that kind of a god. He said, 'I have given you a life and a conscience by which to steer it. Whether you arrive at your destination by way of the Catholic religion, the Protestant religion, or by way of no recognised sect whatever, as long as you recognise you are steering for me, that is all that matters.' She knew He understood all things, her sickness of heart now, her burning desire of a few weeks ago.

Was it only a few weeks ago since she had stood in this room, clasping Rodney's letter to her? It had said: Seven days, beloved . . . Seven days! In a short while, seven days. I can't believe it. We must spend every minute together. Arrange for someone to look after your mother and Annie; offer any sum you like, only get someone. Now don't be silly about this. I read your special letter every night. You'll never really know all it means to me. . . .

Her special letter! The letter which had taken so long to write; hours of thinking and rewriting when a look would have conveyed all there was to say. There had been nothing restrained about that letter; her battered-down emotions had overflowed; and when his reply came the house had become bright with her singing and happy laughter, except when Tim was in.

She had set about preparing herself for their meeting; for nearly two years there had been no time to spend on herself. Each moment was taken up with nursing and work and with washing to eke out their existence. So she had feverishly tried to make up for lost time; her weekly bath had become a nightly affair, the work it entailed on top of the grind of the day becoming a pleasure. After the washing she would fill the boiler with clean water, and a dying fire would heat it sufficiently. The tin bath had to be carried to her room, then the water, bucket after bucket.

Years before she had swung the cracked mirror back and forth and had seen that she was beautiful. Now she swung it again ... but more shyly, for she swung it with the knowledge of what she was searching for. It was eleven years since she had desired to see the reflection of her body. But, as she looked at it now, she knew it had much more to offer than when she was seventeen. It was firm, and moulded like live ivory. From her breast, over the curve of her stomach, down to the rise of her thighs, was a continued modulation. Her face was thinner, but still without a line, and her hair was alive and winging. Only one thing marred the whole, her beauty stopped at her wrists. Her hands were red and coarse—cinders and soda water had taken their toll of them. Nightly, before getting into bed, she sat and rubbed grease into them. In the morning they would look paler, but by evening they were white, with the skin crinkled into little folds. Then, freed from the water and pushing the flat iron, they would harden and redden once more.

Annie hurried into the room.

'The priest's downstairs, Kate.'

'Well,' answered Kate, shortly, 'he certainly knows his way up.'

'But it's Father Bailey, Kate.'

'Oh.' Kate rose and went downstairs.

'Hallo there, Kate!' said Father Bailey. 'I thought I'd look in and see your mother; Father O'Malley is laid up with rheumatism.'

'Oh yes, Father. Will you come up?'

She held the door open for him. Before mounting he turned and faced her: 'You're having a hard time, Kate, aren't you?'

She didn't answer; his sympathy was more unnerving than Father O'Malley's censure.

'Won't you come to mass and try to find peace that way?'

She shook her head: 'I can't, Father.'

'Why not, Kate?'

'I don't believe in any of the things I used to.'

He looked at her, long and steadily.

'You're passing through one of the bad patches, aren't you? And you think you're alone; you don't think any-one's ever been through your particular kind of misery before. But it happens to most of us.... I know, for I've been through it.'

Kate looked at him in surprise.

'Don't let suffering make you hard, Kate. Let it rather be an academy of sympathy.... No man dare look God in the face and say he has never doubted Him, Kate.'

'It isn't that I doubt the existence of God, Father ... it's ... oh, I can't explain it!' She put her hand wearily to her head.

'I know, I know. It's the Catholic way of looking at Him that you are doubting.... Yes, if you think at all, that comes too, sooner or later. But if you'll only keep on praying, Kate, He'll put that right. Keep knocking and the door will be opened ... He'll give you the faith to see clearly and to trust simply, and you'll find that the way He dictates is for your own good. If you rebel against life, struggle against the tide, time and again you will find yourself thrust into black despair. It is as if God wants you to work along certain channels, and either through obstinacy, misdirection of will, or fear, you will not allow yourself to be led. Kate, He knows what makes for your ultimate good ... for the good of the soul, that must live on, if we believe in anything.... Stop fighting, and come to mass, Kate.'

'I can't, Father.'

'What's made you like this, Kate? I've known and watched you since you were a child.'

She was about to answer, 'Priests and teachers have made me like this,' but then she thought, I would likely have come to this way of thinking in the end, in any case. So she remained silent.

He read her thoughts nearer than she guessed, for his patience, too, was tried daily. Sometimes he felt he was earning a saint's halo simply by living with Father O'Malley.

'God bless you, Kate,' he said, and went upstairs.

She stood biting her lip, the tears stinging her eyes; understanding made things worse, it made her ask herself about this question, Can I be right and millions of people wrong?

She thought of Master Bernard's words: 'If you find

faith in God through the Catholic religion, hang on to it with all your might, for the greatest disaster in life is to lose one's faith.'

She was trying to follow the truth, as she saw it; and she had wanted life, full, pulsing life; she had been willing at last to barter all for life. But now she had neither life nor religion, and she was lost.

Oh, she couldn't think.... Why bother to think! What did anything matter? The end was near, she felt; something must happen soon; she couldn't fight this unequal battle against poverty and fear much longer.

'I've finished the brasses, Kate,' Annie said. 'Can I do anything else for you?'

Kate looked at her, and, seeing the anxiety in her face, thought, I'm forgetting about her; I mustn't. I mustn't give in. What would become of her? It would be my early life over again. Place, twelve hours a day, ten if she were lucky, for there wouldn't be any Tolmaches for her ... they happen only once in a thousand years.... She stared at Annie fixedly, thinking, She's too beautiful, she'd be dragged under right away.

'Kate!' said Annie. 'Kate, what's the matter?'

'Nothing, my dear, nothing; I was just thinking.'

Kate shook her head and jumped towards the fire. 'Go on out to play for a while, if you like.'

'Oh, all right. I'll go round to the shops for one more look before they pull the blinds down.'

Kate nodded, and Annie hurried out.

Christmas, and not a thing to give her! If only she could have got her some small thing.... Oh, what was the use of thinking about it; she must conserve every penny she had received for the watch as there was nothing more left in the house which she could pawn. What she would do when the money was gone, she did not know. She would never ask him for any, and she felt she had imposed enough on Mrs. Mullen. There were other neighbours, but she couldn't bear to think of their looks of satisfaction were she to humble herself to borrow from them.... She would know what they were thinking ... 'Lady' Hannigan, brought off her perch at last. She knew that was how they referred to her, and that not an action of hers escaped their notice. With the exception of a few here and there, it was as if improvement or difference in another bred hate in them. They were waiting for her to snap.... There was a street near the docks where it was easy to make money.... My God!

She was in a flurry as she set about laying the tea.... God above, what had put that into her head? What had made her even think of it? Yes, she knew; it was what most of them were hoping would happen.

She had just finished getting the tea ready when Tim came in. She put the teapot on the table and went into the front room and busied herself there.

A little later, hearing his chair scrape, and thinking he had gone to wash himself and that she would be able to slip upstairs without having to pass close to him, she went into the kitchen.

But he was standing in front of the fire, his eyes on the door.

She hesitated for a second. Then, as she went to walk between him and the table, he held out his hand. In his palm lay a number of half-crowns. She stared at them, fascinated but unable to touch them.

He waited; then said gruffly, 'Go on.'

But terror filled her, and she could not move.

Swiftly, he took one of her hands and put the money into it, his fist closing over hers as he did so, and, as swiftly, his other hand moved and pressed hard against the front of her thigh.

She gave a scream and sprang back from him, letting the money fall to the mat.

He was standing staring at her, his lids drooping over his eyes, his hands working a slow movement up and down his trouser legs, when the stair door opened. He turned and gaped in surprise at the priest, having been unaware of his presence in the house, and Father Bailey saw the evil, raw and uncovered, that oozed from him, and the stark terror in Kate's eyes.

The expression on Tim's face fought between resentment and the look of penitence he was wont to keep for the priests, but something in Father Bailey's face showed him the uselessness of pretence. He gathered up the money from the mat, switched his cap off the back door and went out.

The priest stood looking at Kate pityingly for some moments, then, shaking his head in perplexity, hurried out after Tim.

Not a word had been spoken.

Kate sat down heavily, her legs refusing to support her. She was trembling from head to foot.... Something must happen soon.... Something had got to happen soon.

At half-past six Annie came in and asked if she could go to the Baptist Chapel hall with Rosie. The soldiers were there, and were giving a party and presents, and one was dressed up as Father Christmas. And Rosie said they'd get in because they didn't ask if you were a Catholic or not....

She suddenly stopped, and before Kate could answer said, 'Oh, it's all right, I don't want to go.' She saw that Kate looked very white and that the needle in her hand with which she was mending her socks was shaking.

She took off her outdoor things and sat down near Kate.

'The postman's doing a late round, he's loaded with parcels and things,' she said.

Kate looked at her, and Annie hung her head. She didn't know what had made her say it. 'I didn't mean to say it, Kate,' she whispered, her lip trembling.

'It's all right, my dear, but he won't be coming here.'

It was just then the knock came: rat-a-tat-tat, rat-a-tat-tat. They looked at each other, startled.

'I'll go,' cried Annie, and was through the front-room in a flash.

Kate stood, awaiting her return; the socks lay on the mat.

Annie came running back into the kitchen: 'It's a card, Kate,' she said.

Kate read the printed buff-coloured card. She read it again. She turned it over, and back, and re-read it.

She sat down in a chair: 'It's the doctor, Annie. He's safe,' she said in a voice scarcely above a whisper; 'he's a prisoner.'

Annie shivered. She had forgotten what it was like to feel that shiver of delight; the greyness went out of the day, out of all the things that made up her life; everything was bright and shining again.

'Oh, Kate!' she cried, and flung her arms about her. 'Oh, Kate, he'll be coming back! Oh, Kate!'

'Yes, my dear, he'll be coming back,' she said, pressing Annie fiercely to her and rocking her like a child.

Rosie Mullen opened the back-door, unobserved. She stood for a moment wide-eyed before closing it again.

She ran into her own yard, calling, 'Kate and Annie's howling the house down, ma.'

'Oh, my, that'll mean Sarah's gone!' Mrs. Mullen hurried out, with Rosie at her heels.

'It it Sarah?' she asked, bursting in on Kate.

Kate shook her head: 'No, Mrs. Mullen ... it's.... Look!' She handed the card to Mrs. Mullen.

Mrs. Mullen read it laboriously. 'Oh, lass, I am glad. A prisoner! Oh, I am glad. You'll be A1 again now.'

She put her arm about Kate's shoulder and pulled her head to her much-used breast: 'There, lass, there! Have a good cry, it'll do you good.'

Rosie watched her mother in bewilderment; she wasn't only telling Kate to cry, but she was starting to cry herself. Never before had she seen as much as a tear on her face; they weren't a crying lot, the Mullens; only the babies cried, and they soon had that knocked out of them. She didn't cry; not even at that time when her mother had swiped her lug so hard that she had turned a somersault and landed upside down in the bottom of the cupboard.... She looked at Annie ... she was howling awful.

Rosie began to experience a queer feeling, like pins and needles, in her nose, and a bit of brick seemed to have stuck edgeways in her throat. Her face crumpled up, and, try as she might, she was unable to straighten it out.

Mr. Mullen came in, saying, 'Anything I can do, lass? ... Is it Sarah?'

Mrs. Mullen shook her head at him: 'No, it isn't Sarah ... Kate's had a bit of good news, that's all.'

He stopped dead, gazing at the four of them. 'My God! Then what you all blaring for? Crikey! Did you ever see such a lot of bloody fools! I suppose if it was bad news you'd have a damn good laugh, eh? ... And you'—he pointed to his daughter, the daughter who, he prided himself, was a chip of the old block, the male block— 'don't tell me you're piping too!'

'I ain't,' protested Rosie, endeavouring to straighten out her face, 'I ain't . . . it's me nose, it's stopped up.'

She managed to grin at her father, who grinned back. Then, turning to his wife, Mr. Mullen said, 'I'm off for a wet, and I hope I get happy enough to have a damn good cry!'

After he had gone, they looked at each other in silence for a moment, then, one after the other, they began to laugh; Rosie, her face all wet and her mouth wide open, was saying to herself, in relief, 'By, lad, this is better! Me da's a one, ain't he? I wish Annie had a da like him, she'd laugh more then.'


Kate lay and listened to the carol singers; the card was on the pillow, half under her cheek; Annie lay curled into her back, fast asleep.

'While shepherds watched their flocks by night...' the voices rose to her from the street.

'Oh, God, watch over him,' she prayed. 'Make the war soon end; bring him back safely.... And, oh, thank You, thank You, that he is alive.'

' "Fear not," said he, for mighty dread has seized their troubled mind...'

'No ... I will not fear. He will come back. I will fear nothing,' she said to herself, 'not now; not even "him".'

She had lain awake, waiting for Tim to come in, dreading his footsteps on the stairs. She had dragged the big box that had for years acted as a cupboard and placed it across the door, for she felt now that not even Annie was a protection. But he had not come. She wondered if he had gone to Jarrow.... Had the priest said anything to him?

Long after the carol singers had gone from the street she lay awake, waiting. Everywhere was silent; there was no more shouting, no more drunken singing, not even the echo of the carollers from the distance, just that uncanny quiet that seemed full of sound. So, when the footsteps came up the street, she heard them, slithering over the ice. And when they stopped beneath the window she sat up, and, as the knocker banged, she was out of bed and had her coat on in a flash.

It couldn't be him; he always came in the back way. She opened the window and looked down on to a shadowy figure. A white blur was turned up to her, and a voice asked, 'This Hannigans'?'

'Yes,' she answered.

'Well, I've news for you. You'd better come down.'

Sarah called out, as Kate passed her door, 'What is it?'

'I don't know, ma. I'll be back in a minute,' she answered.

She opened the door, to find a policeman standing there. . . .

When she returned upstairs and went into Sarah's room, she noticed that her mother looked strangely alert.

'What is it?' Sarah asked. 'What's the matter, hinny?'

'It's him,' said Kate; 'he's had an accident ... he's in Harton.'

Sarah hitched herself up on her pillows, an effort she had stopped making months ago. 'Bad?' she asked.

'It's his arm and head. . . . I don't know how bad; the policeman says I have to go down.'

'Yes, hinny. Go down. You needn't see him, only find out how bad it is.'

They did not look at each other, and Kate hurried out to dress. She felt lightheaded with relief; it would appear that good news attracted good news as bad bad.

From the moment Kate left the house Sarah began to pray. Not mumbled prayers ... not the prayers that were for ever being repeated at the back of her mind, a jumble of entreaties and requests, but verbal prayers, said aloud into the room, each word distinctly spoken, rising into the air, filling the room with power. The faculties which had been slowly fading during the months past seemed to regain new life. Each word she uttered vibrated with terrible purpose. She went on and on, speaking words and framing sentences that were new to her. Nor did she stop until she was exhausted. Then she lay, wide-eyed, waiting. . . .

When she heard Kate's step on the stairs her bloated body stiffened against the bed and her eyes fixed themselves on the door.

Kate came in panting; she had been gone only an hour and a half.

Sarah brought herself on to her elbow: 'Yes?' she asked.

'He's gone!' said Kate, unable to keep the joy and relief from her voice.

Sarah dropped back on to her pillows, a slow smile spreading over her face.

'Sit down, hinny,' she said; 'you're puffed.'

Kate sat on the side of the bed and took her mother's hand.

'How was it?' asked Sarah.

'They don't know, really. He was knocked down by a tram in Eldon Street. His arm was broken and he received a blow on the head which made him unconscious. But it wasn't serious, they said, and they could not understand him dying. When he came round and asked where he was, and they told him Harton, the nurse said he had a kind of fit, and died in it.'

'Ah!' exclaimed Sarah. 'Harton! . . . That's what he was always feared of, having to end his days in the workhouse . . . it's the only thing that ever worried him; he was mortally afraid of the workhouse. . . . He died of fright, Kate.'

She lay silent for some time, her eyes roving gently round the room, a wondrous peace filling her, like that of carrying a child. It would vanish later, she knew, and there would be the throes of dying, but at present it was here and she hugged it to herself. She smiled at Kate: 'Do you think we might have a cup of tea, hinny, it's Christmas Day?'

## ALWAYS FLIGHT

John Swinburn and Stella faced each other in the drawing-room. Swinburn's face was white and drawn, and his thin nostrils moved in and out in little jerks.

'Do you mean to say, Stella, you don't want to get a divorce ... ever?' His voice was harsh, and deep in his throat.

'Must we have it all over again, John?' Stella made an impatient movement with her shoulders. 'I have told you already I have no desire to be a divorced woman.... Anyway, if I were divorced, I shouldn't marry you.'

'You're a fiend, Stella, a heartless fiend!'

'Then why do you bother with me?'

'I don't know,' he said despairingly.

'John, don't act like a boy. I have told you things can go on just as they are.... We can be together now and again. He'll live his life and I'll live mine.'

'I couldn't do it,' said Swinburn, turning away and beating a fist in the palm of his hand. 'I know how many different kinds of a swine I am, nobody better, and I have no love for Rodney, I think him a prig, but I couldn't work with him and have you at the same time ... not the way I want you. I couldn't do it. He's coming home smashed up, and, after a year as a prisoner, he's not going to feel very bright ... I tell you, I couldn't play that underhand game ... I could go to him and lay my cards on the table and ask him to divorce you, but not the other way.'

'You'll do nothing of the kind,' rapped out Stella. 'Should you attempt it I wouldn't even look at you again.'

'But what about him?' Swinburn turned on her. 'What

189

about the Hannigan girl? Have you thought about her? He may want a divorce.'

'He won't get it.... And please don't shout,' she added coldly.

'How are you going to stop him living with her then, if he wants to? ... Tell me that.'

'He won't live with her, I'll see to that,' said Stella, her lips folding into a thin line.

'What do you mean to do? What are you up to?' he asked.

'Never mind.... He won't live with her! He will live here, and things will go on just as they did before he left.'

'You're a cold-blooded devil.'

'Really!' She raised her eyebrows, tauntingly, at him.

'Oh, you'd drive a fellow mad!' He made a grab at her.

'Please, John,' she commanded; 'not here.... I have told you ... not here!'

'Hell!' He turned from her and flung out of the room.

Stella listened to him stamping across the hall. The front-door banged, and she went to the window and watched him stride away down the garden. She stood, biting her lip with vexation.

Something must be done, and at once ... things seemed to be getting swiftly out of hand. Why had she gone so far with him, anyway? she wondered. Why had she started it? She had never intended it to reach this stage. In the beginning she had used him to play off Herbert, who was demanding too much. But she had found John wasn't like Herbert, she couldn't keep him in line at all. The week-ends they spent together were nerve racking and exhausting; she had been made aware that Rodney, even in his passion, had been tender; and now John was proposing divorce, and marriage to him ... a struggling doctor, with not a penny behind him; it was ridiculous.

Stella admitted to herself that she had been foolish, very foolish, but whatever happened there must be no divorce. The Hannigan girl would have to be dealt with; she should have done it months ago, when that old hag had brought her those letters.

Her face stiffened at the thought of them, and jealously rose in her like a corroding acid.... To think Rodney would write letters like that to a maid! Of course, she admitted, she had herself to blame, she had played him too tightly.

She wondered if she could regain her lost ground.... He would be sick, and would doubtless respond to sweetness. She would devote herself to him; it wouldn't be her fault if she failed to establish at least a friendly footing. She still hated him, and desired nothing but to humiliate him for his spurning of her that memorable Christmas Eve. Well, the opportunity might yet come. But, in the meantime, if she didn't want a terrific scandal and wished to keep her head above the social waters, then Rodney was her only hope. But the Hannigan girl must be dealt with at once, she must be placed out of his reach.

She went to her desk and unlocked a drawer, and took out a bundle of letters. She fingered them as though they scorched her flesh.

Why, she wondered, did that old hag hate Rodney so? She evidently did, to go to the lengths she had in stealing these letters; her tale that she had found them in the street was paltry.

Stella felt that she had made a mistake in paying for them. Yet the old witch had played her nicely, leaving her no other way of getting them. And, although she had dismissed her some time ago, she wondered whether she had seen the last of her. Still, she had provided the means of putting the Hannigan girl where she wanted her; and she must lose no further time in doing it.

Annie was playing at the corner of the street; she stood in a circle with other children, all hopping from one foot to the other to keep warm. A child in the centre stabbed a finger at each in turn, shouting:

> 'Iccle occle, black bottle,
> Fishes in the sea,
> If you want a pretty girl,
> Please choose ... me!'

Annie knew that the first stab could be regulated to choose whichever one you liked. The unfairness of the system did not trouble her; she felt gloriously happy ... the sun was shining, the frost was sparkling, it was Christmas Eve and she was going to hang up her stocking, she had a secret present for Kate ... and oh! oh! oh! the doctor was coming home, the doctor was coming home, the doctor was coming home ... she beat out each word with her hopping feet. Everything was lovely and bright and shiny, Kate was lovely and bright and shiny. She sang all day. They both sang together in the kitchen at night, and Mrs. Mullen knocked on the wall at them, and they laughed because they knew it was only in fun. Oh, they were so happy! They missed grandma at times, but she had been so happy before she died that you did not feel sorry for her now ... it made you feel she had gone straight to Heaven like that ... nice and happy. Oh, wasn't everything lovely! No granda, no more carrying washing for Kate went out to work now, most days, and the doctor, doctor, doctor was coming, coming back! She was still hopping when the circle broke up.

'Count a hundred before you look, mind, Jinnie Taylor!' a little girl was admonished. Jinnie turned her face to the wall and started to count quickly in a loud voice.

Annie dashed into the main road, she knew a lovely place to hide.... It was then she saw the car. It was gliding slowly forward and the chauffeur was looking up at the names of the streets. A woman in the back leaned forward and spoke to him; and Annie stopped running for a second. Turning, she dashed back the way she had come.

Running up the street, she knew that the car had turned the corner and was behind her. It was almost upon her when she reached the door. As she thrust open the door the car stopped. She ran into the kitchen, whispering hoarsely, 'Kate! Kate!'

Kate was not there, so she dashed into the backyard and found her in the wash-house.

'Oh, there you are,' she said. 'I'm getting the steps to put the chains up, you can come and help me.'

'There's ... there's a lady outside, Kate,' Annie panted.

'I think she's coming here.'

'A lady?' Kate asked, knowing that any of their usual visitors would have had the term 'woman' affixed to them. 'Do you know who it is?' she went on, straightening her dress, one of the faded and washed out Quaker-grey dresses she had worn at the Tolmaches, and smoothing her burnished hair up the back of her head with a sweep of her hand.

'It's ... I think it's...' But Kate was already in the kitchen, and Annie let her go through the front-room without adding, 'the doctor's wife.'

To say that Kate was surprised at the sight of her visitor was to say the least. She looked at this beautiful, magnificently-dressed woman, with the background of the car behind her, and found herself incapable of uttering a word.

'Miss Hannigan?' Stella asked.

Kate inclined her head slowly.

'May I come in? I should like to talk with you.'

Stella, poised and calm, felt she already had this woman at a disadvantage. She took in, at a glance, the poverty of Kate's attire, shutting her mind to the beauty that it clothed.

At the second motion of Kate's head she stepped into the front-room, and barely suppressed a shudder as she looked around at the horse-hair suite and the bamboo table standing on the bare wood floor.

Kate found her voice: 'Will you come into the kitchen, it's warmer there?' She led the way, and indicated Tim's chair to the visitor. To Annie, who was standing wide-eyed, she said, 'Go into the front-room, dear, and close the door.'

Stella experienced a sense of irritation at the sound of Kate's voice; she must, she conceded, be suffering a shock, yet her voice was strangely controlled and well modulated; there was none of the raucousness that, to her mind, accompanied the Tyneside speech. She remembered vaguely having heard that one of the old Tolmaches had educated the girl, which increased her irritation. But her voice was cool and level when she spoke: 'You wonder why I am here, Miss Hannigan?'

'No,' answered Kate surprisingly.

'Oh!' said Stella, slightly nonplussed. 'Then that does away with the need of an introductory opening.... Sit down,' she spoke as if commanding a servant; 'you'll be tired before we finish, no doubt.'

'Thank you; I don't wish to sit down,' said Kate. She stood with one hand resting on the kitchen table and holding the middle button of her dress with the other.

'Very well!' Stella suppressed her annoyance with difficulty, for this attitude was unexpected. 'I shall come to the reason for my visit right away,' she said. 'My husband is, as I suppose you know, expected home any day now. I understand he is a very sick man and will need careful nursing for some time, as I expect the surgery was rough in a prison camp, especially with amputations.'

She was allowed a pause, while they stared at each other.

'He will,' she went on, 'need peace, and rest from worry.... Whether or not he gets it will depend on you, Miss Hannigan.'

Kate did not answer, but her eyes widened slightly and became dark.

'I want you, Miss Hannigan.' Stella continued coolly, 'to leave the district, and promise in no way to get in touch with my husband. If you do this he will have a chance to get well and strong again, and to resume his career, which means so much to him.'

'And if I don't?' put in Kate quietly.

'Then, if you don't, he will not have a career to resume ... for I will sue for a divorce.'

'There are no grounds for a divorce,' Kate said evenly. 'And, anyway, divorce does not end a man's career.'

'To the first ... I can prove there are grounds for divorce.'

Stella opened her bag and took out the bundle of letters.

'These are six of my husband's letters to you. In one of them, he speaks of "our beautiful Annie", and that he has loved her since the day he brought her into the world; in another, that to him you are more than a wife, and he makes reference to a week you are to spend together,

194

which he refers to as "heaven".'

The button Kate was holding snapped across, making a loud twang in the silence.... Her letters! ... How? ... Where? ... Mrs. Mullen? ... No. Who, then? ... Dorrie Clarke! Last Christmas Eve.... Yes, sending Annie out so that she could search.... Annie hadn't told her of that until after Christmas, knowing she was so worried and it would only have annoyed her to know.

Kate's voice trembled as she said, 'He's not Annie's father ... you know he's not.'

'Whether I know it or not everything points to it. I can do my best to prove it. But I am not going on that alone.... Rodney made no secret of his attachment to you; he never does when he has these strong attachments for women. You start, Miss Hannigan,' said Stella, with a smile. 'Surely you didn't think you were the only one. Dear, dear! I've had to straighten out these affairs all my married life. But that's beside the point.

'The Christmas Eve before last he spent the night here, and most of the following week. You don't deny that?'

Kate did not answer.

'Also, previous to that, you were seen in a field....'

'In a field!' Kate exclaimed in amazement.

'Yes. Somewhere near Felling. That was at Christmas time, too.'

The night of the drive! Kate thought; walking across the moonlit green hill.... Oh, Rodney.... But to put it like that ... in a field! How sordid it sounded.

'Mrs. Richards, Doctor Richards's wife, told me of this; she felt I should know.... Candidly, I think she would like to see a divorce, and would help me to get it. Anything that would endanger Rodney's career would be beneficial to her husband's practice.... Women are strange creatures, aren't they?' she said, smiling stiffly.

Kate just stared at her, at her beautiful unlined face and her eyes, as cold as the sea.

'You remarked,' continued Stella, 'that divorce does not end a man's career. But this one would. For, should I divorce him and he does not marry a certain lady ... namely, Gwendoline Cuthbert-Harris ... she will immediately bring up a case against him for seduction, when she was his patient.'

'You must be mad!' cried Kate. 'I don't believe a word you say.'

'It does sound mad, doesn't it?' said Stella calmly.

'Lady Cuthbert-Harris is a sick woman,' said Kate, 'she's neurotic. You know she is.'

'Aren't we all!' Stella retorted. 'Tell me who isn't suffering from nerves after going through this war.... But she has asked me to divorce Rodney when he returns. She says that she's crazy about him, which, of course, I know, and so do most people. And, she states, he loves her, and that I am the only obstacle in the way of their happiness.'

'You're lying!'

'Why should I lie about such a thing?' Stella opened her bag again and, taking out another letter, she said, 'Please notice the crest on the envelope and also on the paper.... Now, would you mind listening to this?'

Stella read the letter aloud, raising her eyes every now and again to Kate's white face.

It was the outpourings of a sex-ridden woman, and, as Stella had said, was asking her to divorce Rodney on the grounds of what had taken place between them.

Kate felt sick. She knew it was the letter of a woman who was mentally ill; but she also saw what could be made out of this letter if brought before the public notice. And whether it was or not depended on her.... How was it, Kate thought, she had always sensed disaster would come to him through her?... And she fully realised that this woman before her meant every word she said. She was as dangerous as an adder; nothing would stop her reaching her object, and her object, Kate knew, was to have Rodney once more. And if she couldn't get him she would ruin him.... Oh, God, she cried voicelessly, is there no end to it? What must I do?... But, even as she asked, she knew.

But first she would tell this woman that what she had said about Rodney had no effect on her; it was what she would do to him that was forcing her hand.

'You needn't continue!' she interrupted, her voice quivering. 'I don't believe a word of it.... No, not a word!'

'You don't?' Stella folded the letter carefully and returned it to her bag. 'However,' she continued, 'whether you believe it or not, Miss Hannigan, is beside the point. Should Lady Cuthbert-Harris bring up a case of such a nature on top of my suing for divorce, and she will bring up her case, I'll see to that, what chance do you think Rodney's career will stand? The Medical Board is rather puritanical about the members of its profession, and, should nothing even be proved, Rodney wouldn't be able to stand the strain of it ... it would break him.

'I have the advantage in the knowledge I possess of my husband, Miss Hannigan. His affairs were always numerous, but never serious enough to damage his career; and his affairs were secondary things in his life ... his work came first.

'Have you realised, Miss Hannigan, that nothing matters to him so much as his work? His one aim before the war was to specialise in children's diseases and child psychology. Should you bring about the end of his career, do you think you would be capable of replacing it in his life? ... Remember, once he is struck off the medical register, that will be the end. Sex is not all a man needs. But perhaps you have that to learn.... You undoubtedly will learn it should you force my hand, Miss Hannigan.'

'What if I refuse to fall in with your plans?' cried Kate, momentarily driven to defiance. 'If I stay he will come to me, and you could do your worst. You lost him years ago.... Even if you get your way and you share the same roof for the rest of your days you'll never have him; I know that. You don't exist for him!' she spat out the last words.

Stella stood up, her face bloodless, and they confronted each other in silence.

Then: 'How dare you!' Stella said between her teeth.

She fought to gain control, forcing a smile to her lips. 'Of course, it's foolish to lose one's temper with people of your class. Your speech at any time is apt to be crude.... It only proves to me how soon Rodney would tire of someone having nothing but the flesh to offer him.'

Kate remained silent, refusing to be goaded.

'Well, Miss Hannigan; you know my terms,' said Stella, hunching her fur coat around her. 'Should you be here the day Rodney returns, which will be in about a week's time, then I will not stay my hand a minute. And you will be surprised at the number of people who will come forward to help me obtain the divorce. I have found that the people who dislike Rodney are equal in number to those who like him. For instance, there's Mrs. Clarke. It was she, incidentally, who found your letters in the street. It was careless of you to drop them, Miss Hannigan. She thought I ought to know; very good moral sense, don't you think?'

'Have you quite finished?' asked Kate.

'Nearly,' said Stella. 'You will need money for such a hasty withdrawal. Here,' she said, placing a roll of notes on the table, 'is enough to take you quite a distance from this county, and to keep you and your child until you find suitable work.'

Kate stared straight at Stella: 'Would you mind picking up that money?' she asked, with dangerous quiet.

'We don't want any heroics, Miss Hannigan; nor hypocrisy,' said Stella firmly. 'I am sure you know the value of money. You will no doubt need . . .'

She did not finish; for Kate's hand shot out, and, picking up the roll, threw it into the heart of the fire.

The effect on Stella was paralysing for a second. Then she cried, 'Are you crazy, you fool? Pick it out! . . . There's twenty pounds there, get it out!'

'It's your money,' said Kate. 'It's there for you to take.'

The bundle of notes was well alight. Stella made an effort to put her hand towards them, then drew it back. She lifted the poker and tried to flip then out, but only succeeded in fanning the blaze. She stood watching them helplessly, venomous rage consuming her. . . . There was a swelling of flame, and they were gone. Pieces of black charred paper broke away and floated up the wide chimney.

It was not the loss of the twenty pounds, for it would have been a loss had Kate accepted, but it was Kate's spurning of it that infuriated Stella.

She turned a white, contorted face to Kate: 'You'll be sorry you did that.' She gave a short, bitter laugh. 'It was foolish of me to offer it. Why, I should have known; Rodney was ever generous where his fancy led him. Your great gesture has been lost, Miss Hannigan. But I am afraid from now on you'll find your source of income cut off. So I repeat, you'll be sorry you did that.

'I will take my leave, Miss Hannigan.' She waited for Kate to precede her through the room, but Kate stood stiff and staring.

Kate knew she dare not speak, a hate she had never experienced before was raging within her, and she was afraid of it. She wanted to throw herself on this woman and rend her; there was an overpowering desire to beat her fists into that cold, sneering face. She knew that if she spoke all the work of Bernard Tolmache would be destroyed in a second. One word would release this fury, and she would act worse than any woman of the fifteen streets; the self she had created through constant observation and study would perish in the flame of this hate. Not even Tim Hannigan had aroused such a destructive urge.

After waiting a moment, Stella raised her eyebrows and walked past Kate, so close to her that their skirts touched. She went through the front-room, passing Annie, who was standing with her hands up her sleeves, without a word. She found difficulty in opening the door, and Annie came forward shyly and undid it. Stella gave her no word of thanks; she did not even look at her, but stepped down on to the pavement and into the crowd of children who were surging around the car.

From the window, Annie watched the car drive away, with the screaming children hanging on behind. She watched the curtains being put back into place at the windows opposite and dark figures disappearing into doorways. She watched until the street became quiet again, for she couldn't go into the kitchen ... the lovely bright, shining light had gone from the day. She did not want to look at Kate, for she knew that the light would be gone from her too. She stood trembling, cold inside and out.

Kate remained standing where Stella had left her; the feeling of rage was dying away and a terrible ache was taking its place.... This had been bound to happen; why had she blinded herself all these months? What had she expected? That he would just come back? Come straight to her and they would live happily ever after, while she, his wife, would sit back and let it happen?

Stella, she realised, had not only the law on her side but she had Rodney in the hollow of her hand; that she could break him and that she would, rather than allow him to go free, was evident, and that she had struck the right note when saying that man needed something more than passion, Kate knew. Rodney loved his work, it had been his life for so many years, and, without it, he would be lost ... and lost he would eventually become if she stayed here; for she knew that, no matter what Stella threatened, he would come to her, throwing everything to the winds.... She leaned against the wall and beat it slowly with her fist.

Annie, hearing the dull thuds, crept to the kitchen door, and stood, horrified, watching. Kate made no sign, and Annie could not go to her. This crying, this sorrow was different from any she had ever seen; it frightened her and created a sorrow inside of her which was unbearable. She crept back into the room again.

Mrs. Mullen let an hour elapse after seeing the car drive away, and she wondered if it would look nosey if she were to go in and see Kate now. She had been behind her curtains, like the majority of the women in the street, waiting to see the 'lady' come out. It was Doctor Prince's wife, Rosie had told her; everybody in the street knew who it was. Oh, poor Kate! ... Poor Kate! She had been over the moon these past few weeks; and now what would happen? It should never have started in the first place, he was a married man. Kate should have known what she was letting herself in for.... But there, these things did happen. God knew why! And the doctor was a fine chap, and he seemed to think the world of Kate. But he was a doctor, and he was married, and his wife was a big bug. And, after all, in spite of all her learning, Kate was only a working lass.... Aw, but poor Kate ... poor lass! ... She would pop in now and see how things were; she would take in Annie's Christmas box, it would serve as an excuse.

Before she had time to get it there was a knock on the back door, and Kate herself came in, taking her utterly by surprise; for Kate rarely visited anyone ... even her.

Mrs. Mullen looked quickly at her, and away again ... whatever had happened, it had certainly taken it out of her.

'Sit down, lass,' she said awkwardly.

Kate shook her head. 'Willie's saving up to buy furniture, isn't he, Mrs. Mullen?'

'Yes, lass,' answered Mrs. Mullen, perplexed.

'Do you think there's anything next door he'd like?'

Mrs. Mullen stared at her.

'I know the stuff's not much good,' Kate went on, 'but there's the chest of drawers and one good bed and the lino. Then there's the saddle and chiffonier and kitchen table.'

'What are you talking about, lass?'

'Selling up,' said Kate, in a rush. 'I'm going away and I must have some money. I've only twenty-two shillings in the world. If I could get about ten pounds ... but the stuff's not worth that, I know. Could you lend me a few pounds, Mrs. Mullen? I'll soon get work and let you have it back.'

'Lass, sit down and calm yourself. What do you want to go away for like this?... Why, I thought ... well ... the doctor will be here any day now!'

Kate shook her head from side to side: 'I can't tell you why I'm going, Mrs. Mullen ... only I've got to go.... Do you think Willie will take some of the things?'

'It's very likely; I'll ask him, lass, as soon as he comes in. But what's your rush? When are you going?'

'As soon as I possibly can. Only don't ask me any questions, Mrs. Mullen. If I could tell anybody I'd tell you, you've been so good to me ... but I can't.'

'But it's Christmas, Kate! You can't go rushing off at Christmas.'

'Christmas!' said Kate bitterly. 'Christmas is the very

time for me to go. Anything that's going to happen to me waits until Christmas.... I loathe Christmas! I hate it! Goodwill to men!'

She went out, leaving Mrs. Mullen gazing at the kitchen door in amazement.

# WAITING

Rodney stood leaning on his stick and looking out of the Davidson's sitting-room window. Below, the river Don at low tide ran sluggishly between its slimy banks; to the right lay the Salt Grass, a barren stretch of mounds, bordered, in the far distance, by the houses of Jarrow. Of all the dreary views in the world, he thought, this was the worst. God! if only he could get away from it and never see it again.

Peggy Davidson came into the room, carrying a tray in her hand.

'Oh, Rodney,' she exclaimed, 'why will you stand about? Do sit down and put your leg up ... Peter will be furious with you.'

'I loathe your view, Peggy,' he said, turning from the window.

'Yes, it is awful, isn't it. But I don't seem to see it any more.... Do sit down, Rodney.... Here; come on.' She patted the cushions on a long chair.

'You can live with a thing until you neither see it nor feel it, then?'

'Yes. Yes, I suppose so.... Look here, I'm not going to become involved in one of your arguments at half-past ten in the morning. Sit down and drink this beef-tea. And remember, you induced Peter to let you come downstairs on the solemn promise that you would take things easy for another week or so.'

Rodney smiled at her and sat down. 'I wonder what would have happened to me without you and Peter,' he said. 'I often wonder that, you know.'

'God provides,' she answered.

'Oh, Peggy, you sound like an old Irish woman! You're

a real Jarrowite, you know.'

'And I'm proud of it too.'

Peggy was relieved that his tone, even for a moment, could be bantering. She was worried, and Peter was worried, about him. As much as they loved him, they wished he would go away for a change. Nothing, however, would induce him to talk about it. A few months ago, when he had been at breaking point, he had gone to his people, presumably to stay the winter. But he had returned within a fortnight and had just escaped a severe breakdown.... Oh, Peggy thought, if only she knew where that fool of a woman was! Why didn't she come back?

Rodney sat thinking.... Peggy doesn't see this view because she's happy. Happy! ... The word plunged him into weariness again, and his mind echoed the persistent cry, 'Kate, where are you? Why don't you come back? You must know that you can come back now.' Last night he had dreamed the same old dream again. He woke from it sure that she was lying beside him, and lay taking in the peace and ecstacy of her presence for some moments before realisation came, bringing with it its despair. He first experienced the dream after his foot was amputated. He had only to doze off and Kate would be with him, and he would wake up calling her name. The other fellows around made no comment; the calling out of names was a stage which most of them reached.

Being a prisoner was a hell at any time. But to lie helpless and to have them chopping away at you, knowing that nothing you could say would make any difference, was an indescribable Hell. He did not know why they had not amputated his left arm too; they prepared him for it, and the thought of what it would mean nearly drove him mad. He looked at it now, lying practically useless by his side. Its delayed action irritated him beyond all words; to all intents and purposes it was off, dead. It gave him no pain at all, whereas the foot which was no longer there ached like mad.

The sight of a man striding down the street could fill him with envy; a work-stained drunk, rolling along, brought up the eternal 'Why?' He needed his arms and legs; they could accomplish so much that was good; yet he was left practically useless.

During these spasms of self-pity he would tell himself it could have been two arms and two feet.

When the terrible necessity of having to amputate both arms or both feet had been thrust upon him his mind had shut down on itself, his pity refusing to form thought. At such times pity could wreck you and those around. You used it only in subtle form; you laughed, you cursed, you swore and badgered; and it kept your hand steady. The German doctor, he remembered, neither cursed nor swore; he was polite, and cold and in a hurry.

What effect the happenings of the past year would have left on his enfeebled system if Peter and Peggy Davidson had not been at hand to sustain him he dreaded to think. Stella's changed attitude, on his return to England, was disconcerting; her sweetness and solicitude left him embarrassed and at a loss. She pooh-poohed the idea of a nurse and insisted on looking after him herself. Her constant attention and anticipation of his every need, far from setting a spark to his dead affection, created an uneasiness in his mind. No correspondence had passed between them until just before he embarked for England, when he received a most charming letter from her. Thinking along the lines that a leopard doesn't change its spots, he had asked himself the reason for her attitude.

He had been in a fever to see Kate, but being dependent on someone posting his letters he could not even write to her. So he laid the situation before Peter, who showed no surprise nor offered any advice, but said he would go personally to see Kate and fetch him word of her.

The news Peter brought was so alarming to Rodney that against all advice, he was soon making frantic efforts to walk on his artificial foot. Stella did everything in her power to restrict his movements, only falling short of locking him in his room.

When Rodney eventually reached the fifteen streets Mrs. Mullen made clear the reason for Stella's attitude and also for Kate's disappearance.

'She must have got work right away, doctor,' she said, 'for I got this letter yesterday, with the four pounds she borrowed. There's no address, as you can see, but the postmark's London.'

From Mrs. Mullen's he had gone straight to Peter and asked if he could stay with him for a time, knowing that, feeling as he did, he could not cope with Stella. However, Stella showed no reaction to this move until she found that John Swinburn had come to Rodney, asking him to divorce her.

Rodney had not been prepared for Stella's visit. She was like the embodiment of white-hot lava; raging, she denied all Swinburn had said. Her cool poise was thrown aside and he saw a woman who, even with his knowledge of her, was new to him. She said she would ruin him, that he would never practise again. He had replied that it was doubtful whether he would in any case.

'There are other avenues in the medical line you will want to take up, remember?' she said. 'But I have the power to close them all to you. Apart from your illicit amours with a maid, which are the talk of the town, there is this!' And she showed him what she said was a copy of Lady Cuthbert-Harris's letter.

Rodney was shocked and visibly staggered.

'You know it's a lie!' he said.

'Of course,' Stella answered. 'And you'll prove it to be a lie. But only after I have made that mud stick so hard that you'll never be able to scrape it off.'

The contents of this letter and the talk it would arouse, should it be made public, had hung over him like a black cloud. When Stella mentioned the other avenues which were open to him she was drawing on her knowledge of the plans on which he had often spoken to her and which, she realised, he would be more likely to take up now that he was disabled. The plans concerned sick children, sick not only of body but of mind. Child psychology, he had recognised for some time, was more important to him than the attending of worn-out bodies held together by acid-encrusted bones. If he could prevent some of the children of today from becoming those dimmed and troubled people of tomorrow then he would achieve something. This was the avenue Stella could block.

Yet, in spite of her threats, he went ahead on the evidence Swinburn supplied and petitioned for a divorce. It was strange that he liked Swinburn at this time better than at any other time during their acquaintance; not because he was supplying the means of freeing him from Stella, but rather because he knew Swinburn to be under great stress and that he was trying to do the right thing, as he saw it. Swinburn said he could not help his love for Stella. Try as he might it was no use; his feeling for her swamped everything. His career meant nothing to him without her, and he proposed starting afresh somewhere abroad.

Rodney pitied him from the bottom of his heart. He knew Stella had nothing to give any man; what she offered was a mirage. But it had the power to drive a man mad, as he knew only too well.

That it drove Barrington mad was made tragically evident, for, although Barrington knew that he was supplanted by Swinburn, the canker of desire for Stella seemed to grow with the hopelessness of its fulfilment. It reached its climax when he visited her after reading the notice of the divorce proceedings. The result of this meeting which gave Rodney his freedom by Stella's death instead of by divorce shocked him so much that, for a time, he thought he too would lose his sanity.

At dinner-time Rodney spoke less than usual. Kate was filling his mind again. He felt tied to this place because of her; something beyond reason said it was to here she would return, even to the fifteen streets.

He was recalled to the effect his silence was having on the others by Peter saying, 'Do stop jabbering, Cathleen!'

Rodney roused himself: 'Good heavens, Peter! Don't keep her quiet on my account.... Look here, don't you think it's about time you stopped treating me as an invalid? Go on, Cathleen.'

'Who said it was on your account? You flatter yourself, man. I've had a devil of a morning, and now I want a little peace while I'm eating my dinner. For her tongue never stops wagging.'

'Uncle Rodney doesn't mind, do you?' asked Cathleen.

'Of course not.' He smiled at her and winked his eye.

'Uncle,' said Michael, 'you should see the Meccano set working in a shop in King's Street in Shields. It's wonderful. They've got cranes unloading ships and filling wagons, and it's all set up in a miniature dock. Oh, it's great!'

'It sounds great,' said Rodney. He did a stage whisper across the table: 'What about asking Doctor Davidson to take us round that way in his car this afternoon?'

'Not on your life!' cried Peter. 'Oh, no. And me up to the eyes and you hardly out of bed!'

'O ... oh, daddy!'

'It would be just what a sensible doctor would order,' said Rodney, 'a change of scene. And I'm sick of looking at your filthy river.'

'Be quiet you two,' shouted Peter to Cathleen and Michael. 'And if you want a change of scene, look out of the back window,' he said to Rodney. 'And, woman,'—he glared at Peggy—'if I can't have peace with my dinner I'm going to eat out.'

She smiled at him serenely. 'If Rodney wrapped up well, and we made him comfortable in the back of the car, these two could squeeze in the front seat'—she indicated the children. 'Then, I don't see why not. And, after all, it's Christmas Eve.'

'I have calls to make, woman.'

'Well, they wouldn't stop you; they could sit in the car and wait.'

'No, I just can't do it! If those two want to go to Shields they can take the tram. And as for you'—he nodded at Rodney—'you should have more sense, man.'

They looked at him in silence for a few moments.

'Oh, all right then,' he said, his old smile breaking out, 'But I can't take you till after tea; I'm packed with calls in Jarrow this afternoon.'

The gaily dressed shop windows, the alive and teeming market-place, and the excitement of the children, lifted Rodney out of himself for a time. But only until he thought of what it would have meant to him had he been driving down here with Kate and Annie. However, he maintained an air of excitement in order to please the children and to allay any unrest in Peter's mind. But during the homeward drive to Jarrow he felt very tired and lay back in the car, feeling his strength seeping from him.

Half turning, Peter said: 'Do you mind if I make a call in the fifteen streets; there's a woman there I'd like to see? It might save me coming out later on.'

'No, of course not,' said Rodney. 'Don't worry about me. Go ahead.'

'I'll leave you here, on the main road,' said Peter, bringing the car to the kerb; 'the house is only a few doors up Slade Street.'

Cathleen slipped into her father's seat and was arguing with Michael on who would learn to drive the car first when Michael suddenly exclaimed: 'Look, Cathleen! Look at that old woman along there. She's drunk! She's hanging on to the lamp-post.'

'Oh, so she is! She isn't half drunk, too. And she's coming this way,' said Cathleen, peering through the windscreen. 'Look at the boys following her. Look, Uncle Rodney, she's nearly falling!'

Rodney bent forward. Then swiftly he leant back again as he recognised the figure reeling into the circle of light to be that of Dorrie Clarke. He prayed that she would pass on and would not come near the car; this was the woman who had read his letters. He could still hear Stella's voice quoting extractions from them and telling him how they came into her possession.

The children sat silent, watching the woman. She was harrying the boys. When she was abreast the car she stumbled against the radiator and let out an exclamation: 'God blast yer! Burn an old woman, would yer?' she cried.

Cathleen and Michael started to giggle, and Dorrie Clarke waved her fist at them shouting, 'You would laugh? That's a Christian for yer!' She brought her face close to the window and spluttered, 'Young upstarts, that's what you are.' Her head rolled round, nodding on her fat neck, and she stared into the back of the car.

Rodney, head bent, was pretending interest in a paper, but the light from the street lamp shone on him.

'God Almighty!'

Rodney did not look up, the children sat silent, their eyes wide with mingled amusement and fright.

'Ah, you can bow yer head,' cried Dorrie. 'Yes, bow yer head. Yes; go on, bow yer head. I've seen me day with you. By God, I have.... I said I would, didn't I? And what Dorrie Clarke says she does.... God looks after his own. You thought you were a doctor! Ha, ha! Why, you weren't fit to lick Doctor Kelly's boots! An' what are yer now?... Yer not even half a man!'

Rodney lowered the paper and sat staring straight ahead, his face pallid. Two women came out of Slade Street and, hearing Dorrie, hurried towards the car.

'Come away, you old fool,' said one; 'you'll get yersel' into trouble.'

'What!' she turned on them. 'Me get into trouble for tellin' that sod the truth? Take yer 'ands off me; I'm goin' to tell him some more ... about his fancy piece.'

'Come away, woman.'

'Leave me alone! Get yer 'ands off!' She wrenched herself free and fell heavily against the car door. Steadying herself, she turned her face to the window again: 'Went off and left yer, didn't she? High an' dry! No half man for Kate Hannigan. An' yer put notices in the paper.... God Almightly, it was a laugh!

'Come back to Erin, mavourneen, mavourneen,' she sang, beating time against the window with her hand. 'What would jer give to know where she is, eh? Yer other leg, eh? Dorrie Clarke could tell yer. Yes; I could tell yer. What d'yer think about that?'

Suddenly she was wrenched away from the car, and Peter was saying, 'Mrs. Clarke! If this happens again, I'll put the police on you.'

He got into the car without another word and drove away.

Dorrie Clarke stood leaning against the wall where he had flung her. 'Another bloody upstart! Polis on me, indeed!'

'Ye'll get yersel' in the cart, Dorrie, mind,' said one of the women.

'Do yer really know where Kate Hannigan is?' asked the other.

'Of course she doesn't,' her companion said; 'it's the gin that's talkin'.'

'Gin is it!' yelled Dorrie. 'Gin is it! Yer think I don't know where she's gone! A ... ah! A ... ah! It's me that knows a thing or two.'

'The doctor'd likely pay a pretty penny to know, Dorrie,' the woman persisted.

'Me take his dirty money!' cried Dorrie. 'Not me. Why ... if I was starvin', if I was crawlin' in the gutter for a crust, like this....' She went to get down on her knees, and the women pulled her up, saying, 'Don't be such a damned fool, Dorrie!'

'If he was handin' me a plate of golden sovereigns, I tell yer, and going down on his one good leg to do it, I'd ... spit in his eye! And he'll never get Kate Hannigan ... never! 'Cos yer know why?... She's dead! Dead as a doornail!'

'Dead!' exclaimed the women.

'Yes, dead,' said Dorrie. 'Yer think I'm drunk an' it's the gin talkin' ... but I can still use me head.... She's dead this long while.... Can't yer see? If she wasn't dead she'd've been back and snaffled him. But she's dead, I know for certain she's dead, an' in Hell, sizzling, where she should be.'

One of the boys who had followed Dorrie suddenly cried, 'Ee, look there!' He nudged the woman nearest him and pointed to the tram which had stopped across the road.

'My God!' she exclaimed. 'Well, of all the things that could happen!'

Dorrie Clarke blinked her bleary eyes at the approaching figures; her slack jaw wobbled from side to side and, as the tall woman and girl walked past the group, she slowly slid down the wall to the pavement.

# THE RETURN

Annie lay staring into the dark, waiting for the alarm to go. For some mornings past she had woken up long before the alarm had gone and lain quiet, thinking about Rosie Mullen and the north. Early last Christmas Eve morning she and Rosie had been down to Jarrow slacks to gather wood; there had been a rough tide during the night, which always meant there would be wood and lots of other things, including rotten vegetables, lining the bank. It was funny, but she imagined she could smell the stinking cabbages now. Perhaps it was just the smell of this house, for, no matter how Kate cleaned it, it always smelled like old cabbages.

She had forgotten what Rosie Mullen's face was like. She could see her as a dumpy whole, but her face was never clear. Would she ever see Rosie again? she wondered. Always there was a sick longing within her for Rosie and all that she stood for, the docks, the slacks, the fifteen streets, the Borough Road church and the children.... The children in this town of St. Leonards were not like the children in the north. Apart from speaking quite differently, they didn't play the same games; and the ones who were supposed to be poor didn't look poor. A girl had taken her round an old part of Hastings, which was as close to St. Leonards as Tyne Dock was to Shields, and pointed out the slums to her. The slums had appeared houses of moderate affluence and very quaint, some even beautiful. She couldn't see how those people could be poor, not poor, anyway, like the poor back home. She longed to be able to talk to Kate about it, but whenever she mentioned the north Kate turned the conversation. On her evening off, last week, when they stood on the promenade and watched the moon's reflection gleaming like molten silver on the water, Kate had remarked, 'It's very beautiful, isn't it?' And she had answered her by saying, 'Do you remember, Kate, the glow that used to come over Jarrow when the blast furnaces tipped at night?' Kate had not answered, and they walked on in silence. And that night she heard Kate crying; the quiet, still crying that often went on and on. She always pretended to be asleep when Kate cried, for Kate's tears formed a barrier of pain which she found impossible to surmount.

In that dreadful house where Kate worked in London and they slept in the basement, and where people's feet were continually passing over the iron grating above the small window, even into the dead of night, Kate cried often, and her face always looked swollen. The basement was very damp, too. She remembered how ill she felt one night, and how she went to sleep, feeling a pain in her chest, and woke up to find herself in a ward with a lot of other children. When she was better, Kate had not taken her back to the house, but came here, to this house which smelt of cabbages and was so full of old furniture and pictures that you could hardly move.

Miss Patterson-Carey, who owned the house, liked to tell her all about the furniture and pictures; they had belonged to her grandmother and her mother. She said that if they knew she was reduced to taking in guests for a living they would turn in their graves. She had explained that when she was a little girl they lived in The Square and kept eight servants, and that her father drove his prancing bays up and down the front. But now she had been reduced to living above The Square, in this house which was called Wide Sea View. Which was very funny, Annie thought, since the only place from which you could view the sea was the attic window.

Miss Patterson-Carey told her all these things. She didn't tell Kate, because that would have kept Kate from her work, and she had the guests to see to and all the house. The guests were all old people, and seemed to wear a lot of clothes.

Annie didn't like Miss Patterson-Carey; she was mean

and religious and was always giving her tracts to read. All the guests read tracts, too. Sometimes the house seemed to be full of all kinds of tracts. Miss Patterson-Carey had called her a naughty girl for reading comics; she said they weren't 'holy reading', and she didn't allow anything in the house that wasn't 'holy reading'.

Now it was winter and there weren't so many guests, Miss Patterson-Carey sometimes came into the kitchen at night and talked to Kate. But it was all about God and a thing called ... retribution. Kate never answered her, which seemed to annoy Miss Patterson-Carey, who usually brought up the subject of how difficult it was to obtain a situation where you could keep a child.

The alarm gave a warning bur ... rrr, but before it could get fully going Kate had switched it off; so Annie knew that she had been awake, too. Kate got up immediately and started to dress by the light of a candle, and Annie whispered, 'Kate, can I come down with you?'

'You should be asleep,' said Kate. 'And it's cold down there. Wait until I get the fire on.'

'I don't mind the cold, Kate. I don't like staying up here alone, and I could help you.'

'Very well,' Kate said. 'But be quiet, mind.'

Annie got out of bed and hurried into her clothes; she was ready almost as soon as Kate.

Leading the way down the bare attic stairs, Kate whispered, 'Be careful of the torn carpet on the second flight, mind.'

They crept past Miss Patterson-Carey's door on the first-floor landing and down the last flight into the kitchen. It struck icy cold, and Kate busied herself in cleaning out and lighting the kitchen fire.

Annie asked, 'Shall I do the sitting-room fire for you, Kate?'

'You'll never be able to light it, dear, there's hardly any paper left.'

'I've last week's comic,' said Annie. 'And, oh, I know where there's some paper, Kate. In the bottom of the vegetable basket; I saw it sticking through the slats yesterday, when the man left it. Shall I take the vegetables out and get it?'

'Yes, you can do that,' said Kate. 'I'll light the gas, and then you can get on with it. But try not to make a noise.'

Annie emptied the box and took out the folded newspaper. She picked up some sticks and went into the sitting-room and set about doing the hearth. She opened out the newspaper and crumpled it loosely, as Kate had shown her, and laid it in the grate. She was laying the sticks in a criss-cross pattern on it when a large black-printed word caught her eye. Something about it was familiar. She looked more closely. It said TYNESIDE. She knelt, her head bent sideways, drinking in the word. It was like a fresh breeze in this stuffy, cluttered room. She sat back on her heels, her head still bent sideways, and gazed at the word. She wondered, abstractedly, what the paper could have to say about Tyneside. She lifted two sticks away, and disclosed the word TRAGEDY ... TYNESIDE TRAGEDY.... Somebody had been knocked down, she thought; they always said that in the paper when anyone had been knocked down. She wondered who it was; would it be anyone whom she knew? Hurriedly, she pulled away the sticks, and, lifting out the paper, smoothed it on the hearth. She was reading intently when Kate came in, saying, 'Oh, my dear, haven't you got it on yet? Get by, out of the way, and let me do it.' She pushed her gently to one side and crumpled the paper again.

Annie knelt for a second, as if dazed, watching her. Then she cried out: 'No, Kate! No! Don't burn it.... Look at the paper.... Look what it says.'

'For goodness' sake, child, be quiet! What are you yelling like that for? Do you want her to come down?'

For answer, Annie pulled the paper from Kate's hands and spread it out on the hearth again, and pointed to it.... 'Look!'

Kate knelt back and read for a few seconds. Then her body jerked forward, and, with hands grasping each side of the paper, her eyes moved swiftly down the column.

She sat back slowly and turned to Annie. They stared stupidly at each other. Annie suddenly shivered, the inward shiver of delight. Kate took her hand, and they both rose to their feet.

'What are we going to do, Kate?' whispered Annie.

Kate just stared at her, with that dazed look still in her eyes. Then it seemed to lift like a curtain, taking with it the drawn, dead look that Annie had seen there for so long.

'We're going home,' she said.

'When?'

'Now. Now.'

'Now?'

'This minute!' cried Kate.

'Oh, Kate!' They clung together for a second, their arms gripping each other tightly.

'Come on. We'll get packed.'

They hurried upstairs, yet went softly, through habit; and in ten minutes they returned again, dressed for the street and Kate carrying two cases.

In the kitchen Kate said, 'I'll take her a cup of tea, it will lighten the shock.'

Annie, who still held the dirty newspaper in her hand, asked, 'Kate, can I keep this?'

Kate touched her cheek tenderly: 'Yes, darling; you can.'

As Kate hurried out, Annie opened the paper and read the report again. It was dated April 24th and read:

### DOUBLE TYNESIDE TRAGEDY
#### ON DAY FOLLOWING DOCTOR SUING FOR DIVORCE NAMING ASSISTANT AS CO-RESPONDENT WIFE SHOT BY FORMER LOVER

Stella Dorothy Prince, wife of Doctor Rodney Prince of Conister House, South Shields, was today shot dead by her former lover, Herbert Barrington, who afterwards shot himself. Only yesterday it was made public that divorce proceedings were pending between Doctor Prince and his wife, and naming Doctor John Swinburn, Doctor Prince's assistant, as co-respondent. Barrington called at the home of Mrs. Prince, and, after heated argument, overheard by a servant, shot her. The servant, Mary Dixon, stated . . .

A blur of tears hid the print. It seemed awful that the

216

doctor's wife was dead; although she wasn't nice she had been beautiful.... But, anyway, they could go back home.... Oh, they could go back home now!

Kate came hurrying into the kitchen. She took some money from her bag and laid it on the table. She had hardly done this when the kitchen door burst open and Miss Patterson-Carey entered, her hair under a high night-cap and an old dressing-gown draped around her angular body.

'You can't go like this!' she cried. 'You just can't do it!'

'But I can,' said Kate quietly. 'There is the money in lieu of notice that you say you require.'

'You're a wicked woman to leave me like this.'

'I have just read some news,' said Kate, 'which has altered everything for me, but had you treated me even once as a human being I should not have left you so suddenly. Anyway, you are neither old nor sick, and, as you have often quoted to me, idle hands are armchairs for the Devil. So it will be a change for him, in your case, to be made to stand this Christmas.' Kate picked up the cases and motioned Annie to the door. There she turned and delivered her Parthian shot: 'This, Miss Patterson-Carey, is what is known as ... retribution!'

Annie opened the door and they went out into the dark morning.

The long journey from St. Leonards was nearly over. Kate and Annie, with the compartment to themselves, sat close together in one corner. The reaction from almost hysterical joy had set in, and Annie was sobbing, long, shivering sobs that shook every bone of her slight frame. Kate soothed her, saying, 'There, there. Come, darling; stop it. You'll only make yourself ill.'

'I can't help it, Kate, I ... I keep thinking, if I hadn't seen that paper we might never have ...'

'Sh...h!' said Kate. 'Just let's thank God you did see it. And there now; stop crying.... Listen! We'll soon be coming to the tunnel. Remember the tunnel?'

In the dark of the tunnel they sat with their arms about each other, and Kate kissed Annie almost passionately.

When they got out at Tyne Dock station, Kate stood for a moment on the dimly lit platform and looked around her. She was home ... home! For years she had longed to get away from the north and never see it again, but now she felt it held all that she wanted in life. She did not know where she would find Rodney; she might have to move on again in search of him; but she knew that she would return here eventually. For this was her home; the people here were her people ... good, bad and indifferent, they were her kindred.

At the dock gates they took the Jarrow tram. And Kate felt she would not exchange the hard slotted seat for one in Paradise. After they got out of the tram at the fifteen streets, they passed a group of people standing at the corner of Slade Street, and Annie asked softly, 'Did you see who that was, Kate?' And Kate answered, 'Yes, I saw. But she can do nothing more to us.'

Kate's eyes were dry and bright, and her hand trembled as she knocked on the Mullens' door. It was opened by one of the younger children. He peered at them through the gloom, then darted away without a word, and they heard him yell, 'It's Kate and Annie Hannigan!'

Before they could cross the threshold Mrs. Mullen was there. 'Kate lass! Kate! In the name of God, where've you sprung from? Come in, lass; don't stand there, come in.... Oh, lass ... where've you been?' They were borne into the kitchen on her welcome and into a surge of the Mullens, all talking at once and clamouring about them. 'Sit down. Sit down, Kate,' cried Mrs. Mullen. But before Kate could do so, she had gathered her and Annie into her embrace, and they all clung together for a moment, half laughing, half crying.

Annie turned to Rosie and they stood staring at each other, awkward and embarrassed, not even touching hands.

'Oh, Rosie!' was all Annie could murmur.

'Ee, Annie, ye've come back!' said Rosie.

'All the way across the country in one day!' Mrs. Mullen was saying. 'Why, lass, you must be famished! I'll have you something to eat in a coupl'a shakes of a lamb's tail.'

Kate drew Mrs. Mullen to one side: 'Where is he, Mrs. Mullen? Do you know?'

'He's at Doctor Davidson's, lass; he's been there all the time.'

Kate stood silent a moment. 'Do you think I could have a wash and do my hair, Mrs. Mullen? I won't have anything to eat, just a cup of tea.'

'Well, just as you like, hinny,' said Mrs. Mullen. 'Aw, lass'—she squeezed Kate's arm—'I'm glad to see your face again. And just wait till the father sees you,' she said, referring to her husband, 'he won't half get a gliff.'

Annie was saying to Rosie, 'We lived in a place called St. Leonards, with an awful woman.... She reads tracts.' Annie caught Kate's eye and they both began to laugh. Kate laughed as she had not done for a year, and in a moment the whole of the Mullen family had joined in. And Rosie thought, It's like that night in Kate's kitchen when we all cried and me da was funny and old Tim died.

Kate walked from the fifteen streets to the house on the Don. She had the urge in her to pick up her skirts and run. She felt her heart would burst through her flesh; her mind was crying, 'In a few more minutes I'll see him. In just a few minutes I'll be able to touch him.' She crossed the Don bridge, and thought, It all seems beautiful. But when she pressed the bell of the Davidson's door she felt faint and weak.

The door was opened by Peggy, who said, 'Yes?' then stood staring in wonder at Kate. She had seen Kate only a few times before, but had never spoken to her.

'I'm Kate Hannigan,' Kate said. 'Could I ... Could I see Doctor Prince?'

Peggy drew her inside and into a room off the hall before speaking. Then she exclaimed, 'Oh, I'm so glad you've come! Oh, you don't know how pleased I am to see you at this moment.'

'I never knew what had happened until this morning,' Kate said; 'Annie, my daughter, saw the report in an old newspaper.'

They appraised each other in silence for a moment; then smiled, as if each liked what she saw. 'Really, I can't believe it's true that you are here!' exclaimed Peggy. 'Excuse me a moment. I must tell my husband.' She darted into the hall and called, 'Peter!'

Peter's voice came from the sitting-room, saying, 'There! I bet I'm off again. Now do as I say, won't you? Go to bed, and I'll look in on you when I return.'

With a finger on her lips, Peggy motioned him to silence. She closed the sitting-room door which he had left open, and whispered, 'It's Kate! She's come.'

'What! No! Where?' Peter's eyebrows almost disappeared into his hair in surprise.

'Ah!' warned Peggy. 'In there.' She pointed to the door.

'Well!'

When Peter went into the room and saw Kate standing wide-eyed on the hearth-rug, whatever he had intended saying was never said. This was not the Kate he remembered; she had always appeared to him a very young girl, even when well into her twenties. But here was a woman, beautiful still, yet in a widely different way from the other Kate; more finely drawn, more poised, but strung up, at this moment, to breaking point, if he knew anything about it. His treatment of her was studiously casual: 'Where on earth do you think you've been?' He spoke as though she had left the house at seven o'clock promising to return at eight, and now it was nine.

She smiled faintly.

'Nice dance you've led everybody ... haven't you?'

'Take no notice of him, Kate,' Peggy said. She turned to Peter: 'She found out about it only this morning from an old newspaper.... Isn't it strange?'

'Strange!' said Peter. 'Of course not; you couldn't expect her to act like a sensible person and read the daily paper. Anyway, Kate, where have you come from now?'

'From St. Leonards in Sussex,' Kate said. She understood what his off-hand manner was aiming to achieve, and his efforts were succeeding, for her tense nerves were easing, even as he spoke.

'When? Today?'

'Yes; we left early this morning.'

Peter's voice became softly sympathetic as he said, 'He's in the next room, Kate; but you'll find him somewhat changed. He's never given up hope that you would return.'

Kate said nothing. Now that the moment had come she wished she had more time, time to control the trembling of her body and the racing, whirling expectancy of her mind.

Peggy took her arm. 'Come, Kate,' she said, giving an intonation to the name, which brought a flash of gratitude from Kate. 'Let me have your hat and coat,' she added.

Kate took off her things in the hall, and Peggy, pointing to the sitting-room door, gave her arm a gentle pat and left her.

As she opened the door Kate did not know what she expected to find. But when she saw Rodney looking to all appearances whole she experienced a slight shock; she had not expected him to look whole. He sat lost in brooding thought, his head bent and his hands lying idle on his knees. At the sight of him all her senses seemed to rush from her body. In the second before he looked up she experienced the acute pain of incredulity that accompanies any feeling nearing ecstasy; she was alive to the overlapping of the emotions, for this joy which filled her was also suffering. He lifted his head, and the remark he was about to make to Peggy died on his lips as he beheld Kate standing with her back to the door. The air between them seemed to vibrate; emotion winged back and forth; but neither of them moved. He closed his eyes, and when he opened them again and Kate was still there he breathed her name ... a small sound, so inadequate, expressing nothing of the wonder of this moment. He made a hasty and clumsy effort to rise, grabbing for his stick and knocking it out of his reach. His bad arm gave way under his weight as he tried to assist himself from the chair. He floundered back, despair and rage at his helplessness and inadequacy to meet this occasion tearing at him.

In the second that it took Kate to reach him, she saw

that he wasn't whole, nothing about him was the same; his hair was grey at the temples and his face was unnaturally pale, with the bones showing prominent under the skin, and his body seemed broken.

She was at his feet, and her arms were around him, straining him to her. As only one arm returned the pressure she was choked by a rush of feeling, so poignant that no words could express it.... Love and tenderness seemed small parts of its ingredients; there was a protective and maternal urge mixed with her passion for him; all so intertwined that they were inseparable. And, as his lips gropingly sought hers, her whole being was transported, even while her heart was rent by his tears which were wetting her face.

# CATHERINE COOKSON NOVELS
# IN CORGI

WHILE EVERY EFFORT IS MADE TO KEEP PRICES LOW, IT IS SOME-
TIMES NECESSARY TO INCREASE PRICES AT SHORT NOTICE.
CORGI BOOKS RESERVE THE RIGHT TO SHOW AND CHARGE NEW
RETAIL PRICES ON COVERS WHICH MAY DIFFER FROM THOSE
ADVERTISED IN THE TEXT OR ELSEWHERE.

THE PRICES SHOWN BELOW WERE CORRECT AT THE TIME OF
GOING TO PRESS (NOVEMBER '80).

| | | |
|---|---|---|
| ☐ 11350 6 | THE MAN WHO CRIED | £1.25 |
| ☐ 11160 0 | THE CINDER PATH | £1.25 |
| ☐ 10916 9 | THE GIRL | £1.75 |
| ☐ 11202 X | THE TIDE OF LIFE | £1.75 |
| ☐ 11374 3 | THE GAMBLING MAN | £1.25 |
| ☐ 11204 6 | FANNY McBRIDE | £1.25 |
| ☐ 11261 5 | THE INVISIBLE CORD | £1.25 |
| ☐ 11571 1 | THE MALLEN LITTER | £1.35 |
| ☐ 11570 3 | THE MALLEN GIRL | £1.35 |
| ☐ 11569 X | THE MALLEN STREAK | £1.35 |
| ☐ 11677 7 | ROONEY | £1.25 |
| ☐ 11391 3 | PURE AS THE LILY | £1.25 |
| ☐ 11676 9 | OUR KATE | £1.50 |
| ☐ 11674 2 | FEATHERS IN THE FIRE | £1.50 |
| ☐ 11203 8 | THE DWELLING PLACE | £1.95 |
| ☐ 11260 7 | THE INVITATION | £1.25 |
| ☐ 11365 4 | THE NICE BLOKE | 95p |
| ☐ 11675 0 | THE GLASS VIRGIN | £1.75 |
| ☐ 11366 2 | THE BLIND MILLER | £1.25 |
| ☐ 11434 0 | THE BLIND MENAGERIE | £1.25 |
| ☐ 11367 0 | COLOUR BLIND | £1.25 |
| ☐ 11448 0 | THE UNBAITED TRAP | £1.00 |
| ☐ 11335 2 | KATIE MULHOLLAND | £1.95 |
| ☐ 11447 2 | THE LONG CORRIDOR | 95p |
| ☐ 11449 9 | MAGGIE ROWAN | £1.25 |
| ☐ 11368 9 | THE FIFTEEN STREETS | £1.25 |

*All these books are available at your bookshop or newsagent ; or can be ordered direct from the publisher. Just tick the titles you want and fill in the form below.*

CORGI BOOKS, Cash Sales Department, P.O. Box 11, Falmouth, Cornwall.

Please send cheque or postal order, no currency.

**U.K.** Please allow 30p for the first book, 15p for the second book and 12p for each additional book ordered to a maximum charge of £1.29.

**B.F.P.O. and Eire** allow 30p for the first book, 15p for the second book plus 12p per copy for the next 7 books, thereafter 6p per book.

**Overseas customers.** Please allow 50p for the first book plus 15p per copy for each additional book.

NAME (block letters) ...........................................................................................

ADDRESS ...........................................................................................

(NOV. 1980) ...........................................................................................